Todd wasn't having fun anymore. Oh, the clowns had tried to keep him from feeling homesick. They'd brought him toys and books and candy. And two orders of french fries with his Big Mac and chocolate milkshake every day. One of the clowns had even taught him to use the remote control for the computer.

At first he'd had a good time, but that was just until the clown who'd brought him here had locked him in. That clown wasn't as nice as the other one who'd given him picture books to look at and told him a bedtime story so he wouldn't be scared.

There were no windows in the place, so Todd couldn't tell if it was day or night. But he could count to twenty. The bedtime-story clown had tucked him in three times in a row, so Todd knew three nights had passed. And he could recite the days of the week by heart. Wednesday, Thursday, Friday. So today must be Saturday. Maybe Mommy would come for him tomorrow night, the way she did on Sundays when he went to visit Daddy.

He tried not to think about that. He didn't want to cry the way he had when Daddy went to stay away from the house. He was bigger now. And maybe if he was good and he did everything the clowns told him to—even brush his teeth before bed—Mommy and Daddy would take him home and they could all be together again. . . .

CATCH A RISING STAR!

ROBIN ST. THOMAS

FORTUNE'S SISTERS   (2616, $3.95)
It was Pia's destiny to be a Hollywood star. She had complete self-confidence, breathtaking beauty, and the help of her domineering mother. But her younger sister Jeanne began to steal the spotlight meant for Pia, diverting attention away from the ruthlessly ambitious star. When her mother Mathilde started to return the advances of dashing director Wes Guest, Pia's jealousy surfaced. Her passion for Guest and desire to be the brightest star in Hollywood pitted Pia against her own family — sister against sister, mother against daughter. Pia was determined to be the only survivor in the arenas of love and fame. But neither Mathilde nor Jeanne would surrender without a fight. . . .

LOVER'S MASQUERADE   (2886, $4.50)
New Orleans. A city of secrets, shrouded in mystery and magic. A city where dreams become obsessions and memories once again become reality. A city where even one trip, like a stop on Claudia Gage's book promotion tour, can lead to a perilous fall. For New Orleans is also the home of Armand Dantine, who knows the secrets that Claudia would conceal and the past she cannot remember. And he will stop at nothing to make her love him, and will not let her go again . . .

SENSATION   (3228, $4.95)
They'd dreamed of stardom, and their dreams came true. Now they had fame and the power that comes with it. In Hollywood, in New York, and around the world, the names of Aurora Styles, Rachel Allenby, and Pia Decameron commanded immediate attention — and lust and envy as well. They were stars, idols on pedestals. And there was always someone waiting in the wings to bring them crashing down . . .

Available wherever paperbacks are sold, or order direct from the Publisher. Send cover price plus 50¢ per copy for mailing and handling to Zebra Books, Dept. 4435, 475 Park Avenue South, New York, N.Y. 10016. Residents of New York and Tennessee must include sales tax. DO NOT SEND CASH. For a free Zebra/ Pinnacle catalog please write to the above address.

STAR BABY
ROBIN ST. THOMAS

ZEBRA BOOKS
KENSINGTON PUBLISHING CORP.

ZEBRA BOOKS are published by

Kensington Publishing Corp.
475 Park Avenue South
New York, NY 10016

Zebra and the Z logo Reg. U.S. Pat & TM Off.

First Printing: January, 1994

Printed in the United States of America

for Jeffrey and Vikki
and
to the memory of Michael Fardink,
whose laugh lives on

ACKNOWLEDGMENTS

Five people offered expert help and information "above and beyond the call." Without them, STAR BABY's denouement could not have been written. They are:

> Mary Beth Minton LoVecchio
> Angela Fagan
> Detective John Fagan
> Detective John O'Boyle
> Detective Steve DeGregorio

With thanks and appreciation,

                                        Robin St. Thomas

One

The door to Todd's nursery was ajar, probably so that Jill, his nanny, would hear him over the sound of the TV set in the den when he awoke from his nap.

Wearing sneakers had been a good idea; even though tile floors didn't squeak, you could never be sure about wooden stairs.

Another good idea was the timing. With Todd's mother at the studio and his grandmother at a charity function, it was perfect. No fear of Todd's daddy showing up, either. Even during breaks, there was no rest for the director. So, as long as Jill stayed glued to her soap opera, there was no one else to interfere.

The first priority was to gain Todd's trust; sure, he was precocious, but with a four-year-old you never knew. The whole thing could go up in smoke if he suddenly got scared and cried out for help.

A quick glance in the mirror outside Todd's room offered reassurance that the kid wouldn't cry out. The clown disguise was brilliant. The silly face and bulbous red nose would convince *any* kid that it was all a game.

But it wasn't a game. And if second thoughts had appeared—which they hadn't—it had gone too far to back out now.

A falling light crashed to the floor and ended the take before the AD could yell "Cut!"

"Goddammit!" Ansel Kline leaped from his chair in a fury that silenced more than a hundred voices at once.

A gaffer quickly set about replacing the lamp, and in a few minutes they were ready to go again.

"Background! Take your positions!" bellowed the AD.

The extras with less experience began pushing forward; the old-timers knew better and edged out of camera range, mindful that a close-up would kill them for the rest of the picture—and a Kline-Hemmings picture meant plenty of overtime, because Ansel Kline was known to shoot around the clock to get what he wanted.

"No wonder he and Stevie are getting a divorce," whispered one extra. "Who could live with a perfectionist?"

The woman next to her laughed. "A perfectionist like my ex, no way. But Ansel's net worth must be at least twenty million. I could live with that."

The first woman nodded. "Hey, did'ja hear that Stevie got custody? I'll bet her momma-in-law is seething!"

"Yeah. Carolyn Kline makes Nancy Reagan look like a saint."

Their gossip was interrupted by Ansel Kline's angry voice addressing the script supervisor.

"What do you mean, you forgot, Tanya? On a forty-million-dollar budget, you don't *forget!* Your oversight means we have to reshoot the entire last scene!"

"Ansel, I'm sorry!"

"I am, too, Tanya, but if it happens again, you're off the picture."

The script supervisor was visibly shaken. Ansel Kline was a man of his word. One more slip-up and she was out.

She was deep in concentration and didn't see Stephanie Kean until the actress was standing beside her.

"I owe you an apology, too, Stevie," she said. "You'll have to go through your big breakdown scene again."

"Hey, it won't be the first retake of my career," said Stevie. "At least we have the luxury. I remember when Ansel's budget didn't allow reshooting. So relax. He's under a lot of stress."

"As if you're not," said Tanya.

"Well, don't beat up on yourself. Ansel wants the world to think and behave exactly the way he does. If he could bend half an inch, we wouldn't be splitting up."

Stevie spotted Ansel and took a deep breath. Her Adonis of a leading man left her absolutely cold, but a single glance from her estranged husband still turned her knees to Jell-O.

She passed one of the grips, who offered a thumbs-up and a, "How's Todd?"

"He's terrific, Hal. Napping before his grandma takes him shopping." She made a mental note to call Jill during a break; she'd forgotten to tell the nanny that Carolyn Kline would have Todd for the afternoon. A shopping trip would keep her from dropping by the set and spreading her own brand of tension, but Stevie couldn't help feeling uneasy whenever Todd was out of her sight. Especially with the recent celebrity kidnappings becoming as commonplace as drive-by shootings on the freeway.

Stevie still hadn't shaken the memory of her overreaction to Todd's "disappearance" only the week before.

They'd spent all morning at the Beverly Center, outfitting Todd with clothes to replace those he'd outgrown. He'd dragged his larger-than-life Bugs Bunny from store to store.

Stevie was signing her autograph for the salesclerk. By the time she'd written her name, Todd was gone.

"Todd? Todd!" She didn't see him anywhere. *"Todd!"*

"Mommy! Over here! Peek-a-boo!" came the small voice.

She whirled around. Three dozen or more identical Bugs Bunnies smiled back at her. The left ear of one rabbit moved and Stevie heard a whisper. "Psst! Here I am, Mommy!" Todd flung the other bunnies aside and threw himself into his mother's arms. She hoped he didn't feel her heart racing.

"I didn't mean to scare you, Mommy!" he said, hugging her.

How could she reprimand him for her own irrational fears?

"Didn't you know I was hiding behind Bugs, Mommy?"

"Well, I wasn't sure," she said. "And I couldn't tell which Bugs was yours, because they all look alike."

When they returned home, Jill was gone for the day, and Todd and Stevie were alone for the evening. They'd finished their chili and Caesar salad. Todd had eaten the anchovies—a definite first—and been unusually quiet throughout the meal.

"I'll be right back, Mommy," he said, climbing down from his chair. "I have to fix something and it's important."

"Okay, sport. Then what d'you say to a movie before bed?"

"Yes!" Todd clapped his hands. "Can we have popcorn?"

"Yessir. With melted butter and cheese."

"Okay!" He bounded from the kitchen.

Stevie had popped the corn, but Todd was still upstairs. Well, he'd had a full day; maybe he'd fallen asleep.

He hadn't. She found him sitting cross-legged on the nursery floor with his Magic Marker pens strewn about him.

Bugs Bunny lay across his lap, but it was no longer the same stuffed rabbit Uncle Lyle had given Todd for his birthday.

Bugs's ears had been painted purple. Telltale ink smudges covered the artist's chubby little fingers.

"Todd?" said Stevie from the doorway. "What's all this?"

His smile was pure love. If that hadn't melted her heart, his answer would have.

"It's so you'll never be scared again, Mommy. With purple ears, Bugs won't look like any other rabbit in the world!"

Two gaffers broke in on Stevie's thoughts with a wave and a mimed greeting, and she waved back. The guys at the prop table smiled encouragement.

Thank God for the crew! Everyone on the picture—not to mention most of Hollywood and half the country—was privy to the more sensational aspects of the Kline-Kean divorce proceedings. The supermarket rags were busy inventing reasons for the split-up because incompatibility wasn't shocking or scandalous enough. No drugs. No kinky sex or clandestine affairs.

So the rumor mills were having a field day. Stevie felt as though she were parading around naked from the moment she said good morning to the guard at the studio gate.

It was different with the crew. The electricians and carpenters, the hairdressers and makeup people, had adopted her from the start of her career and had remained loyal ever since. They more than compensated for the family she'd never known.

Most of them had worked with Ansel for longer than Stevie had been in the business. Maybe that was why they weren't taking sides. Ansel wasn't a villain, after all. Just a genius. And a genius wasn't easy to work with.

Or to live with.

Ansel was trying to ignore his reaction to Stevie, but God, she looked more gorgeous than ever! Was this the effect of their separation? Her long auburn hair cast a golden-red halo above her head—unless it was simply Jay-Jay's lighting magic casting its spell. Christ, the way those suede pants hugged her slim hips and long legs, the fit of that angora sweater—hell, she could turn him on without even trying! All it took was a glance at her violet eyes.

Ansel forced himself to study an extinguished cigarette butt next to his shoe until the effect of Stevie's "spell" passed. He thought he'd succeeded until he looked down at his fly. So much for mind over matter. He turned to see two gaffers making an effort to ignore what they, too, had seen.

Great, thought Ansel. Life in a fishbowl called Hollywood.

"But where are we going?" Todd asked the clown.

"Well, your mommy and daddy are on location for a few days, and they want you to have a special celebration while they're away.

"Did you tell Jill?"

"Your mommy told Jill."

"And G'andma?"

"And your grandma."

"And you're sure Mommy said it's okay?"

"I'm sure. She said you're to have all your favorite foods and toys and games. And guess what?"

"What?"

"I'll show you how to play with a magic computer."

"Magic? What kind of magic?"

"You'll see."

Todd clapped his hands in delight. "Are we almos' there?"

"Almost, so get ready for a big surprise. In fact, I'm gonna blindfold you so the surprise'll be even bigger, okay?"

"Okay!" squealed Todd.

The actors had taken their places. Three groups of dress extras had been given their cues for action. Jay-Jay's lights were set. The sound man signaled that he was ready.

The director of photography, Chuck Breem, and his cameraman were ready, too. Stevie was given a last hair check and powder-down. The clapper moved in front of the camera and lifted her chalkboard.

Suddenly, Barbara Halsey, the assistant producer, came charging toward Stevie through the forest of cables and equipment.

"What the—!" Ansel yelled. He stopped when he saw Stevie's face.

Stephanie Kean, the consummate pro who could summon or suppress her emotions according to the demands of a role, was breaking down before the cameras rolled.

"It's Todd," she said in a choked voice. "He's . . . missing."

Two

A break was called. Stevie, Ansel, and Barbara rushed to Stevie's dressing room. Inside were two uniformed policemen and Carolyn Kline. Her jaw was tight, her manner more authoritative than usual.

Stevie was too upset to speak. The matter-of-factness of the policeman's words made little or no sense. In a way they made things worse.

Words like "probably wandered off" and "playing children's hide-and-seek games" fell numbly on Stevie's ears. Todd hadn't just wandered off. And he wasn't hiding—although that had become one of his favorite pastimes lately. No. Games didn't involve the police. Or Carolyn Kline. Or words like *missing*. *Missing* had to be a substitute for a word no one wanted to use.

The more softspoken of the two policemen was explaining what had brought them to the studio.

"The child's babysitter—"

"Nanny," corrected Carolyn Kline.

The policeman nodded. "The nanny, Miss Jill

Denson, was watching television and didn't hear or see the child when he awakened from his nap."

Stevie's head was beginning to throb. This couldn't really be happening. It was only a scene in a movie. So, what would she say if she were acting the role of a mother whose child was missing?

"Officer," she said. "Todd likes to hide in the cabinet under the sink in the kitchen."

"We checked there, ma'am."

"Yes, well, there's also the breakfront in the dining room. Sometimes he takes his stuffed animals and sits inside with them. The first time he did it we were sick with worry."

"Ma'am, the sitter—I mean, the nanny, Miss Denson—showed us all his favorite hiding places. He has quite an active imagination."

"He's . . . he's very bright," said Stevie, her throat catching. Pretending to be filming didn't work. They were talking about Todd, her child. Where could he have gone?

Or been taken?

The policeman had said something else to Stevie, and Carolyn was answering for her. Before Stevie realized it, she blurted out, "Carolyn, *why* are you here?"

"Well, Stephanie, that should be obvious. I went to collect Todd, and when Jill and I couldn't find him anywhere in the house, I telephoned a friend at the Beverly Hills Police Department, and he agreed with me that it might be wise to seek local assistance."

"Why? What do they think has happened?"

When there was no reply, Stevie turned to Barbara Halsey. "Barb, what's going on? What is it that no one's telling me?"

Barbara shrugged helplessly at Stevie.

"Look, I have a right—we both do—to find out what this is all about! The LAPD doesn't send police to investigate a child who's only been missing for a few hours, even when they're asked to by a meddler who has friends in high places!"

"Now wait a minute, Stephanie!" said Carolyn.

"No, Carolyn, *you* wait! You discover that your grandson isn't sitting on his bed with bated breath when you come to take him shopping, and the very first thing you do is call the police—"

"It was *far* from the very first thing, Stephanie, I assure you. Miss Denson and I made a thorough search of the premises, inside and out. After which"—a glance at the two policemen—"these officers did likewise. When Todd was nowhere to be found, I felt—*we* felt—that Ansel and you should be notified."

Carolyn adjusted the frosted wave over her left ear and then continued. "This is not the appropriate time, Stephanie, but I'll say it nonetheless. If Todd were in his father's care—or mine—instead of yours, he might not be missing now!"

"Goddammit, Mother!" Ansel exploded. "You really have a knack!"

The door, which was ajar, opened fully, and Lyle Hemmings entered Stevie's dressing room.

"One of the grips told me about Todd," said Ansel's partner. "Hey, listen, guys, I know my godson. Todd's one smart kid, and smart kids get into

18

all kinds of mischief. It's never anything serious, though, so . . ." His voice trailed off when he saw no response.

Stevie turned to him. "Thanks for trying, Lyle, but the truth is, Todd's an obedient child. He wouldn't just wander away from the house without telling Jill where he was going."

"My point exactly," said Carolyn. This time she was examining her perfect manicure.

Stevie wanted to remind Carolyn that she, not Todd's grandmother, had been granted custody. But she was too upset to enter a sparring match with her ex-mother-in-law-to-be. Instead she asked, "What do we do now? Just wait?"

"Yes, ma'am," answered the softspoken policeman. "If he's just lost, he'll probably get scared around nightfall and ask someone for help."

If he's just lost. Was that supposed to be reassuring? What if he asked the wrong person? There were always stories in the news about children who were abducted by pornographers and perverts, cases never solved and children never found.

Stevie shuddered. Sometimes they were found, but seldom alive. A sudden image in her mind triggered a release of her worst fears. She looked down at her wristwatch and saw that an hour had passed.

An hour beyond whatever time Todd had been missing.

No, he wasn't lost. And he wasn't playing hide-and-seek. A mother knew these things.

19

Three

Eppie Goldwyn parked her pink Cadillac alongside the gunmetal-gray Mercedes she recognized as Carolyn Kline's car. So she didn't have a reserved space; neither did Carolyn. Okay, so her least favorite person happened to be the director's mother. But what the hell, that old phrase about sauce for the goose still applied.

Just for appearances, though, Eppie placed the card marked PRESS under the windshield window. The last time she'd parked in a producer's spot, sign notwithstanding, her Caddy had been moved. And since she always leased rather than buying, the dealer hadn't been exactly thrilled by the scratches incurred.

Before alighting, she checked her hair and makeup in the rearview mirror, then rehearsed her repertoire of facial expressions: empathy, confidentiality, and compassion.

She practiced her smile and noticed a smudge of bloodred lipstick on a tooth. Wiping it away, she laughed. What a crock, she thought. Oh, she wasn't happy that Stevie Kean's kid had disappeared—

even if he was Carolyn Kline's grandson—but shit, Eppie couldn't be bothered by sentiment; she was here to get an exclusive. She patted her mobile telephone as though it were her best friend, positioned the tape machine inside her purse to Record, and set out to get her story.

She hadn't needed the anonymous tip to find the principals; everyone in or around the soundstage knew where to find the Klines. By the time Eppie reached Stevie's dressing room, she had taped enough background comments to fill three columns.

But it always helped to be on the safe side. That was why she'd stuffed a copy of *Probe*, the supermarket scandal sheet, into her tote bag. Usually Eppie shied away from such trash—it made the tabloid she wrote for, *Scoop*, high class by comparison.

Today, however, it might serve a purpose. The four-inch headline cried out: SATANIC CULT DUE TO STRIKE AGAIN; WHICH STAR'S CHILD IS NEXT? It was accompanied by a black-and-white photograph of teen idols Dana and Jim Travers at the funeral of their murdered fourteen-month-old son.

Ghoulish, Eppie admitted to herself as she reached for the doorknob. But hey, she had a job to do. And sometimes props helped people to open up.

* * *

The moment she stepped inside Stevie's dressing room, Eppie saw that someone else had taken the same precaution. The current issue of *Probe* lay on top of a script on the floor beside the flowered chaise longue. Was it possible that the magazine had gone ignored?

Eppie's entrance drew disapproving looks from everyone present and undisguised hostility from Carolyn Kline.

"The press has no business here," said Carolyn.

"Hell, darling, I'm not here as press. I'm here as a concerned *friend.*" Eppie made a beeline for Stevie and planted a noncontact kiss on her cheek. "Honey, you poor thing! I came as soon as I heard!"

Stevie seemed dazed, or numb.

Eppie blinked until tears formed, then asked, "Have the police made any progress?" She glanced at the two officers while making a point of settling her eyes on the telltale copy of *Probe.*

Lyle Hemmings stepped forward and took Eppie's arm. "I don't know how you got past the guards, Eppie, but I'll escort you to your car."

"Lyle, darling, I've just arrived."

"And you're just leaving." Following her gaze, he crossed to the chaise, picked up the magazine, and tossed it into the wastebasket next to Stevie's dressing table.

"What's that?" asked Stevie.

"Nothing," replied Lyle. "Garbage. That's what it is and that's where it belongs." He was starting for the door when Stevie suddenly came alive and darted to the wastebasket. She withdrew the magazine and stared at the cover.

Part of her brain refused to connect with the headline or the photograph.

"Well, what *is* it?" asked Carolyn Kline.

Ansel took the magazine from Stevie and handed it to his mother.

Stevie felt nausea rising inside her. "I don't read *Probe*. What's it doing in my dressing room?"

Eppie loosened Lyle's grip on her arm and moved toward Stevie. "Honey, don't get worked up. That story probably has nothing to do with Todd, and—"

"How did it get here?" Stevie demanded. To the policemen: "What is it you're not telling me!"

Eppie backed off, and as Lyle once more led her toward the door, he whispered to Ansel, "I have an old detective buddy at LAPD. Mike Galvin. I'll give him a call."

But Stevie had heard him, and what little remained of her composure now crumbled. "Mike Galvin!" she cried. "I know that name from the newspapers! He's—he's the detective in charge of . . . that special task force . . ." She couldn't finish the sentence.

"What's she talking about?" asked Carolyn Kline. "What task force?"

Ansel pointed to the copy of *Probe* in her hands. "The task force that's investigating a Satanic cult, Mother. Read it. Maybe you'll learn something." Then, turning to Eppie, he said, "And you—when I ordered the set closed to reporters, that meant *all* reporters."

"But Ansel, sweetie—"

"Don't sweetie me, Eppie! I want you out of

23

here!" He grabbed Eppie's arm, and the tote bag she was hugging began sliding from under her elbow. Catching it to keep it from falling, Ansel's hand felt an unmistakable outline inside the soft pink kidskin.

"You bitch!" He pulled the purse open and revealed Eppie's busily whirring tape recorder. Ansel yanked out the cassette and thrust it hard against the wall. "If you *ever* come sneaking around like this again, Eppie, I'll see to it that your job is history—no matter *who* you screwed for it! Now get out!"

Stevie's sobbing didn't stop until the studio doctor had given her a sedative and everyone else but Ansel had gone home for the night.

"I'll drive you home," he said, helping her into the car.

She nodded.

"I know the police will be watching the house, but I can stay over if you like," he said.

She shrugged.

Ansel knew that Stevie's indifference was probably due to the sedative, but he also saw irony in the situation: the disappearance of their child had thrust them together.

"I'll sleep in the den," he said.

Stevie was curled up in the passenger seat, and her eyes were closed. Ansel couldn't tell whether she was awake and ignoring his offer or whether she had dozed off without hearing a word.

Four

Stevie knew she shouldn't try to fight whatever it was the doctor had injected into her arm. Disembodied voices seemed to be whispering to her as someone—was it Ansel?—helped her into bed and covered her with a light blanket.

"Let yourself float, Stevie," the voice said. "Just float away as if your limbs are made of driftwood." But another voice—her own, she was sure—hissed, "Don't give in! You know what's happened! Don't think you can shut it out!" Stevie wanted to cover her ears against this voice, but her arms felt weighted, less like driftwood than like lead.

Her eyelids were the heaviest weights of all. The draperies were drawn, and the room was shrouded in black. Not unlike her thoughts.

Better not to think. But how to draw a drapery across the mind? Why wasn't the tranquilizer working? Where in God's name was Todd?

She repeated his name over and over as though it were a mantra, until finally she felt herself letting go. The terror that earlier had made her its victim at last loosened its hold, and she succumbed to the rhythm of her own breathing.

At first she found it soothing. But soon the soothing was gone, and Stevie began sinking into a dark and horrible void where everything was surrounded by black. Images glided past, faces without features, a blank and meaningless horizon against a pitch-enveloped sky.

Slowly, fragments, jumbled props and actors, came hurtling through time and space, posing a terrifying riddle in black.

The noncolor penetrated Stevie's consciousness even as she plunged deeper. Why? she wondered. Why all this black?

People, young and old, varying in size and shape. Why was everyone dressed in black? The faces drew closer, then dissipated into the ether. People Stevie knew, people she had worked with. Some of the faces were famous. Were they in mourning? Had some Hollywood dignitary died?

The children were also wearing black. Even the youngest among them—Dana Travers's little boy. And now he was . . .

Wait! whispered the faraway voice. *Don't you remember?*

Stevie tried, but the image that came to her was of a party. A strange party.

Why couldn't dreams unfold in logical sequence? What was her brain trying to tell her?

The shower . . .

Yes. The ridiculous party Carolyn had insisted upon giving for Stevie. And the ridiculous "guest," the obsessed fan who'd conjured thoughts of the uninvited witch at Sleeping Beauty's christening. *Can you remember her name, Stevie?*

Tammi. The fan-witch. Stevie could visualize her now as clearly as though she were standing beside the bed. The wild, Brillo hair, the pimples; the stocky figure whose stubby hands had dared to touch Stevie's swollen belly. Stevie shivered beneath the covers.

She'd never forget. Tammi had spoken to her.

"Star baby!" In a trancelike, otherworldly voice. Then her ejection from the house.

And Eppie Goldwyn's taunting promise: "I'll get my exclusive story yet, Stevie, you'll see!"

What exclusive? *What story?*

What news in another fan crashing another "power shower"? A stupid fad. Everyone, everything, in black—down to the organza and lace of the baby-to-be's christening robes. More like a pagan, anti-Christian ritual, turning the celebration of pending life into a mocking celebration of death. *Oh, God . . . !*

The sedative came to Stevie's rescue. The shower faded, immediately replaced by the memory of another night.

Stevie suppressed a hollow laugh, not unlike the laugh she'd suppressed on the night of March 29 four years before.

The night Todd was born.

The night Stevie missed the Academy Awards.

Ansel hadn't missed the Oscars. He'd missed the birth of their child.

27

And Carolyn Kline still held a grudge. Not against Ansel. She blamed her daughter-in-law for going into labor on the most important night of her son's career. She probably blamed Stevie for Barry Levinson's win over Ansel.

Did she blame Stevie for Todd's disappearance, too?

Even in a somnolent state, Stevie couldn't handle that. She tried stifling her sobs, although there was no one to hear them.

Her hair was damp, her left arm had fallen asleep beneath the weight of her head against the pillow. Without coming fully awake, Stevie turned. The tingling sensation made her arm a limp and useless appendage. The way her mind and body felt.

She continued drifting in and out, wanting to capture the happier images that danced through her head, wishing she could banish those which bore an ugliness she feared to acknowledge by name.

Those babies. She knew the Landaus and the Traverses, but until now she hadn't understood what they'd gone through.

And the children. Had they suffered terribly? Why was Freddie Travers the only one found? Who would want to harm such innocence?

And what about Todd? The others were too small to recognize danger, but Todd was four. He'd remember his captors' faces.

There you go again, Stephanie! hissed the voice. *You don't really care about the others, do you? "Stephanie Kean brings such empathy to her roles." That's what the reviewers say. Maybe you've been fooling them, is that it?*

Stevie's tearful "No!" was muffled by her pillow. Her eyes were tightly shut, as if to hide a shame she felt but didn't understand. Unlike earlier, when she'd been unable to recall the face of little Freddie Travers, she couldn't erase it now.

He'd been the last child taken. How long ago, a month? Damn the media, raking it up again just when Dana and Jim were trying to put the pieces of their lives together.

Freddie blurred, and another child, his face unknown to Stevie, came into view. His outstretched arms beckoned her, his mouth formed a soundless *"Mommy!"*

"Stop it, stop it!" Stevie screamed, her breathing shallow, her words as silent as the child's voiceless cry. She gasped for air, fighting her own fear of suffocation.

Maybe Carolyn was right, Stephanie. If you hadn't left Todd alone with Jill, if you hadn't insisted on custody, if you weren't so stubborn, too proud to "go Hollywood," you'd have hired a bodyguard for your precious child, your "star baby," and he wouldn't be . . . missing. Maybe, just maybe, if you and Ansel had taken the time to talk things through . . .

Strangely, Stevie's indictment of herself had induced the sedative's intended effect. A forgetful hand reached out to Ansel.

Of course he wasn't there.

Then, as the voice of her mind whispered, *It's too late, Stephanie,* she sank into a deep and mercifully dreamless sleep.

Five

"Sergeant Galvin, please."

"That's *Lieutenant* Galvin, sir," said the switchboard operator. "Just a moment, please."

It took longer than a moment, but finally Lyle heard the familiar gravel voice. "Galvin speaking."

"Well, my old buddy's moved up in the world," said Lyle.

"Hemmings? Well, for Chrissake, talk about moving up."

Lyle had expected sarcasm. He wasn't disappointed. "Hey, Mike, gimme a break. A producer's life is more hectic than a doctor's!"

"Yeah, or a cop's, right?"

"Okay, okay. I've been meaning to call. There just doesn't ever seem to be any time, y'know?"

"There used to be in the old days," said Galvin.

"C'mon, Mike, those quickie slash-and-tears wrapped ten minutes after they started—and looked it. Nowadays we're talking budgets of forty million!"

"And all those A-list parties. Somehow I feel a certain nostalgia for the old days, Lyle."

"Mike, I promise, as soon as this one's in the can, we'll get together."

"Yeah," said Galvin. "We can do lunch." A pause, during which Lyle heard the click of a cigarette lighter. Probably Mike's old Zippo. He made a mental note to send his friend a little gift, maybe a Colibri malachite and gold, like his own.

"Listen, Mike, I didn't call to schmooze. I need your help. That is, my partner and his wife need your help."

Galvin flicked the lighter lid again. He'd recently given up smoking, but not the habit that had always helped him concentrate.

"You know my partner Ansel Kline and his wife, Stevie Kean," said Lyle.

"*You* know them. I know *of* them."

"Their kid is missing, Mike."

Galvin stopped clicking his lighter. "Since when?"

"Today. Sometime in the afternoon."

"It's only seven-thirty. How do you know he's missing?"

"Look, the kid's grandmother has connections. They've already got cops on it."

"So why call me?"

"C'mon, Mike, I read the papers. You're heading the task force that's investigating the satanic cult kidnappings."

"What makes you think the cult has anything to do with your partner's kid?"

"Mike, the cult goes after kids of famous stars. Todd Kline's parents are famous. I figured you might be interested in the possible connection."

31

There were noises in the background, then Galvin's voice. "I've gotta go right now, Lyle. I'll do some checking and get back to you."

"I consider it a personal favor, Mike. So will Ansel and Stevie."

"Yeah. Later." Lyle heard another clicking, but this time it was the sound of Galvin hanging up the phone.

Six

In the darkness of the room, the blue digits on the clock read 5:00 A.M. Officially morning. It meant that Ansel no longer had to try to sleep. It also meant a beginning of the first full day of knowledge that everything had changed. He gave in to another wave of emotion. Despite hours of practice, it wasn't much easier to control.

He sat up and cursed the pain in his lower back, a souvenir from the fold-out sofabed in the den. The ache followed him downstairs to the kitchen, where he strained the muscles even further while reaching for the jar of coffee beans in the cabinet above the sink.

It wasn't there. Then he remembered; Stevie had always left the jar on top of the refrigerator. Ansel was the one who'd always put it away.

While the coffee perked, he drew back the living-room curtains and looked out. At first he saw only his reflection in the glass. The swollen eyes, the wrinkled clothes he'd slept in. A wreck, but so what?

A police car was still parked at the foot of the drive. To the right, the shadow of a uniformed cop stationed at the front door.

Ansel was suddenly blinded by the glare of flashing lights. Then more, causing him to shield his eyes. When the blinking green-and-red dots cleared, he was able to see a photographer running down the slope of the lawn and climbing into a black sedan.

Two more squad cars appeared, and the cops were out on the street within seconds. So were the backup media people. There were new camera flashes. Lights from camcorders. Men and women lined the curb, some speaking into mikes, others into tape recorders, still others shouting Ansel and Stevie's names so loudly they could be heard over the police bullhorn commanding them to keep back.

Ansel allowed the curtain to fall across the window. The fishbowl had turned into a shark tank.

Upstairs again, he quietly entered the master bedroom. Stevie lay on the far left side of the king-size mattress. Her side. The sheets and blanket he'd covered her with last night now lay in a tangle around her. The room was too cool, but the air-conditioner's hum diminished the increasing noise from outside. Ansel pulled the draperies tighter, stopping the thin sliver of first light before it touched her face, although he doubted whether that, or even the circus forming downstairs, could disturb her drugged sleep. Whatever the doctor had given her, Ansel was grateful—and sorry he'd turned down a dose for himself.

He showered and put on an old pair of jeans and shirt he'd left in the closet next to the john. He checked the medicine cabinet for a razor, was secretly relieved at not finding one, and dispensed with thoughts of a shave. He noted the absence of a "guest" toothbrush, too. God, had the supermarket rags infiltrated his mind, after all? What did he expect, a pair of men's silk pajamas hanging from the brass hook beside the towels? He was reminded of his mother's unfunny remark about the large monogrammed "K" on their linens and bathrobes.

"Such a practical idea," Carolyn had said. "In case of a divorce, the two of you can divvy things up and go your separate 'K's." What did his mother have against Stevie, anyway?

And why was he thinking about any of it now? What did any of it matter?

Ansel crept out of the bedroom, gently closed the door, and headed along the landing that led to the nursery and the upstairs den—a distance of less than seven feet separating Jill and her goddammed soap opera from Todd and his abductors.

Ansel's hand rested on the doorknob. He couldn't go in. He'd lose it completely if he saw his son's room with its happy painted clown faces peeking out from around the windows or shelves. And he couldn't bear to look at the empty bed.

The front doorbell chimed four times before Ansel reached the foot of the stairs. The phone rang at the same time. He opened the door to a blast of humid July heat.

"You know her?" one of the cops yelled.

"Mr. Kline!" the girl with him cried. "It's me! Carla!"

The crowd out front had more than doubled. Ansel heard the whirring of countless cameras. The phone was still ringing and everyone seemed to be screaming, including Carla Franzen.

"Close the door, Mr. Kline! Please!" She ran past Ansel, stopping at the banister and leaning against it for support. She jumped like a frightened cat when the door slammed shut.

"Hello!" Ansel barked into the receiver as the bank of telephone buttons began blinking like Christmas tree lights. He answered the one farthest to the right.

"Ansel Kline?"

"Yes! What?"

Ansel looked over at Carla, who was still cowering near the stairs. He snapped his fingers and pointed to the three blinking buttons on the phone, then to the kitchen. Carla nodded and ran from the foyer.

"Lieutenant Galvin, Mr. Kline," said the scratchy voice at the other end of the line. "This your private number?"

"Yes."

"Good. Don't make any outgoing calls on it. Your wife up yet?"

"No." Ansel felt a twinge at Stevie's being referred to as his wife.

"Good again. Keep her away from a TV set."

"Great—but they're broadcasting from right in front of the house."

"That's not what I meant. We found another body this morning. Not your son, but it won't make things easier on anyone. I'll be there within the hour. You be there, too. And Mrs. Kline. I'll need to talk with her."

The line went dead. The incoming calls had subsided for the moment; only one button was still lit.

"No, Miss Goldwyn," Ansel heard Carla saying into the kitchen extension. "I take care of Todd on Jill's day off. . . . Yeah, I know . . . I just thought maybe if I came over anyway, I could do something to help. . . . Oh! I didn't realize you were such close friends! Sure, if there's any news, I'll call right away. Lemme have your number in case I—"

Fucking airhead! "Carla!" Ansel bellowed. "Hang up!"

Seven

Ansel took the stairs two at a time and stopped to tiptoe only when he reached the bedroom door. He thought he heard voices coming from within. He knew he heard the unmistakable sounds of Stevie's sobbing as the voices went dead. He flung open the door and immediately understood.

The television was on, the anchorwoman pantomiming her story while the word MUTE posed on her left shoulder. Stevie was still holding the remote control; apparently she'd heard enough.

He went to the TV set and switched it off. Then he turned to Stevie.

With her tousled hair, her nightshirt disheveled from sleep—or from the lack of it—she looked so vulnerable, not unlike a child herself. He wanted to go to her, but she seemed to be gazing past him, or through him. The director in him, the always self-assured, in-control Ansel Kline, suddenly gave way to the helpless father, and he felt himself unraveling. For an instant he envied Stevie her tears. He wished he could permit himself to cry.

Stevie's words were unintelligible at first. Ansel

moved closer to the bed, and Stevie reached for his hand. Her fingers were like ice, her words came in short spurts.

"I dreamed—Ansel—the baby! I saw him—the picture—"

"Shh," he whispered. "I didn't want you to see it, but you turned on the set before I got back up here."

"No!" Her knuckles were white from clasping his fingers so tightly. "Not the TV—I mean—my *dream!*" Her breasts, through the silk of her nightshirt, were heaving. "Ansel—I saw"—she covered her eyes with her free hand—"I *saw* it—*before* it was on TV. Oh, God, it was horrible!" The floodgates burst once more, and she was shaking and sobbing so violently that Ansel, without thinking, pulled her to him in a fierce embrace. He was rocking her in his arms and searching for words to comfort them both when there was a knock on the bedroom door.

"What now?" He jumped up and rushed to open it. Big help, the cops. If they couldn't keep the press out of the house, how would they ever find Todd?

But it was Carla at the door. She was carrying a tray.

"I brought breakfast for Stevie. She should have something in her stomach, it'll make her feel better. And a detective is here from LAPD to see you, Mr. Kline. Lieutenant Galvin."

Ansel saw Stevie's reaction to the name, then remembered the telephones. He turned to Carla. "You stay with Mrs. Kline till I've spoken with"—a

39

glance at Stevie—"the detective. I'll need you to field calls today, Carla. Can you handle that?"

"Sure thing, Mr. Kline. It's my regular day to be here, anyway, and since—"

Ansel cut her off. "Fine, Carla. Stevie, I'll try to keep it short. We'll talk later."

"Sure," she said, her eyes not on him but on the blank gray of the television screen. "Business as usual."

Ansel didn't hear her; his thoughts were already projected downstairs to the waiting Lt. Galvin.

"Listen, Stevie . . ." Carla said when they were alone. "You gotta eat. I fixed scrambled eggs and a toasted English."

"That was nice of you, Carla, but . . . I'm just not hungry right now." The thought of food made Stevie want to throw up.

"Well, take a sip of coffee, at least. And maybe a bite of the English. Really, my ma used to tell me bread soaks up all the bad juices in your system, no matter what's happened."

Stevie pushed the tray away and Carla took the hint. She removed the tray from the bed, wishing she'd had time for her own breakfast that morning. But under the circumstances it would be tacky to ask if she could eat Stevie's.

Carla glanced over at the telephone with its blinking buttons. "Mr. Kline said I should take care of calls, but the phone isn't ringing. How d'you know who's calling and who's on hold?"

Stevie had never realized that Lyle's part-time

maid was such a space cadet. Carla must be on something, or the girl was incredibly slow on the uptake. And right now Stevie had insufficient patience for either.

"Carla, there's a volume-control key under the unit. We—that is, I—always turn the volume off at night."

"Oh, y'mean it rings on all the other extensions, but not up here?" Carla turned the unit over and started searching, but before she could find it, Stevie had swung herself off the bed and reached for the unit. "Here, I'll do it. Why don't you have my scrambled eggs before they get cold?"

"Well, if you're sure you're not—"

"I'm sure, Carla. Go ahead. I hate waste." Stevie closed her eyes. Her own words had made her think of the murdered child she'd seen on that morning's newscast. A wasted life. Was there anything more terrible?

She didn't want to consider the answer.

A quarter of an hour passed. Fifteen minutes in which Carla straightened the bed to an accompaniment of her own incessant prattle.

"Listen, Stevie," she was saying, "I know you're worried sick about Todd, but he'll be okay, you'll see."

"I wish I were as certain as you, Carla."

"Well, he's not the kind of kid to go off somewhere with strangers, y'know? I mean, like, maybe he went looking for his grandma or one of his friends, and just got lost. Kids get lost all the time, and they don't wanna admit they're scared, so they hang out till they get hungry, then they knock on a neighbor's door, y'know?"

"He's only four years old," said Stevie.

"Yeah, but he's very grown up for his age. Independent, too. Todd won't let anybody hurt him, not if he has any say about it."

But would he have any say about it? Did Carla have any idea that each word she uttered upset Stevie even more?

And then there was Ansel. Everything was changed, yet nothing was changed. Start a conversation—mundane or life-and-death importance—and Ansel had to take a call. Or a meeting. Or do lunch. So it usually involved deals. Now it involved their missing child. She prayed he'd recognize the difference in time to save their son. He hadn't seen it in time to save their marriage.

Stevie was seated on the edge of the chaise longue. It offered two views: the grounds outside that had become a media campsite, and the TV set, which seemed, if possible, more ominous without its picture than during the earlier special news bulletin with its terrifying images.

With the telephone volume adjusted, Carla was managing to intercept calls by the second or third ring. Although she accidentally disconnected several callers—including Carolyn Kline, who immediately called back—and continued to make inane remarks, Stevie was grateful for the company as well as for the temporary distraction.

42

After half an hour, however, the novelty was wearing off. Stevie was beginning to feel that she was a prisoner in her own home, her bedroom akin to a cell shared by a sitcom secretary who didn't have the brains or tact to know when to speak and when to shut up.

The aftereffects of the doctor's sedative, on top of the reasons for it in the first place, were taking their toll, too. Stevie felt as though her entire nervous system were poised on the surface of her being and ready to explode at the slightest provocation.

"I was thinking," Carla said during a lull in the phones, "that maybe some of this is like the war thing in the Persian Gulf, y'know?"

Stevie wondered if Carla had fallen to earth from Mars. "The war thing?" she repeated.

"Yeah. What I mean is, like, everybody was glued to the tube for a month. Even if you didn't want to watch, you couldn't tear yourself away, y'know? So maybe you'd feel better if you turned on the TV."

Stevie shrugged. Obviously Carla had hit on a brainstorm. And obviously she'd tell Stevie, whether Stevie wanted to hear it or not.

"Why will the TV make me feel better, Carla?"

Jill's stand-in reached for the remote control and handed it to Stevie. "Because," she explained, "you'll watch the news and there won't be anything about Todd, so you'll know he's okay. Like that old saying, 'No news is good news.' "

"Oh." Stevie pressed ON, but not from belief in proverbs. Having the TV on would preclude further conversation with Carla. It wasn't much, but it was something.

Eight

Eppie Goldwyn checked her reflection in the smoke-tinted glass entrance to Hubert Braddock Publications, Inc. She wasn't displeased with what she saw, although she wished she'd had time for her hair appointment that morning. Never mind; by the time the hordes of media vultures woke up and smelled the coffee, Eppie would have time for touch-ups and leg waxings and nail wrappings *and* the glory. Hell, she'd probably wind up with the Pulitzer for writing the story of the decade.

And there was an added incentive by the name of Carolyn Kline. Neé Carolyn Stein, "altered" to Stone. Accuracy, Eppie, if you want to cop the Pulitzer.

The thought of that extra perk put a swing in her step as she alighted from the elevator and headed for her publisher's office.

"Hubie!" she gushed, ignoring Braddock's secretary and breezing into the inner sanctum. "Have I got a story for you!"

She seated herself on the black tufted-leather sofa and waited for Hubert Braddock to come to her. He rose from the chair behind his six-foot slate desk and approached the sofa, where he and Eppie greeted each other with air-kisses.

"You're looking well," he said.

"Likewise, Hubie. As always." She flashed her pollinated lashes and took the position of a lady-in-waiting, crossing her legs at the ankles and posing at the edge of the sofa cushion.

Hubert Braddock was accustomed to the range of ploys in Eppie's repertoire. Since the long-ago day on his yacht when a guest had died mysteriously. According to published reports, Hubert Braddock had gone ashore to interview an ambitious young reporter named Iphigenia Gold, who subsequently added a syllable to her name and a job to her résumé.

A job for life. Her employer understood that the contract included an unwritten rider: Eppie could have whatever she wanted.

So he couldn't help wondering what she wanted this time.

Their meeting had gone as Eppie expected, and she was beaming with satisfaction. "Hubie," she said, tucking her pink-and-gold pen back into her purse, "you're an absolute doll. You always make me feel like the luckiest reporter in town."

"And you always make me feel as if I have a choice," he answered.

Eppie tried her best to look coy as she said, "I'm really a terrific person, Hubie, once people get to know me."

That prompted a smile, although Braddock carried so much facial tension that his grin could be mistaken for a smirk.

It had no effect on Eppie either way. She had no romantic interest in Hubert Braddock—his lips were too thin for her taste—but every now and then it was fun to flirt. Flirting had a way of making her feel young. Just now, though, she felt it was a waste of time and energy, so she turned strictly business.

"Much as I'd love to sit and schmooze, Hubie darling, I'll be running along. After all, my exclusive won't get written here, will it?" She pressed his arm with unfelt affection and waited until she reached the doorway to offer her exit line. "This will make the Lindbergh kidnapping pale by comparison, I promise!"

"I don't doubt it, Eppie," said Hubert Braddock.

He watched her teeter down the corridor on her spindle-thin patent-leather high heels and marveled. Whatever else she was—and she was a lot of things he despised—there was no getting away from the fact: Eppie Goldwyn *was* one helluva reporter.

And he wouldn't envy anyone who tried to stand between Eppie and her story.

Nine

The sun's glare reflected in the mirrored lenses of Galvin's glasses. A great opening shot, Ansel noted, except that it had been done before. He pushed the image from his mind. This was a hell of a time to be thinking pictures.

Without asking, Galvin readjusted the sun umbrella and eased his generous frame into the delicate wrought-iron garden chair.

"That's better," he said to Ansel. "I can see you now."

"Sorry. This is the only place we can get away from the phones."

Galvin nodded. Kline was right, but the house was much cooler. From the pocket of his rumpled suit he withdrew a pen, a small pad, and a Zippo lighter, each item landing with a *clink* on the round glass table between them.

"Lieutenant, about this morning's . . . news."

"I'll be getting to that, Mr. Kline." He took a sip of the coffee Ansel had prepared, and with the mug gestured toward the pool. "Bet that comes in handy on a scorcher like this."

Ansel glanced at his watch.

"In a hurry?"

"To find my son? Yes. *Asshole.*

"We are, too. I'll want a look at the nursery."

"Your people found nothing up there."

Okay, Mr. Kline. We'll play this your way. Galvin proceeded in a more formal tone.

"You no longer reside here. Is that correct?"

"Yes."

"But at present you're making a film with Mrs. Kline." Galvin reached for the pad and pen.

"The contracts were signed before our separation."

"Would you say, then, that you feel forced to work together?"

"Stevie's a very good actress, Lieutenant, and . . ."

"She was granted custody of your son, right?"

"Wives usually are."

"Jealous?"

"I felt badly."

Galvin was writing as he spoke. "Your mother notified the police?"

"You know that."

"Yes, I do. I'll be talking to her later. Does she get along with your wife?"

"What are you asking?"

He'd struck a nerve. "Just routine. Your father?"

"Deceased."

"And your wife's family?"

"She was orphaned in infancy."

"Tough break. She do any drugs, Mr. Kline?"

"Now, look—"

"What about you, Mr. Kline?"

Ansel took a moment to calm himself. "Years ago. When everybody did. A little grass once in a while. This is Hollywood, Lieutenant."

"I was born here. You?"

"New York."

"The nanny." He leafed through the pages of his notebook. "Jill Denson. You trust her?"

"We did. She came from the Van Heusen Agency."

"The good ones do. Miss Franzen, too?"

"No. She works part-time for my business partner. That's how we found her."

"Were you on the set all morning yesterday?"

"Yes. I never left."

"Who did?"

"There were over a hundred people working, Lieutenant. Ask my ADs. Or Mr. Hemmings. You know him."

"I do. And I will." Galvin picked up the lighter. "Now. Who hates you, Mr. Kline?"

"No one I can think of."

"Think harder. A couple as successful as the two of you don't get this far without making a few enemies."

"You mean this might not be cult-related?"

"We're just covering every angle. I'm not talking only acquaintances here. Anybody. Strangers, weirdos."

Mike Galvin was an irritating son of a bitch, but Ansel had to concede that he might have a point. And anything—almost anything—seemed preferable to the thought of Todd in the hands of satanists.

"Weirdos," Ansel said suddenly. "There's one. Come with me. I'll show you."

Galvin followed Ansel through the glass doors back into the house. It was a relief to be out of the heat. They passed a dressing room and bath, then entered a large study. The phone rang, and Ansel stopped dead. It rang once more, then fell silent.

"Carla's got it." Ansel went directly to the wall lined with shelves of film books and videotapes. Galvin leaned against the large oak desk covered with scripts. "Have a seat, Lieutenant," said Ansel, gesturing Galvin to the tweed sofa that faced the forty-inch TV monitor while he pushed a tape into the VCR.

"This is a tape of our baby shower."

Galvin remembered when showers were for the mother-to-be, no men allowed. He also remembered that movie people belonged to a different species.

Ansel fast-forwarded on the remote until he found the spot. "Here, Lieutenant, keep your eye on the entrance hall."

Galvin noted that the house had been redecorated since the shower—maybe since the separation. Not overdone, but not what he'd call a dump, either.

The camera panned a crowd of famous names and faces. Everyone in black. Close-up on a three-year-old girl in a studded leather jacket and black chiffon skirt. Trendy. Creepy, too. Cut to a long shot of the room. In the foreground, a very pregnant Stephanie Kean was waving at the lens. She wore dusty rose, the only color.

Galvin finished the last of his coffee, then placed the mug on the table beside the sofa. He recalled hearing about "our shower" from Lyle Hemmings, during a then-weekly poker game at Lyle's house in West Hollywood four years ago. The poker games had ended with Lyle's move to the thirty-room mansion in Beverly Hills, the place that Galvin had yet to see.

Galvin studied the screen as an elegant woman, sixtyish, stepped into the frame. She looked like Ansel Kline with a nose job and frosted blond hair.

"Stevie, darling!" she gushed, crushing her daughter-in-law with her embrace. "My grandchild will watch this one day! Say something to him—or her!"

Stevie hooded her eyelids and, in a decent imitation of Garbo, murmured, "I vant to be alone." She leaned closer into the lens and added, "Vith your father—if I could find him!"

"You didn't shoot this?" asked Galvin.

"My cameraman." Ansel hesitated, then added, "I was busy." He'd been in this very room, with Lyle, closing a deal with the head of production at Touchstone. Stevie hadn't let him forget it.

The guests' backs now faced the camera, their attention focused on a disturbance in the entrance foyer. Sounds of raised voices in the background, then a short, overweight woman in her early or mid-thirties rushed to the center of the room—and center stage. Zoom in on the acne-scarred face, the prematurely gray hair. Wardrobe in keeping with the theme: black overalls.

"That's who I was talking about," Ansel said to Galvin.

She offered a manic smile and said, as if to them alone, "My name is Tammi—with an *i!* And I've seen *Off Season* nine times! Stevie, you deserve an Oscar!" The shot pulled back in time to capture Tammi as she moved toward the guest of honor. Stevie's features were frozen. Tammi reached over and placed her hands on Stevie's stomach, as if discovering a treasure. Her lips moved, but her words were covered by someone yelling for the police.

"What'd she say?" asked Galvin.

"Star baby," Ansel replied.

The lieutenant said nothing, but jotted down the answer on his pad. The mother of each abducted child was a star.

From off-camera, a hand came to rest on Tammi's shoulder. A deep male voice spoke to her, and she turned to him.

"You got here late, Tammi. The party's almost over." His tone was gentle, polite. "Won't you let me escort you to the door?"

She nodded and took his arm. The crowd cleared a path. As Galvin watched the man lead her out of camera range toward the entrance foyer, he thought he recognized the face.

"Quite a freak show," he said. "Who's the guy?"

"One of the bodyguards we'd hired for the day. We figured something like Tammi might happen. She'd bothered us before."

"The guy's name wouldn't be Joe Madden, would it?"

"Matter of fact, it is. Why? You know him?"

"Knew him. Used to be on the force. Booze."

"He was sober that day. The other times, too. We hired him whenever we entertained on a large scale. We . . . I haven't seen him in a while."

"Well, I hope he pulled himself together," said Galvin. "Otherwise he's cheating his clients. I hear he's got himself a PI license these days." He put away his pad and pen. "Let me borrow that tape. I'll get stills made so I can circulate photos of Tammi." He made a mental note to talk to Joe Madden about her, too.

Ansel hit the Rewind. "I don't know if this helps, but whenever Stevie has a new picture opening, Tammi shows up out of nowhere. And a couple of times we've caught her rummaging through our garbage."

"How recently?"

"About six months ago."

"January," Galvin said.

Ansel knew what he meant. "That's when the first child disappeared."

"The Delaney boy. It all started in January."

The tape came to a stop. Ansel removed the cassette and handed it to Galvin. "Do you mind if we get some air?"

It was even hotter now. Galvin didn't need air. He needed a cigarette. With elbows propped on the glass table, he flipped the lid of his Zippo.

53

"Okay," said Ansel. "What about these murders?"

Galvin had put his sunglasses back on, and through them he glanced at Ansel Kline's trembling hands, then at his face. The jaw muscles were tightly set, the veins in his neck tense. "Well, we're fairly certain this morning's discovery was the first victim. The Delaney boy. It fits the Travers case."

"You mean the condition of the bodies?"

"More than that. I'll explain to you, Mr. Kline, but the less your wife is told—"

"She's already seen it on TV. I couldn't help it."

Galvin muttered "shit" under his breath, then said, "At least they don't have enough to spell it out."

"Spell what out?"

"It's pretty grisly stuff. Both of the bodies appear to have been, to varying degrees, dismembered."

Ansel went white. Galvin waited for him to take several deep breaths before he continued.

"The Travers body was . . . in better shape. We found him after two weeks. It'll be tougher with this one. The Delaney boy has been missing since—"

"January," Ansel supplied.

"Right. But there's a glitch in all this. It could work in your child's favor."

"What do you mean?"

"We haven't given it to the media, but there was a ransom note for the second victim, Andrew Landau."

"A ransom note?" Ansel repeated. "You just said he's still missing."

Galvin nodded without replying.

"Lieutenant, why would they kill only two of the three kids?"

"We don't know."

"Did the Landaus pay?"

"They paid. A quarter of a million. Without telling us."

Ansel was having difficulty processing the information. "Wait. How do you know the Landau boy isn't dead?"

"We don't. It's a possibility."

"There's an awful lot you don't know, Lieutenant."

"And a lot we do."

"Let me get this straight," said Ansel. "You're saying that a ransom note would be a good sign?"

"It could be." Galvin flipped through his pad. "With the Landau boy's disappearance, except for the ransom note, we saw a pattern emerging. Brought in some experts. Worked out some dates."

"Experts on what?"

"Demonology." Galvin found the pages he was looking for and began reading aloud. "Freddie Travers. Age fourteen months. Missing since June ninth. Found June twenty-fifth, buried at a construction site. Estimated time of death on or about June twenty-third." He glanced up. "That's the Eve of St. John the Baptist on the Christian calendar, but it's the spring sabbat for devil worshipers." He went back to his notes.

"Andrew Landau, age eleven months. Missing since April sixteenth. April thirtieth, *Walpurges-*

nacht. It's another satanic holiday. The ransom note was received on April twentieth."

"And this morning, Donny Delaney," Ansel said.

"Age one year. Gone since January nineteenth. Found partially buried in a landfill." Galvin closed and pocketed his notepad. "February second is called Candlemas. A witches' winter mass."

"This is nuts!" cried Ansel. "Stevie's half out of her mind already! What the hell do I tell her?"

"As little as possible." This time it was Galvin who checked his watch. "I'll want to talk to the substitute nanny while I'm here. Then I'll have some questions for your wife."

"Stevie's smart. She'll have questions of her own."

"I'll answer them, without the graphic details."

"Such as?"

Galvin removed the sunglasses to rub his eyes and to buy time to measure his words. "Our experts think these children are being used as human sacrifices to Satan. Part of a ritual in which certain body parts are . . . devoured."

"You don't mean—"

"Cannibalism, Mr. Kline."

Ansel's head began to swim. His mind raced through an instant replay of the whole crazy nightmare.

"Today is July eighteenth," he said at last. "Every child has been kidnapped two weeks before a black mass, right, Lieutenant?"

"Yes."

"What's the next one?"

Galvin didn't need to consult his notes. "Lamas Day. The summer sabbat."

"That's August first, isn't it?"

"Yes, Mr. Kline," said Galvin. "We've got fourteen days."

Ten

Fourteen days. If Ansel's nerves were frayed before Lt. Galvin's visit, they were in shreds after his disclosures. How much had the lieutenant told Stevie? Ansel should be with her; she'd wonder why he hadn't come back upstairs the moment Galvin was gone. And she must know he'd left; his car had been parked in the driveway directly below the master-bedroom windows.

Galvin had probably come up with a story that was somewhere between the truth and the TV reports. Ansel hoped the detective had demonstrated more subtlety with Stevie than he had with him.

Ansel felt dizzy. No, he *was* dizzy, his physical reaction to the fear and horror he felt.

He needed to calm himself before he went upstairs. He was somehow able to tune out the sounds of the ringing phones, even the babble of the army gathered outside the house. But Galvin's words kept repeating in his ear.

He remembered what he and Stevie had jokingly called their pharmacy. It was a drawer under one of the kitchen cabinets, in which they kept the usual store of over-the-counter medications and vitamins. Maybe Stevie had, over these past months, added Valium to her cache of cold remedies and headache pills.

Ansel had. He'd never used tranquilizers or sleeping pills, but since the separation, especially after a heavy, stressful day on the set, he'd considered it. His doctor had given him a prescription—only five milligrams worth—just in case. Until now, he'd opted instead for a brandy before bed, and the little bottle still sat, unopened, in the medicine cabinet at his half-furnished "bachelor digs" in Westwood.

It was too early in the day for brandy, so Ansel opened the kitchen drawer.

No luck. All he found was children's aspirin.

As he was leaving the kitchen, Ansel noticed that the phones had stopped ringing. He glanced at the unit alongside the electric coffeemaker and saw that all the lights were blinking except for the one on the far right. That meant someone, Carla or Stevie, must be using the private line.

Galvin had said not to make outgoing calls from the private number. But of course it wasn't Ansel's private number anymore, and maybe the lieutenant had forgotten to tell Stevie to keep the line free. Better remind her now. It was one way to begin, as good a way as any other.

Ansel was halfway up the stairs when the doorbell rang. He started to shout for Carla, realized that Stevie might be asleep, and went to the door himself.

Lyle Hemmings was peering into the camera on the security TV that was mounted on the wall inside the entrance.

Christ! Ansel had forgotten that it was a scheduled workday. The reaction shots from yesterday's shoot. Wait. They'd closed down immediately following the news of Todd.

Ansel hoped Lyle had remembered to call a temporary halt in production. Or rescheduled to shoot around Stevie. She'd be out of commission until they found Todd, and only then if these satanic psychos hadn't—

Stop it, Ansel! Just open the goddammed door!

"Jesus, man, you look like death warmed over," said Lyle over the crescendo of reporters' voices as Ansel hurried to shut the door.

"Thanks. That's exactly what I don't need to hear."

"How's Stevie?" asked Lyle.

"How do you think? Sorry. I didn't mean that the way it sounded. She's holding up, I guess. Maybe better than I am."

"Have the cops made any progress?"

Ansel shook his head. "Your pal Galvin just left."

"And?"

"The way he sees it, there are three main possibilities. The cult he's investigating, or Tammi-the-nut-case-fan, or me." He tried for a laugh, but it stuck in his throat.

"That's a joke, isn't it? About Mike suspecting you?"

"I'm not sure. His manner didn't read like comedy."

"Sometimes Mike has a slight attitude problem," said Lyle. "But he's one sharp guy."

"Good. Maybe if he doesn't let attitude interfere, he'll find Todd." Ansel was reminded that he still needed to talk to Stevie. He lowered his voice to make sure it wouldn't carry up the stairs. "Come into the study."

On the way down the long terra-cotta-tiled hallway, Ansel filled Lyle in on Galvin's theories. When they reached the room where Galvin had viewed the baby-shower tape, Ansel felt as though he himself were trapped in a limbo of instant replay.

Lyle was usually revved up like one of his three-hundred-thousand-dollar custom-made Italian racing cars. This morning, he listened without interruption.

When Ansel had finished, Lyle sat back on the tweed sofa and said, "I didn't realize there was an actual pattern in these kidnappings. I wouldn't have reacted so casually at the studio yesterday."

"I didn't even notice, Lyle. I'm sure Stevie didn't, either. Besides, none of that's important. The only thing that matters is getting Todd back. Safe and . . . unharmed."

"Look, Mike is right. The ransom note sounds

hopeful. If Todd was kidnapped by a cult that's started demanding ransoms—"

"Only in the case of Andy Landau, so far," Ansel cut in.

"Yeah, but he's the kid who's still missing!" Lyle's energy was moving into high gear again. "Don't you see, Ansel? If the cult is going for bread all of a sudden, it means they're more interested in money than in sacrificing kids." He looked away, as though he'd said too much.

"It's all right, Lyle," said Ansel. "You weren't about to say anything I haven't thought of already."

"No, it isn't that."

"What, then?"

Lyle was tapping his manicured fingernails on the table beside the sofa.

"D'you mind, Lyle? That drives me nuts."

The tapping stopped. "Okay. Call it lousy timing, but . . . I'm a little short of cash."

Lyle was right; it was lousy timing.

"Something wrong, Lyle?"

"No. Well, I just overextended myself a little."

"By how little?"

Lyle hesitated.

"I need thirty-five hundred. Just till Monday."

It was already Thursday.

When Ansel didn't answer, Lyle said, "If you can't do that much, a few grand would be okay."

The hell with timing. "For Chrissake, Lyle, you spent fifteen thousand last week on a ship's figurehead for your den!"

"Ansel, it's not for me. I owe this guy."

"Look, I know we agreed not to interfere with each other's personal lives."

"Yeah, well—"

"Lyle! I'm your business partner! Don't pull this crap with me! I see you making all those trips to the john. If you've got a bladder problem, see a doctor!" Ansel's face was red with anger. "On top of that, you've got the balls to come here and ask me for money when my son—your godson!—is who-knows-where!"

His outburst silenced them both.

Lyle rose slowly from the sofa. "You're right, Ansel. I'm sorry. I didn't mean to drag you into it, with Todd still . . . well, with so much happening. I'd better get over to the studio. I'm setting up a meeting with the cast-insurance people to check out our options. Don't worry about it. I'll handle everything, including my . . . problem. Love to Stevie."

Lyle started for the door.

"Wait a sec," Ansel said, pulling out some bills from his money clip. "I can give you three hundred. It's all the cash I've got on me."

"Thanks, Ansel, but . . ."

"Hey. You're my partner."

Eleven

The reporters were still leaning against their cars or news vans as they schmoozed and speculated and waited for something to break in the Todd Kline story. They were so intent on watching the house, they didn't notice Carolyn Kline's gunmetal-gray Mercedes, which stood, its motor idling, a short distance down the road.

Carolyn was waiting, too. She didn't think Eppie Goldwyn would dare show her face—and the hideous pink Cadillac was nowhere in sight. But she'd spotted Lyle Hemmings's red Ferrari parked in the circular driveway. Carolyn wanted her son's full attention, and wasn't about to share it with his business partner. She was counting on Lyle's customary wired energy to speed him on his way.

She wasn't disappointed. Five minutes later, she saw the red Ferrari zoom by. Carolyn slowly inched her own car past the news vans. Even though she wore dark glasses and a straw hat, the Hollywood paparazzi weren't fooled. Shouts of "Hey, there's Momma!" were heard as she drove by. Carolyn offered the cameras an imperious scowl, a visual reprimand for their having recorded her importance in the drama. Tragedy.

Stevie had refused another sedative injection from Dr. Fuller, but she accepted a prescription for Valium. Jerry Fuller left a week's supply on the dresser, but Stevie put the bottle into a drawer the moment he left. She didn't want to take the pills unless it became absolutely necessary. The blur from last night's medication had begun to lift during the interview with Lt. Galvin, and she had no desire to return to a zombielike state.

Just now she felt like a different kind of zombie. Everyone around her was handling whatever needed handling—except Stevie. While she was grateful, she couldn't help feeling resentment toward this sense of uselessness being forced upon her.

Because the thought of a long soak in the tub appealed to her, she rejected it. With Todd gone—missing—the smallest pleasure seemed like an act of betrayal. But so did inaction. It was going on noon and she hadn't done a goddam thing.

She hung up the damp towel Ansel had left on the bathroom floor. Before the separation, it had been a daily source of annoyance. Now it was just a damp towel on the floor.

Stevie watched through the window as Lyle drove off. Carla was downstairs juggling calls. The police were outside keeping the media at bay. If no one else showed up for fifteen minutes, she and Ansel could talk. She was showered and dressed in ten.

* * *

"Mr. Kline!" Carla called from the kitchen. "Miss Halsey's on line two and your agent's on three!"

"Fuck," Ansel whispered. Then, speaking into the cordless phone, he said to his production manager, "Myron, I've got to go. It's been crazy for the last hour. . . . Look, I *know* we've got to move on what to do . . . Lyle just left to meet with the studio and insurance people. . . . No, he was here. . . . Well, just stall them till Lyle gets back with some answers."

He hung up and added another reminder to the two pages of notes for Lyle. He glanced at the nearby phone unit on his desk. Its blinking lights told him that his assistant and his agent were still on hold. The private-line button remained dark. Was that good or bad?

He took a quick sip of tepid coffee as a third line lit up.

"Mr. Kline!" shouted Carla. "It's your publicist!"

"Tell Al that Barbara will call him back!" Ansel yelled, going to the desk unit and pushing line two. "Barbara? It's a madhouse. . . . No, I want you here at the house. Carla's helping out, but she needs a breather. . . . Yeah, so do I . . .

"I don't know. Look, call Gary and map out a statement for him to give the media, maybe that'll get them off our necks. I'll want to read it before it airs, and I want it here within the hour."

66

He pushed line three. Line one began to ring again.

"Hi, Sue. No, I *can't* say how this affects my November schedule, and . . . I don't speak for Stevie."

He felt a slight movement of air and looked up. Stevie was standing in the doorway of the study. She was holding on to her coffee mug as if its grip represented her hold on life, but the color had returned to her cheeks. Without makeup, and her still-wet hair hanging loosely around her face and shoulders, she looked like a child who had stayed up past her bedtime.

"Sue," said Ansel, "I'll call you later. Just vamp with Universal for now."

He hung up.

"Well," Stevie said, closing the door behind her. "That's a first."

Ansel was still clutching the cordless phone. He laid it on its stand alongside the desk set and offered a tired smile. "I guess it is. How do you feel?"

Stevie shrugged and flopped down on the sofa. "As if I've been run over by a steamroller." She curled up with her feet under her. "I'm glad you're here. Any word?"

Ansel shook his head.

"I didn't think so."

"We'll find him, Stevie."

"Talking with the lieutenant helped. It gives the whole thing—"

The phone rang again, and conditioned reflexes made Stevie stop in midsentence, just as Ansel's reflexes made him reach for the receiver. But he jerked his arm away. Carla could get it.

"—a kind of reality," Stevie continued, as though they hadn't been interrupted. "I've got to start facing the reality."

"What did Galvin tell you?"

"Everything he told you, I imagine."

Ansel hoped not.

"They're questioning the neighbors."

"Maybe that'll turn up something."

Stevie's expression all but said, "It won't and we both know it won't." Ansel reminded himself not to patronize her; she wasn't a fragile hothouse flower.

"Ansel," said Stevie, "I've got to say this, just once."

"What?"

Her eyes rimmed with tears. "I'm sorry."

"Me, too."

He wanted to go to her. But he didn't. Couldn't. And knew she understood.

"Stevie," he began, "when this is all over . . ."

She held up a hand to silence him. "Ansel . . . we don't know . . . what that . . . will mean." She took a piece of Kleenex from her jeans pocket and dabbed at her eyes. After several swallows, she almost managed a smile. "God! I didn't think I had any tears left!" She blew her nose into the rumpled tissue. "All right. Now. What can I do?"

The doorbell chimed. Once, twice, with an impatience seemingly its own. Then voices from the foyer.

Stevie looked at Ansel. "Timing really *is* everything, isn't it?"

He wasn't permitted a reply. The study door opened and Carolyn Kline made her entrance.

Twelve

The last person Stevie felt capable of dealing with this morning was Ansel's mother. She fumbled with an excuse, all the while aware that she owed Carolyn none and reprimanding herself for making the attempt.

"I'll be upstairs," she said to Ansel and the space that separated him from their perfectly coiffed, immaculately dressed intruder.

But upstairs was worse. With Carla in the kitchen playing secretary, the twenty-two-foot-square bedroom was suddenly as stifling as a closet. Funny, this room was four times bigger than the cubicle Stevie had shared with three other girls as a child, yet today it was short on space.

She walked to the double-thick, bulletproof windows that had until yesterday offered the illusion of safety. Nothing could enter, but nothing could escape. Hermetically sealed and still no guarantees. She'd pointed that out more than once to Ansel. Healthier to breathe the air, polluted or not—at least have the option. Wasn't that the original idea behind the move to Beachwood Canyon?

To steer clear of the hedge-hidden fortresses on the tour-bus route? The grounds were carpeted with gorgeous flowers, but how could their perfume penetrate such modern-day "security"?

To be fair, Ansel hadn't gone paranoid about security before Todd's birth—not Hollywood-paranoid, at any rate. But ten thousand dollars' worth of electronic surveillance equipment hadn't kept a party-crasher named Tammi out, had it?

Lt. Galvin had mentioned several possibilities, no doubt to veer Stevie away from the cult. Probably why he'd asked so many questions about the pending divorce and her custody of Todd—as if *Ansel* would ever kidnap his own son!

The detective had also hinted that perhaps it was an inside job; someone had to know the numeric keypad combination in order to disable the alarm system. But Stevie had a simpler answer. Jill Denson was dyslexic. She couldn't memorize the combination. So, during the day, the system wasn't activated. Stevie hadn't told Ansel—he'd have fired Jill on the spot. Stevie, however, knew that Jill compensated for her difficulty by never letting Todd out of her sight.

Until yesterday.

Again Stevie couldn't shake her own feeling of blame.

Do something! urged the voice that was becoming a constant companion. *It's the only way you'll ever assuage the guilt. And the only way you'll ever find Todd.*

* * *

71

The house was under siege as it had been all morning—on the inside by the police, then by Carla, Lt. Galvin, Lyle, and now by Carolyn Kline; outside, the reporters hadn't budged. And weren't likely to until they had more news.

Stevie had to get out. She'd lose her mind if she didn't.

But where would she go? To Barbara's? No, Barb was coming to the house to help Ansel. Besides, how could Stevie leave without being seen or followed?

Wait. She could impersonate Carla. Stevie was an inch or so taller, but they were both slim and she wouldn't stand still long enough for comparison. Carla was dishwater blonde, but Stevie could hide her own auburn hair under a scarf.

She chose the most unglamorous silk square she could find—a long-ago gift from Carolyn in muddied yellows and greens, two of Stevie's least favorite colors—and a pair of sunglasses with oversize frames and darkest bottle-green lenses. She exchanged her silk shirt for a cotton tee; the jeans were fine, and with flat-heeled sandals, she'd even match Carla's height.

Next. How to tell Ansel without getting an argument from him, let alone God-knew-what from his mother?

She could leave a note. She was hunting for paper and pencil when she reconsidered. A note was cowardly. She'd call him on the private line from the mobile phone in the car.

Which car? Ansel's vintage Jaguar was parked in the front driveway, but his Range Rover, even after the separation, was still sitting alongside Stevie's Lexus in the garage. The Rover had neither radio nor phone, so the Lexus was the only choice. Stevie wished now that she'd opted for a standard color, something nondescript like sky-blue or gray, instead of a customized metallic bordeaux.

Forget the color. Forget the car. She had yet to make it down the stairs—unnoticed—then get to the garage—also unnoticed—and *then* drive past the SRO crowd outside.

Without being seen? Who the hell was she kidding?

By inching her way along the walls and crawling on all fours to the indoor garage entrance across Todd's playroom floor, Stevie finally reached her goal.

She was exhausted. From worry and inaction, but most of all from the absurdity of having to sneak out of her own home. The situation bore tragi-comic aspects and confirmed what Stevie had always suspected: that despite her filmed portrayals of women in peril triumphing over incredible odds, her screen terrors didn't begin to approach the real-life fears she'd experienced in the twenty-four hours since Todd's disappearance.

She timed her opening of the automatic garage door to coincide with her turning of the ignition key, so the moment the car had overhead clearance, she could gun the motor and be on her way. Funny, Ansel was the one who'd insisted on the ES 250 because of its extraordinary power; Stevie had agreed only because the Lexus was less extravagant than some of the other sports sedans she'd seen. Now she was grateful for the added horsepower; it offered freedom.

Freedom for what, Stevie?

To think. Even though sometimes it seemed better not to think.

Stevie was halfway down the winding road before any of the reporters recognized her or the car she was driving. And by then it was too late.

She slowed only so she wouldn't be stopped for speeding. She had no particular destination in mind as she turned on Franklin, then on through downtown Hollywood, which looked far seedier than when she'd come to town ten years ago.

She passed Mann's Theatre and the rose-colored walk with its eight decades of celebrities' names engraved on brass stars. One of them bore her name. It always amazed Stevie the way tourists flocked here.

And fans. Stevie watched through her rearview mirror as a group of them surrounded a tall, lanky brunette. From the wild mane of jet-black Carmen curls and the black leather ensemble, this had to be Cher in the flesh or a perfect double. Stevie had met the genuine article, but just now even she wasn't sure. The shutterbugs raised their cameras to shoot. One of them, a sloppily clad woman who was short and stout, bore a strong resemblance to the Tammi-wacko Lt. Galvin had questioned Stevie about.

The woman turned. Her face was unfamiliar, but Stevie's uneasiness increased at the thought that one of these fans might be obsessed enough to kidnap a star's child. Or worse.

Stevie waited for the traffic light to change at the intersection of Hollywood and Vine. There was a print shop at the corner. In the window was a framed copy of the Hopper-inspired painting. There they were: Monroe, Dean, Bogart, and Presley. She remembered the title: "Boulevard of Broken Dreams." Never had it held such meaning.

The sign read: SANTA MONICA FREEWAY.

The freeway? Christ, this must be what losing it was about. She hated the freeways, went out of her way to avoid them whenever she could, and here she was, driving toward . . .

The ocean. *Didn't you know you were headed there from the moment you left the house?*

It wasn't so crazy, after all. Since childhood, the ocean had calmed her when nothing else could. The single joy still remembered—still treasured—from her first eighteen years was the Home's proximity to the ocean. She'd hiked miles, climbed walls and fences, to reach the water, only to be found, reprimanded, punished for running away. Yet the forces within her were stronger than those without. It was as if part of her life's blood came from the ocean.

If she stayed on the freeway, she'd wind up at

Malibu; she was almost there now. She hoped she wouldn't be recognized or bump into anyone she knew.

It was hotter, despite the ocean breezes. Stevie parked the car in a spot that was shaded by the rear-entrance awning of a roadside café. She checked the name out front so she'd be able to retrace her steps later. She was surprised—and at the same time not surprised—to find that it was the same place where she and Ansel had come on Oscar night six years before.

The restaurant had changed, just as everything in their lives had changed. Then, the adobelike facade had been painted coral; now it was turquoise blue.

Stevie smiled to herself. They hadn't been able to see the color until sunrise the next morning. They'd sneaked away from Swifty Lazar's post-Oscar party at Spago just the way Stevie had always sneaked away from the Home. The way she'd sneaked off today.

"I've got an idea," he'd said, leaning over to whisper in her ear. "Let's cut out of here."

"But it's early," she'd said.

"It won't be, all night."

"I know . . ."

"C'mon, it's not as if this is your first trip to the Oscars."

Couldn't he see that it was? That she was only here because the studio had fixed her up as the date of a gay male star who was afraid of what

coming out might do to his career? He and another actor were already conspicuously absent from
the table.

Ansel seemed to read her mind. "He's not coming back, you know."

"I know."

"You've said that twice."

She started to say it again, stopped herself, and
they both laughed. "Look, Mr. Kline—"

"Ansel. Mister is pompous. And I'm not famous
enough to be pompous. I will be, though."

"Famous or pompous?" She was starting to enjoy the banter. Something in Ansel Kline's manner
made her trust him. Maybe because he didn't seem
to be asking her to. "Trust me" was the Hollywood
euphemism for "fuck you," synonymous with "I
can keep a secret" at the Home. Stevie hadn't come
to Tinseltown completely unprepared.

"I've been dreaming about this night since I was
five," she heard herself say aloud. Christ, she'd
meant it, but she hadn't planned to *voice* it!

"Dreamed of what?" he asked. "Of attending
the awards? Of Wolfgang's pizza? Or of sneaking
off with a director who's going to win that statue
next year and who's trying to use that to lure you
out of here with him?"

His eyes twinkled with intelligence and humor,
and either he sensed that she was smart, too, or
he was clever enough to flatter her into thinking
he did.

"Stephanie Kean," he said. "I must hear it from
your lips. Is my attempt to impress you having any
effect at all?"

Stevie made a purposeful show of carefully considering his question.

"Well, I'm not sure. Maybe I should stand up. If my knees buckle under me, your answer is yes."

"Otherwise?"

"Otherwise, you're better off with someone else. As you said, it won't be early all night."

She did stand up. And her knees, while not buckling under her, did tremble. Not from passion but because her shoes were pure torture. Since four-thirty that afternoon her toes had been trapped inside sandals teetering on four-inch, spindle-thin heels. In retaliation, her feet refused to support her now.

Ansel offered his arm, she accepted, and they left. Simple as that. She wasn't sure whether to take him seriously—God knew she didn't take most of tonight's "performance" seriously—but she'd been smiling since stepping from the limo at six that evening, and her back teeth had begun to lock. Ansel Kline, interestingly enough, had made her smile without the slightest tension in her jaw.

They drove to Malibu because it was that kind of night. And they stopped alongside a roadside café not because they were hungry—the café was closed—but because Ansel's Jaguar had developed a cough.

With anyone else, Stevie would have been suspicious about the engine rattle, but Ansel Kline didn't come on like any of the guys she usually had to fend off. A director who didn't promise a girl instant stardom to get her in bed was worth investigating further—at least to find out whether he was real, or if his honesty was just another form of strategy.

They took off their shoes and walked along in silence under the starlit sky.

"Just like in the movies," Stevie said, wiggling her toes in the damp sand.

"Almost," he said, extending his thumbs and four fingers to form a rectangle and holding it up to his eyes. "We could use a moon."

" 'Oh, Jerry,' " she recited, " 'don't let's ask for the moon; we have the stars.' "

"Your Bette Davis is pretty good."

"My Katharine Hepburn's even better."

Now, Voyager," he said. "Would you believe it, my mother sobs buckets—goes through a whole box of Kleenex—every time it's on TV."

"Me, too," Stevie admitted.

"Well, that's probably the single thing you and my mother have in common." He laughed, then added, "At least I hope so."

"Why?"

"Because I'm going to marry you."

That stopped her. The damp night air, or the champagne, or the excitement of the evening made her heart race, and for a moment she couldn't speak.

Then she recovered. "You sound awfully sure of yourself. The same as when you talk about winning the Oscar."

"You think it's too direct?" he asked.

"Maybe not with the Oscar. Definitely with the lady."

"But I'm going to win."

"Which?" she asked.

"Both," he said.

At the post-Awards party at Spago the following year, Stevie teased him, but not unkindly. "Look at it this way, Ansel. One out of two isn't half bad."

They'd been married for ten months, and although Ansel had received his first nomination for best director, he hadn't copped the statue. Nonetheless, Kline-Hemmings Productions was becoming known as a team to be reckoned with, and Stephanie Kean was establishing her own name in the industry. They talked of making movies together, but Stevie still had commitments with other studios.

Making a baby was easier. By the time she was contractually free to star in a film directed by Ansel, she was pregnant.

"I'm due at the end of March," she said. "If it's a boy, we can name *him* Oscar."

Over her mother-in-law's dead body.

They named him Todd.

"It's Ansel's middle name," Carolyn insisted, rehashing again the way, years before, the famous Mike Todd had saved Ansel's father from ruin.

Stevie capitulated. Still, Carolyn couldn't resist. "The baby's name shouldn't hold any importance for you, anyway, Stephanie dear. After all, it's not as if any of us knows who your people were."

Strange to be thinking about petty matters now. And maybe not. This place, this very beach at Malibu, was where the story had begun.

Thirteen

The blue '87 Honda had stayed several car lengths behind Stevie's Lexus all the way to Santa Monica. There was too much history with the Klines to let anyone, especially the cops, catch sight of her or the car. They'd lock her up and never ask the right questions. Shit, if people would only ask the right questions, they might begin to find the answers.

Poor Stevie. Must be a mess over this! After all those years wanting a kid. Tammi knew. She'd lost a baby, too. Except that hers had been stillborn. Not the same as seeing your child, holding and loving him, then losing him.

Amazing how alike they were, she and Stevie! Oh, not on the outside, but where it *really* counted. In their hearts they could be twins. Imagine, their birthdays even matched—well, maybe not the same *dates,* but identical month and year was getting it pretty close, astrologically speaking.

She had less sympathy for Ansel Kline. Kinda hard to feel sorry for someone who's had the world handed to him—including the most beautiful, talented, and loving wife any guy could want. Especially in the movie business. And what had he done? He'd gone and blown it.

Wrong words. *Blown it* applied to his partner. Man, Lyle Hemmings had probably *spilled* more than Tammi had ever snorted! What was it with some of these guys at the top? Was Lyle Hemmings trying to see how far was too far?

Hey, okay, maybe there'd been times when she'd blown it, too. Like crashing the baby shower and hanging around when that nice guy Joe had told her not to. But she wasn't just another fan—she *loved* them! She'd do anything to see them back together! Didn't anyone get it? Ansel and Stevie—and Todd—were her *life!*

No, not a soul would understand. They wouldn't even listen if she tried to explain. They'd call her crazy and put her away again. It was smarter to stay in the background.

At least for now.

Stevie had expected the ocean to ease away some of her tension, but the day was too perfect. There was too much of everything. Too much sun, too much laughter around her, too much happiness when her own world was falling apart. The random indifference of the universe. No wonder so many people were doing drugs. To numb the pain. She could relate to that.

But not to the opiate. When a yuppie stopped her on the beach and offered her "some high quality blow," Stevie realized it was time to head for home. Escape was as temporary and self-destructive as "blow." She didn't need to be alone; she needed the opposite, to be back at the house with people she knew—even if that included Carolyn Kline.

The sun was slowly sinking toward the water. Despite the smoke-tinted windshield and her dark glasses, there'd be glare if she didn't start back soon. Besides, there was nothing to be gained by staying away.

She returned to the car and telephoned the house for the fourth time. Barbara Halsey answered again. An encore of Stevie's earlier calls.

No news.

And Lt. Galvin hadn't responded to the messages she'd left at the precinct. She gave a moment's thought to Carla's words that morning.

Was no news really good news? Stevie's doubts were growing stronger.

Well, at least Ansel's mother had left. The media were still ensconced, Barbara had warned, and Stevie would have to sneak back into her house the way she'd sneaked out, but once inside, she'd be among friends. There'd be comfort in that.

And tomorrow—whether Detective Lt. Michael Galvin made any progress or not, whether Carolyn Kline invaded her home and life or not, whether there was a God in heaven or not—Stevie Kean was going to do something, *anything*, to find her son!

Fourteen

Friday, July 19

The building was in Silver Lake. Even at eleven-thirty in the morning the neighborhood had an abandoned look. The deserted street did offer compensation, though: a curbside parking spot directly in front of the entrance. Lt. Mike Galvin tucked the large manila envelope under his arm and headed up the walk.

He pushed through grimy revolving doors and saw a rack of newspapers outside the concession stand in the lobby. The dailies, the tabloids in particular, boasted pictures of Ansel and Stephanie separately and/or together. The headlines were interchangeable: THE LATEST SCOOP ON THE CRIME OF THE DECADE. Hawked like an ad for a new TV series. Galvin shook his head; there was sure to be a book in it—maybe a movie—as soon as the case was solved. All that jazz about the public's right to know. Hell, the public couldn't get enough.

* * *

A creaking elevator let him out on four. At the end of a badly lit hallway was a door marked *Joseph Madden, Private Investigator.*

He pushed the intercom button and heard Madden's voice over the squawkbox.

"Yeah, it's Galvin," he answered.

"You're late."

"Not by my watch."

A buzzer tripped the lock, and Galvin entered a small reception area with no windows and no receptionist. A door in the far wall was open.

"In here," Madden called.

That morning's *LA Times* covered a section of scarred wooden desk. Joe Madden sat behind it. Dust particles played through the sunlight and accented the lines around his eyes. Galvin figured him to be about forty now.

Madden remained seated as he gestured to a frayed chair facing the desk. When he didn't offer his hand, Galvin sat down and gave a quick glance around the room.

"How's business?" he asked through a grin.

"It just picked up. What's funny?"

Galvin shrugged. "You. This place. The neighborhood. You're playing the cliché to the hilt."

"It's cheap." Madden picked up a pack of Marlboros and held it out. Galvin shook his head.

"I forgot," said Madden. "I heard you quit." He took a cigarette and lit it. "There's hope for us all." He allowed the smoke to drift toward Galvin, who inhaled what he could before tossing his manila envelope onto the desk. Madden reached for it and withdrew an eight-by-ten photograph.

"Tammi Reynolds," he said.

Galvin pulled out a pad and pen. "You sure of that?"

"It's what she calls herself. She's a movie freak. Debbie played Tammy. Get it? She spells it with an 'i' to be a little different."

"When did you see her last?"

"About two years ago, the last time I worked for Ansel Kline. That's what this is about, isn't it?"

"He led us to you."

"How's Stevie taking it?"

"Stevie?" Galvin looked up from his pad.

Madden stared him down, then looked back at Tammi's photograph. "You get this off the baby-shower video?"

"Yeah. Nice job, that day."

"A compliment? From you?"

"Tell me about the shower."

"You saw the tape. There's not much else to tell. Once I got Tammi out of the house, she ran to her car and drove off. A blue '87 Honda."

Galvin made a note. Two of Stephanie Kean's—*Stevie's*—neighbors had mentioned a blue '87 Honda cruising the area in the last few months.

"You know where Tammi Reynolds lives?" Galvin asked.

"She used to move around. Hollywood, mostly. Local character. People knew her. You don't think she's part of this, do you, Galvin?"

"I'm wondering."

"Fine. But don't be too sure."

"Telling me how to do my job is what helped get you off the force, remember?"

87

"Hey, I vested out after fifteen. Honorably. No thanks to you, remember?"

"Listen, I just put you where you could do the least harm. In an office, behind a desk." Galvin made a show of suppressing a laugh. "From the looks of things, that's still where you are."

"Difference being it's *my* office and *my* desk."

"You still keep a pint in the bottom left-hand drawer, Joe?"

"I stopped after I got back from that month in the country you sent me on. You never believed it."

"One trip to the detox farm didn't convince me."

Madden took a deep drag from his cigarette. "I'm dry as a bone," he said. "And just to set things straight between us, I was dry when I retired, though it's beyond me why I give a rat's ass what you think, after five years."

"You always did like being right, Joe."

"I still do. And I know Tammi Reynolds."

"Forget about her for a sec. What do you think of Ansel Kline?"

"He's okay, for Hollywood. Not like his partner, though. But you must know that already."

"Hemmings and I kind of lost touch." Galvin felt himself coloring as he spoke.

"You're in touch now, I'll bet."

"Getting back to Kline . . . ?"

"What, a guy snatches the kid he didn't get custody of? Is that where you're headed with this?"

"It's a possibility."

"I'd believe that before this 'crazy fan' road you're on."

"I thought you liked Kline."

"Doesn't take away his motive. What's Tammi's?"

"The cult."

"Crap, Galvin. She worships stars, not devils."

"Maybe it's a short step from one to the other." Galvin picked up the newspaper from the desk. "You've been following this thing."

"It passes the time between investigations."

"Yeah. You look real busy."

"They're breaking my door down. I've got a bead on every two-timing husband in LA."

"Including Ansel Kline?"

"No. Is that why they're splitting up?"

"You sound interested."

"It's just that he'd have to be nuts." Madden crushed the cigarette in a tin ashtray with the name of a bar and grill embossed on it. "Well?"

"No," Galvin answered. "I don't think he fucked around on her. But we'll see."

"You didn't answer my first question. How's Stevie?"

"She's pretty torn up."

"Can she finish the picture?"

"Who knows? Doesn't look that way. The press is having a field day. It's getting to her."

"Always did. She likes her privacy."

"Then she's in the wrong business."

"Ah, Galvin. Still the sympathetic soul at heart."

"Did you like the kid?"

"He was in diapers last time I saw him, but, yeah. Nice kid. And lucky."

"You mean the money."

"I mean his mother. Stevie's career took second place once he was born. No matter what she was doing, she made time for the baby. Not so Ansel Kline. Too busy. And Ansel's mother sure as hell didn't help. Put it all together, you've got a divorce."

"Why'd you stop working for them?"

Madden spread his hands to encompass the entire office. "This. I just celebrated my second glorious year in business." He paused, then added, "Besides, no matter how weird the scene gets in this town, I still haven't heard of parties being held to celebrate breakups. Unless it's just that I don't get invited."

Galvin rose and picked up the picture of Tammi. "On second thought," he said, tossing it back on the desk, "I've got more. You keep this."

"You don't think I'm gonna start doing your job for you, do you?"

"Shit, Madden, you can't even do *your* job. Frame it, for all I care."

"But it wouldn't hurt if I had a mind to show it around, would it?"

Galvin walked toward the door. "I think you're a dumb sonofabitch, Madden, but I wish you luck."

"Hey, no regrets, here, Lieutenant. You still gonna follow up on the Kline motive?"

"I've got to, but I think it'll be a dead end. It's the cult, Madden. The case has all the numbers."

"According to what I read, you don't have much time."

"No. And I'm up to my eyeballs with the three other cases, including all the paperwork."

"Just like it was."

"Yeah. I guess you don't miss it."

"I guess," Madden answered.

Galvin looked around the office one last time. A brown pigeon was perched on the windowsill. It took a second to realize it was made of wood.

"You carve that?" Galvin asked.

"I'm still at it. Switched to birds."

"Still OT?"

"Naw. Hobby, now. Even sold a few."

Galvin nodded. "You're gettin' good."

Galvin looked at his watch as he stepped from the elevator into the lobby. It was almost noon.

He headed for the street exit, reviewing the last half hour as he walked. He didn't like Joe Madden any more now than when Madden had been on the force, but he had to admit the bastard seemed to have straightened himself out. Maybe he really was off the sauce. Maybe not. There was one sure fact: Joe Madden had a thing for Stevie Kean.

A driver had just tossed a stack of newspapers onto the pitted linoleum floor outside the concession stand. The papers were still bound by cord, but there was no missing the front page of that day's edition of *Scoop*.

Two photographs filled the upper half-page. On the right, Stevie Kean, wild-eyed and mouth opened in a scream. Galvin recognized it as a still from a thriller she'd starred in.

But on the left was the freeze-frame photo of Tammi Reynolds taken from the baby-shower tape.

The headline was printed in red. *STEVIE KEAN CRIES: DID THIS WOMAN STEAL MY BABY?*

"Goddammit!" Galvin had received copies of the picture only this morning.

Fuming, he pushed past the newspaper delivery-man and stormed the revolving doors. Leave it to Joe Madden to rent space in a building where you couldn't even slam the fucking door!

Fifteen

One of the reasons behind the glass-everywhere design of Hubert Braddock's publishing emporium was so that everyone could keep an eye on everyone else. The disadvantages were obvious, but they were sometimes offset by the positive side, such as Eppie Goldwyn's clear view of Carolyn Kline's approach.

No wasting time, Eppie noted, but no sacrifice to style, either. Carolyn was a meticulously orchestrated symphony in bone Irish linen. The matching sling-backed shoes tipped in black and the quilted bone purse were Chanel. The suit might be Donna Karan, but then again, maybe not. Unless Carolyn had *walked* all the way from Beverly Hills—perish the thought!—there was more than a tad of polyester in the skirt and jacket; the only visible wrinkles were the frown lines at either side of Carolyn's mouth. No, she didn't have to be two feet away for Eppie to spot them. For some things, Iphigenia Goldwyn had X-ray vision second only to Superman's.

Come into my parlor . . . Eppie grabbed a pencil

and began scribbling notes from a telephone caller who wasn't there. She looked up only when Carolyn was standing in the opened doorway—which Eppie had left that way because she'd been expecting this visit since the morning edition of *Scoop* had hit the stands.

"Carolyn. What a surprise." No inflection. No rising to greet her guest.

"Just who the hell do you think you are, goddammit, Kitty Kelley?"

"Don't flatter yourself, Carolyn. You're not in Nancy's league."

Carolyn was breathing miles above her diaphragm. "What right do you have to put this—this *infamy*—in print!"

"First Amendment, darling. Free speech and all that?"

"I'll sue you and your goddammed paper, Eppie!"

Eppie held up her hands as if acknowledging applause. "Before you waste my time and Mort's money, Carolyn, you should know I always double-check my sources." *Well, almost always.* "And I have taped interviews as backup."

"You're spreading lies! That headline—"

"Was *not* a direct quote, darling."

Carolyn removed a nonexistent fleck of lint from her lapel. "I've consulted my attorney regarding libel action."

"On what grounds?"

"Malicious intent, Eppie. The tripe you've written about me." Carolyn cleared her throat. "However, that's not why I'm here."

The hell it isn't. "Really? Is it your concern over Stevie?"

Carolyn was halfway between the doorway, and Eppie's desk. Now she took three long strides until she was standing directly opposite Eppie. She leaned over the desk and splayed her hands on the polished rosewood.

"Damn you, Eppie, you can write whatever you like about my past—although for accuracy's sake, you might include yours as well, since we share so much of the same territory. But this—this *venom* you're spewing about my family can only cause harm. Whoever is responsible for the abduction of my grandson *wants* this disgusting kind of publicity! You're playing right into his hands, and I won't have it!"

"You won't have it?"

"You cannot *use* this story to advance your own reputation—not when the life of a four-year-old child hangs in the balance!"

"Yeah, especially when it's your son's four-year-old child, right?"

"That's not the point!" Carolyn's hands balled up into angry fists.

Eppie was impressed. Either Carolyn had discovered feelings, or she was taking acting lessons.

But Eppie was no pushover.

"Tell me, Carolyn, where were you when the other stories broke? I covered the Landau kidnapping."

Carolyn's tear ducts were actually functioning. She lowered her eyes. "I . . . I don't really know the family."

"They were at Stevie's baby shower."

Carolyn shook her head. "I don't recall."

"Well, darling, I have a photographic memory—
for visuals in particular. And by the way, I left a
lot out—for decorum—if you bothered to read the
whole story." In truth, the article had been cut
because of space requirements.

"You didn't leave enough out. My family's social
and financial status have absolutely nothing to do
with my grandson's kidnapping."

"People are curious."

"They don't give a damn about me."

"They don't give a damn about *you*, Carolyn"—
Eppie had salivated over that line—"except that you
happen to be Ansel Kline's mother. And, at least
for now, Stevie Kean's mother-in-law. In fact, Carolyn, the public is probably more interested in Stevie
than they are about anything else except the case
itself."

"Which brings us back to the reason for my
visit."

Back? "And that is—?"

"I want you to drop this story. Now."

"You. Want. Me. I like that."

"If you don't, you'll be placing yourself—not to
mention your career—in jeopardy."

"You're threatening me? Carolyn Kline of Beverly Hills is threatening Eppie Goldwyn?"

"I'm serious, Eppie. If, as you claim, you have
information the police don't have, and if, by publishing that information, or by withholding it from
me, the police should be hampered in their investigation—"

Carolyn stopped to collect herself. She'd rehearsed most of the dialogue, but not the threat part.

Eppie inadvertently helped her out.

"Look, Carolyn, I hope you know I wouldn't deliberately set out to endanger a child. No matter *who* his grandmother may be."

"Perhaps not deliberately," said Carolyn, her voice for the first time losing some of its steel.

But a moment later the metal returned.

"Just remember, Eppie. If anything you do results in further harm brought upon my grandson, I'll ruin you. And that's for the record."

Eppie remained seated at her desk long after Carolyn's departure. She wasn't thinking about anything in particular, yet at the same time her mind was racing in several directions at once.

She thought about the present. That day's *Scoop*, which had prompted Carolyn's visit, lay on the black-leather-and-chrome sofa to the left of her desk. She made a mental note to call Al, the stringer who'd swiped a copy of Tammi-the-fan's picture for Eppie from the precinct station. Maybe by now Tammi had a surname and an address. And maybe, if she wasn't a total mental twit, she could provide more information about the case. Contrary to Carolyn's suppositions, Eppie tried to substantiate her stories whenever possible. It was one thing to blackmail your way to the top, another when it came to staying there.

Carolyn Kline. Amazing the way she managed

97

to maintain such complete self-involvement, taking credit where it wasn't due and shifting blame to others when it suited her purpose. You'd think that Carolyn had been the one jilted all those years ago, that she'd been the one left waiting at the altar, when in fact it had been the other way around. Eppie had a right to hold a grudge, but Carolyn? Hadn't she gotten everything she'd ever wanted?

Well, maybe not. Sure, she'd landed Mort. And his money. And six months later—no, seven—the reason Mort had broken it off with Eppie, a son.

A son they'd named Ansel Todd Kline.

The irony wasn't lost on Eppie, even now. Carolyn's family had threatened a scandal, so Mort had been forced into marrying the pregnant, cold bitch. If he was back in Eppie's arms within a month, it wasn't her fault.

"Carolyn's mother must have taught her to close her eyes and think of England," Eppie had joked when she learned of Carolyn's distaste for sex. Had Carolyn actually expected Mort to become a monk? Wrong church, honey!

Eppie bristled at the memory of Carolyn's accusation. Imagine *her* using the word *whore!* Carolyn had sold her body for a wedding ring; Eppie had given love, asked nothing in return. And Carolyn would always hate her, because they both knew. Mort had loved Eppie.

Yeah, but he'd married Carolyn.

Well, dammit, that was thirty-six years ago, and she'd come a long way since then. No more giving without getting.

But wait a sec. Eppie wasn't all bad. She'd check around, make some inquiries, see what she could do to help find Stevie and Ansel's kid.

Just so long as it didn't screw her out of a scoop.

Sixteen

"Yes," Stevie said into the receiver, "I'll hold."

Every button on the telephone unit was lit except for the private line.

Another tranquilizer might calm her trembling hands the way it had calmed her before bed last night. But she'd had too much sleep, too many dreams. She hadn't awakened until eleven. No, it was enough to know the pills were there, in the dresser drawer. Just in case.

She looked out the upstairs den window. Reporters were still congregated below. Fewer of them now, but with renewed ferocity since that day's *Scoop* had made good on its name.

"I'm sorry, Mrs. Kline," the desk sergeant's voice said, "Lieutenant Galvin isn't here right now. Is there a message?"

"I left one two hours ago and he hasn't called back."

"Mrs. Kline, we're doing everything we—"

"Just tell the lieutenant that I called—again."

Stevie hung up and her eyes fell immediately on the copy of *Scoop* beside the phone. She observed her own hysterical image and the screaming head-line. They approximated her feelings, but neither explained how Eppie Goldwyn had managed to get that picture of Tammi. How could Lt. Galvin have allowed this to happen?

And where the hell was he, anyway?

With the tabloid in her hand, Stevie left the den.

As she passed the closed nursery door, she thought of Jill. Under normal circumstances, Jill would be at the house today. Of course, these weren't normal circumstances, but Todd's nanny hadn't even attempted to get in touch.

Why not? Fear, most likely. Worry. Guilt. Stevie could identify with all of the above. Maybe Jill needed to have Stevie contact her. She'd get the number from the Rolodex in the downstairs study and call.

An extra phone unit had been installed, and Barbara Halsey was speaking to one caller while scribbling a message from another.

Her brownish-blond hair was knotted at the nape of her neck; just enough makeup covered any tell-tale circles from her own lack of sleep. Her white cotton shirt and faded jeans were clean and neatly pressed.

Stevie unintentionally made eye contact with the wall mirror. I look like hell, she thought. And didn't care.

She turned toward Barbara. "God, I hate phones."

Barbara had just pushed the Hold button, but was still balancing the receiver between her shoul-

101

der and ear. She glanced up at Stevie and smiled. "One day they'll have to surgically remove this thing."

"You're not the only one," said Barbara's secretary from the doorway. "Coffee?" She carried a steaming mug in her hand.

"No thanks, Fran," answered Stevie.

Fran took a seat alongside Barbara at the desk. "I can handle the calls for a while if you need a break."

"I do. I'm on hold with Publicity. Tell them we want no comment on the *Scoop* piece until I talk to Ansel—and I don't know when that'll be, unless *you* can reach him." Turning to Stevie, she said, "Now, lemme outta here!"

Stevie slid into the padded leather banquette in the breakfast nook. She remembered that during her last four months of pregnancy she hadn't been able to squeeze in between the seat and the table.

"Where's Ansel?" asked Stevie.

"At the studio. Fran will keep at it till she finds him. She's good. Too good. Sometimes I think she's after my job. I'm only kidding. Anyway, Ansel's taking meetings with the second-unit people in case we can't close down."

"I can't go back to work, Barbara. Not yet, anyway."

"No one expects you to. If worse comes to worst, we'll shoot around you, use a double, and dub your voice in later."

"Christ."

"But we won't have to," Barbara said too quickly. "Todd will be home safe and you'll be back on the set in no time. I know."

"How?"

"Because I'm right about everything." Barbara pressed Stevie's hand. "So tell me. Any luck in tracking down that cop?"

"No, and it's making me crazy! I realize there are the other cases, that Todd isn't the only child missing. But there must be *something* we can do!"

"Okay, take it easy." Barbara went to the refrigerator and returned with a glass of orange juice. "Here. It's ice cold. Drink it slowly."

Stevie took a sip, then with her other hand held up the copy of *Scoop,* which she'd carried in from the study.

"Look at this, will you? I didn't even realize I've been schlepping it around with me."

"I'm sorry I brought the damn thing over."

"I'd have seen it eventually. Eppie would have messengered a copy to make sure Carolyn doesn't miss it."

Barbara was looking at Tammi's picture on the front page. "Do you think she's the one?"

"She could be. You were at the shower."

"Yes, but the article says the police consider her a new lead. I mean, what if it's Tammi alone?"

"Eppie may have invented that part. But you know, it *would* give me more hope to think it's only Tammi." Stevie paused. "No. I won't cling to false hopes. I don't think Tammi's capable of four kidnappings—not by herself. That leaves the cult. And somehow—" She stopped.

"What?" Barbara asked. "What were you going to say?"

"I don't think Tammi would do . . . the things they say have been done." She swallowed too big a gulp of juice, and the cold made her shudder. "I suppose it's easier for me to believe that Todd is with her."

"Then maybe he is."

"Don't coddle me, Barb. Whoever took those other children also has Todd—whether Tammi's part of it or not."

"Sorry."

Stevie squeezed Barbara's hand before removing it from her grasp. "So am I. I'm just trying to keep some kind of foothold on reality. And I feel like I'm starting to snap."

"Stay close to Ansel on this. Talk to him."

Stevie gave a wry laugh. "That's easier said than done. He's too busy to talk. One of our major problems, of course."

"Then who *do* you talk to, Stevie? I mean, we're friends, but you don't talk to me about 'things.' "

"What 'things?' "

"Stuff you need to get off your chest. The stuff most women tell their mothers."

"Or their mothers-in-law?" Stevie said.

This time Barbara laughed. "That's my point. I hate the expression, but who is 'there' for you?"

Stevie shrugged. "No one, I guess. Not lately, anyway. Ansel and I used to 'be there' for each other, and it was enough, before."

"Before the separation?"

"Before we were 'rich and famous.' Well, before we were *this* rich and *this* famous. I didn't need anyone else besides Ansel. And Todd." Stevie's voice broke. When she felt her eyes beginning to redden, she closed them tightly and shook her head. "Dammit! Here I go again!"

"It's okay. Come on. Talk to me."

"Oh, Barb, I just feel so shut out! As if I'm no more than a governess for Carolyn's grandson! I can't forgive her for calling the police and making this *real!* It should have been *me. I* should have been here, and *I* should have called!"

She had to swallow tears out of the way. Barbara poured two mugs of coffee and handed one to Stevie, who took a sip, then continued. She described the night Todd was born, and the pain that no doctor—or woman—had warned her about. "It was sheer agony, Barb, but I'd swap it in a minute for what I'm feeling now!"

Barbara could hear hysteria wavering just below the surface. "C'mon, tell me more about Todd," she prompted. "Some kids are whiny or colicky from day one, but you're lucky. Todd has such a sunny disposition."

A brief smile flashed across Stevie's face. "It's true. I wish I knew where he gets it."

"Well, obviously from you or Ansel. Definitely *not* from his paternal grandma."

"It's funny," Stevie reflected, "as a child I never felt a burning need to find out who my parents were. I was probably protecting my ego—you know, they rejected me, so I'd reject them. I'm sure it's

105

why I grew up determined to make it on my own."
A sigh escaped but she didn't try to conceal it.

"It's not funny, Stevie; we're talking survival.
Which you've done better than most."

"Well, you're right, it *was* about survival. But
motherhood changed all that. Once Todd was
born, I began wondering—not about his nature or
looks, I mean about important things I'd never
even considered until then."

"You mean his genes?"

Stevie nodded. "I started asking myself if my
parents had any physical problems or susceptibili-
ties that Todd could inherit."

"Did you ever try to find out who your parents
were?"

"Two years ago. It seems my mother wasn't married, so she used a phony name. Mary Jones, gone
without a trace. It's an irony, because by the time
I was ready to take the risk and meet her face-to-
face, I wasn't given the chance."

Stevie's words pressed other buttons, but again
Barbara came to the rescue. "I'll bet Todd gets his
verbal skills from you," she said.

Mental images kept the tears at bay. "God, Barb,
all those nights of nonstop babble from the moment he started talking! I'd come home from the
studio bone-tired and he'd be wide-awake and so
eager! I'd listen till his bedtime, then I'd sing him
a lullaby. And when he fell asleep, I'd tiptoe downstairs in dire need of adult conversation—to find
Ansel not back from location or holed up in the
den going over business deals with Lyle."

She paused, then added, "Ansel's missed so much, and now, if we don't find Todd—!"

Barbara was helpless this time.

"I want my baby back, Barb! I can't take this much longer! Todd must be terrified! *What* have these people done with my baby!" She buried her face in her hands and inadvertently her elbow upset the half-empty mug of coffee.

Barbara quickly mopped it up, then cleared off the damp copy of *Scoop* and asked, "Where'd you put the Valiums?"

"I took one last night, Barb. I don't want to get hooked."

Barbara insisted.

"All right," Stevie said. "Maybe half a pill."

"You rest in here," Barbara whispered, leading Stevie into the living room. "I promise I'll let you know if there's any word."

"I have to call Jill."

"You will. Later. Just now, you need to relax."

Two and a half milligrams weren't enough to induce sleep. But together with her brain's endorphins, they were enough to dull her senses. She stretched out on the sofa and closed her eyes. Even the ringing telephones seemed to fade away.

Seventeen

Stevie imagined hearing Ansel's car in the driveway. Six years had accustomed her to the sounds made by his 1968 Jaguar, even though its engine sputter-cough had been repaired long ago.

Six years. Including the separation. There was no way not to include it.

In the beginning they'd known how to talk to each other—hadn't they? Or had six years amounted to nothing more than a semblance of communication, relayed messages masquerading as conversation but in reality just exchanges of information about meetings, parties, and shooting schedules?

No. In the beginning it had been what novelists called blissful. They'd had something special. Stevie had tried to explain it to Barbara, but no one, especially someone in this business, could understand what made it so special. At first, neither had Stevie.

It hadn't taken long, though, for her to see that what she and Ansel shared, in addition to their passion for each other, was their passion for movies. They *adored* movies. She adored acting, he adored directing, and together they adored the magic of making movies.

Movies had been Stevie's means of escape from emptiness before she found the ocean. She'd identified with her favorite stars and heroines, while recognizing that stories onscreen must never be confused with life. From the start, she'd understood that stardom was the sometimes lucky result of cause and effect. For Stevie, acting was what it was all about.

Ansel, on the other hand, had grown up in the business. His father had been a major force in film distribution; his mother . . . well, Carolyn had probably been born knowing how to give what she called the right parties for the right people.

And all the "right" people had flocked to the Kline mansion in Beverly Hills. Ansel had speculated aloud to Stevie that perhaps it explained his father's marriage to Carolyn. "A wedding of his money to her clout. Like royalty." Carolyn had even referred to their son as her little prince. He hated it.

It wasn't Stevie's imagination. Ansel had pulled into the driveway. And threatened violence when one of the paparazzi came too close. The strain was visible on his face, and the intensity in his voice made the photographer back off. His cohorts quickly moved aside to let Ansel pass.

He still had a set of keys to the house, so he was able to avoid the embarrassment of having to ring the doorbell of his former home. Thank what-ever-up-there for tiny favors down-here.

Between sudden bursts of anger or emotion, Ansel had been burying himself in routine. Meetings, revising scripts and schedules, whatever demanded his personal attention—or didn't—so he'd have no time to think. The problem was, he needed to think. He needed not to *feel*.

He checked with Barbara and Fran, decided that most of the calls could wait, and willed away a headache.

He tried reaching Lyle at the studio, then at home, although Carla sounded even more skittish than ever, so it was probably pointless to leave word. He did anyway.

Next he phoned his partner's buddy at LAPD. Detective Lt. Michael Galvin, the most elusive cop in town. What the hell was it with these guys? Did promotions include Fridays off to play golf?

Barbara anticipated Ansel's question when he looked up from the notepad and papers on his desk. "She's in the living room."

He tiptoed down the hall, but didn't go beyond the archway. Stevie was curled up, and whether she was asleep or just resting, Ansel saw no reason to disturb her.

He watched her rhythmic breathing and then, when he was fairly certain he could take a few steps without waking her, he moved to the phone unit and turned down the volume. He slid out of his loafers, sank onto the suede love seat, leaned his head against a cushion, and closed his eyes.

The low back, tuxedo style was too much for his

sacroiliac. Two nights on the fold-out sofabed in the den had probably ruined his spine for life. The goddammed mattress felt more like a hammock.

He twisted and turned and stretched until he was in a relatively comfortable position. And found himself gazing at his wife.

Wife. Some habits were hard to break.

He was about to doze off, when Barbara crept in from the study. Ansel was up in a shot.

"It's Carla," Barbara whispered. "She says the earliest Lyle can set up a meeting with the insurance people is Monday."

"Dammit to hell!" Ansel quickly lowered his voice, but it was too late. Stevie had opened her eyes.

"I thought I heard your car," she said. "It's a good thing I never tried drugs. I mean, I went out, bingo, like a light."

Light made her glance toward the telephone unit. The buttons, all but the private line on the end, were blinking.

"I'll head back to Fran and the fort," said Barbara. "Why don't you guys leave the volume down? If there's anything important, I'll yell."

"Christ!" said Stevie. "I forgot to call Jill!"

She jumped up and was halfway across the room when Ansel's voice stopped her. "You don't have to."

"Ansel, I do. She's probably feeling responsible."

111

"And damn well should. That's why I called and fired her."

At first it didn't sink in.

"Run that past me again, will you?"

"What, that I fired her?"

Her adrenaline was rising fast. "Why did you do that? What gave you the right?"

"The right? Well, I suppose Jill's negligence that allowed my son to be kidnapped gives me the right!"

"He's my son, too, Ansel—and *I* was awarded custody! Firing Jill—or not firing her—wasn't up to you!"

"I'm the one who's been paying her salary, and she screwed up!"

Stevie was trying to keep from shouting, but she couldn't hide the accusation in her voice.

"Ansel, this isn't really about Jill—or Todd. We both know that."

"Then what *is* it about, Stevie?"

"Blame!" she blurted out. "You and your mother want to blame me—but you can't come out and do that, so you're blaming Jill!"

"That's ridiculous!"

"No it isn't! You and Carolyn are doing it again!"

"Doing what?"

"Ganging up on me! Anything I do, whether it's wanting to live in Beachwood Canyon instead of Bel Air or refusing to spend every cent I earn at fancy stores and trendy restaurants just to impress a bunch of salesclerks and waiters—"

"Stevie . . ."

"I haven't finished yet! I was perfectly ready to

112

take a few years off to raise my child—*our* child—but you and Carolyn decided it would be the end of my career. So the two of you have to share the guilt, Ansel, no matter how your mother tries to build a personal indictment against me!"

"Stevie, I don't give a damn what my mother thinks or says!" He shrugged his shoulders wearily. "This has less to do with Carolyn than with me, doesn't it?"

"Maybe so," she admitted.

"We ought to talk it through."

"Oh, Ansel, we ought to have talked it through for the past three years! Except that every time we ought to have talked it through, you were somewhere else!"

He expected her to bring up the night of Todd's birth.

She didn't.

So he said, "I'm listening now, Stevie."

She shook her head sadly. "It's the same thing it's always been, Ansel. You want to direct everything, whether it's on or off the set. You can't see any viewpoint besides your own. You need to be in control. You're even trying now."

Ansel almost laughed. He'd never felt less in control.

"Stevie, whatever you believe, I fired Jill because she wasn't doing her job." More softly he said, "If she had, Todd wouldn't be missing."

"Ansel, aren't you holding Jill responsible for something you really feel is my fault?"

"Did I say that?"

"You don't have to—I can feel it! You and your

mother are convinced that I've neglected Todd, that if you'd been granted custody this wouldn't have happened! She even said so that day at the studio!" Her voice was beginning to break. "We have to *do* something, Ansel. *I* have to. Otherwise I'll go crazy!"

"Stevie, the police are handling it."

"They're not handling a damn thing! They can't even handle the reporters outside! And what about Lieutenant Galvin? Why isn't he returning our calls? Is he afraid to tell us he hasn't any news—or does he have news he's afraid to tell us?"

This time her voice did break, and Stevie gave in to uncontrollable sobbing.

Barbara and Fran couldn't help overhearing, even from the study.

"I'll be back in a sec," said Barbara, dropping her storyboard and rushing to the living room.

She found Stevie shaking convulsively in Ansel's arms as he tried to comfort her. He glanced helplessly at Barbara, who touched her index finger to her lips and quietly retraced her steps down the hall. She knew the reasons for their outburst, but the enormity of what they must be feeling suddenly hit her in the pit of the stomach. She made a detour into the kitchen, where she poured a glass of water and swallowed the other half of Stevie's Valium.

* * *

Ansel's arm was still around Stevie's shoulder, and she was leaning against his chest. His strong, usually steady heartbeat hadn't stopped racing. In happier days, it would have meant a prelude to lovemaking. Now, though, she knew the palpitations were from his fears, which mirrored her own.

Neither of them had spoken for what seemed like hours. At last Stevie said, "You know what would happen if this were television, don't you?"

Ansel was stroking her hair, another old habit. He caught himself and moved his hand away. "I've never done TV. You tell me."

Stevie recognized his withdrawal. She rose from the sofa and began pacing the floor in much the same way Ansel did when rehearsing a scene with his actors.

"Well," she said, "Act One is the setup, where the crime is committed and discovered. In Act Two, the police investigate. Clues appear to keep the audience's interest, but not enough to solve the case."

"What's next?" asked Ansel.

"Act Three, the wrap-up, in which the private detective puts it all together."

"What private detective?"

Stevie couldn't believe the sudden calm that had, out of the blue—or out of desperation—taken hold of her. And the name that popped into her mind.

"Joe Madden," she said.

"Joe Madden," Ansel repeated. "Do we still have his number?"

"It was on the Rolodex last time I checked." Of course, she hadn't checked in a long time.

"I'll see if I can reach him," said Ansel.

Stevie was about to say that she'd call, but then she remembered Joe Madden's not-too-well-hidden interest in her. It was better, on second thought, to let Ansel make the call.

Eighteen

At the intersection of Sunset and Silver Lake Boulevard, Joe Madden stopped pushing buttons on the air-conditioner and admitted that it was dead. Great. If it was the compressor, repairs would cost as much as he'd paid for this heap.

He made the turn and rolled down his window. He could taste the air. A whole summer of this. What the hell. He was almost home, such as it was. He remembered Mildred Pierce's line, that she lived "where all the houses looked alike." In nearly fifty years, that much hadn't changed. His was the third on the right and easy to find because it was the only one on the street that was still dark.

It was hotter inside the house. The light on the answering machine wasn't blinking. What else was new? He threw off his jacket, turned on the air-conditioner—at least this one was working, thank God—then tossed his mail into the mess on the kitchen table, got a diet Coke out of the fridge, and hit the lights. Stanley and Blanche woke up and started chirping, a noise he could do without.

They were probably screaming because the cage needed cleaning. Yeah. Tomorrow.

Except that starting tomorrow he'd be working for the Klines.

He sat down at the table and took a long pull on the soda, wincing at its sweetness. He'd never get used to this stuff.

He stared at the pile of woodchips and carving tools strewn across sheets of newspaper which covered the table. At the center, where he'd left it late last night, was the block of wood. Thin pencil lines followed the grain to form the beginning of a bird's head. But what kind of bird? Until he decided, it would remain just a block of wood. He pulled at the edges of the paper to clear space on the table.

The copy of *Scoop* was still at the office. No matter. He'd practically memorized it. He smiled at the thought of how pissed Galvin must have been when he saw it. A leak in the department was just the kind of thing that could really throw a wrench into an investigation. And now Ansel Kline and Stephanie Kean were feeling neglected because Galvin wasn't giving them his full attention. Well, who could blame them? It was their kid.

So Galvin's loss was Madden's gain. A new client, a chance to see her again. "Mrs. Kline" to her face, although Galvin had picked up on the "Stevie" slip.

The place was beginning to cool off. So were the birds. Madden lit a cigarette to kill the linger-

118

ing aftertaste of the cardboard enchiladas he'd wolfed down at the diner. He unbuttoned his shirt and pressed the cold can first against his chest, then to his forehead. That was better. In fact, everything was. Ansel Kline hadn't balked at a four-hundred-dollar-a-day fee plus expenses, and the extra money was coming in time to hold off the collection agencies. So why the lousy mood?

He shuffled through the stack of mail. Mostly junk. The rest, bills. All but one envelope.

Madden tore it open. Inside was his first partial retirement check. It would just about take care of fixing the car's A-C. He could look forward to this grand sum once a month till he croaked. Big deal.

He remembered his last day on the force. The story shouldn't have ended like that. And five years shouldn't go by so fast.

"Shit," he said aloud. "I'm only forty."

Well, almost forty-one, but back in shape, since he'd laid off the booze. The spare tire of six months ago was flat and firm. Madden sucked in his stomach while dragging deeply on the cigarette, which resulted in a coughing fit. He pushed the butt into the soda can and listened for the hiss as it died. Christ, if he had to give up smoking, what was left?

Sure. Sex.

It made him laugh. That it actually struck him funny worsened his mood. He could barely recall the last time, or the last woman.

Or the last communiqué from LAPD.

The familiar little red flag popped up and waved in Madden's brain. Last winter he'd fallen off the wagon. All the symptoms were there. He wanted a drink.

Madden looked at the wall clock. If he left now, he could just make the eight-thirty meeting in Echo Park. Fewer drunks than cokeheads there, but a meeting was a meeting.

A shower would be nice, but there was no time. He stood and began rebuttoning his shirt. The decision to go didn't make him feel any better, but it changed his attitude. Yeah. Change your attitude, change your life.

He could hit the automatic teller on the way home and deposit the check. Weird coincidence that the Department, Galvin, and the Klines had all reconnected on the same day. *What goes around really does come around.* Do a good job, some people remember. He wondered whether it was Ansel or Stevie who'd thought to call him.

Stupid. The point was they'd kept the printed Rolodex card he'd sent with the announcement. It didn't matter whose idea it was.

Not much.

Madden switched off the A-C and turned out the lights. The birds went quiet. He reconsidered, then patted the check in his pocket and switched the A-C back on. After the meeting, he'd work on the wooden bird. Let the place stay cool. For a change, he could afford it.

Nineteen

No one had mentioned that the legalities of Stevie and Ansel's pending divorce might be put into question by their having spent three nights in succession under the same roof. That Stevie had slept alone in her bed upstairs while Ansel tossed and turned on the den sofabed was beside the point.

Which was why Lyle Hemmings, when he stopped by to discuss changes in the shooting schedule with Ansel, said nothing to either of them about the "couple aspect" they presented when Ansel answered the door in a striped velour kimono that was identical to the one Stevie was wearing to prepare breakfast.

It was also why Lyle sprinkled his and Ansel's business conversation with inclusive asides to Stevie: "You don't have to be concerned about any of this," or "I'm covering all the bases," whatever was needed to reassure Stevie that neither her role in the picture nor the picture itself was in jeopardy.

She appreciated his attempts, but she couldn't have cared less. In three days' time—four, now that it was Saturday—her priorities had sharpened in focus. If she never made another picture, never acted another day in her life, what did it matter? All she wanted was the end of this nightmare and the safe return of her child.

By the time Joe Madden arrived, Lt. Galvin had phoned with the news that he had a last-known address on Tammi Reynolds. That and several cups of coffee revived Stevie's spirits. And she'd slept without the help of medication last night. No dreams, just flat-out exhaustion. *Rested* wasn't the precise definition of the way she felt, but at least she wasn't jumping like a frightened cat whenever the door chimed or the telephones rang.

She'd even noticed a touch of color on her face, but that was less from sleep than from her trip to the beach two days before.

And now it was two days later! The anxiety started tugging again, but this time she was, literally, saved by the bell.

"I'll get it," she said to Lyle and Ansel as she rushed to the door.

Madden had been tempted to belt the reporters. Or the photographers. Or a combination of both.

He wasn't nuts about the cop on the door, either. The guy looked like something from Central Casting. Hell, maybe he was. Acting gigs were hard to come by; maybe guard-dogging beat out waiting tables.

He flashed his credentials, which the cop eyed suspiciously—probably from watching *Hunter* or re-runs of *Hill Street Blues*—and just to speed things up, dropped Galvin's name. The latter had an immediate effect. The kid all but clicked his heels as he stepped aside.

Madden rang the doorbell and waited. While he waited, he tried to "think cool," even though the shirt under his jacket was stuck to his skin after the drive from Silver Lake. He couldn't help wondering whether Ansel Kline was back in the picture—in more ways than one. If so, he'd answer the door.

He didn't.

It opened just enough for him to see her standing in the shadows, probably to keep out of tele-photo-lens range.

"Nice to see you, Mrs. Kline," he said. Maybe indelicate, considering.

She didn't take offense. "Please, Joe, it's Stevie. And thanks for making yourself available on such short notice."

"For you, anytime." That was the truth, but he'd been careful to say it without laying a heavy number. Stevie Kean was a star, she was accustomed to guys making fools of themselves over her.

And why not? Even with her hair damp and pinned up off her neck—God, what a neck!—and her face scrubbed clean of makeup, not to mention the strain of the past four days, she'd still win any Hollywood contest. It was all in the eyes. Yeah, and the rest looked good, too. And it wasn't just because she was wearing a bathrobe and probably not much underneath it.

Shit. Ansel Kline was wearing one, too. A perfect match.

Ansel had come into the foyer, and now he and Madden were shaking hands. Okay, it was time to put the personal agenda where it belonged. Where it had been for months. On hold.

"So, Mr. Kline," Madden said, all business, "where can the three of us talk?"

It turned out to be the four of them. They went into the study, where Ansel's partner, Hemmings, was waiting. No one asked him to leave, so who was Madden to say boo—even though the hotshot producer seemed even more wired than Madden remembered. Last time he'd seen Hemmings, he'd figured the high came from working the room, getting off on the trip. But who could tell? Hemmings had reached the top rung faster than most, and maybe that rung wasn't all it was cracked up to be. Or what Hemmings had expected it to be. Probably why the main event at so many industry parties took place in the upstairs powder room. As it were.

Having observed all kinds of human-animal behavior during what he called his post-LAPD, freelance period, Madden could spot members of the nose-candy crowd from a distance of two miles. From two feet, at the moment.

Well, that was Ansel Kline's problem. Madden

hadn't been hired to stand in judgment of Lyle Hemmings.

Madden settled into the chair being offered him and turned his full attention to the case for which he had been hired. It was, after all, paying him four hundred a day plus expenses.

Yeah. Lyle Hemmings's lunch money. Or his afternoon's supply of toot.

"And you've received no word about Todd?" Madden was asking.

"Nothing," said Ansel.

"It's your info on this Tammi woman and her Honda that gave the cops a lead on her address," Lyle said to Madden.

"That won't help much. Tammi's the transient type. I think our real lead is tied up with the second kidnapping and the ransom note."

"You mean the Landaus' child?" asked Stevie. "In what way?"

"That's what I hope to find out." Madden was reaching for the pack of cigarettes in his pocket when Carla appeared.

"Stevie, I didn't want to disturb you, but there's a Mrs. Gill on line two from Save Our Children, and, like, she needs to talk to you about some TV charity special you're doing. She says it's, like, real important, because the show, or whatever, is next Wednesday." She was pantomiming apologies as she spoke, and her hands, legs, and eyes moved as if she were a marionette whose strings had become tangled.

Madden took a deep breath. Jesus, for a household that wasn't into drugs, this place was flying! And he'd been dumb enough—or romantic enough—to fall for the media myth: that it had all ended with the eighties, that everyone was "just saying no." Hell, *nobody* was saying no—they were just paying more to say yes.

He was watching Stevie as she riffled through the pages of her Filofax. She looked up when she reached Wednesday, July 24.

"It completely skipped my mind. I'm supposed to do a guest shot on the SOC gala. It's being televised all over the world."

"That's out of the question," said Ansel. "They'll understand if you cancel."

Lyle agreed. "They can't expect you to keep up with your normal schedule." He shot a quick glance at Madden for backup. "Don't you think so, Joe?"

Madden's eyes were still on Stevie. "I think it's Mrs. Kline's—Stevie's—decision."

He could see from her expression of gratitude that he was right. No wonder she was having trouble holding it together. As if the terror of having her kid grabbed by lunatics wasn't bad enough. What was this shit? Treat Stevie like a china doll and be amazed when she breaks into pieces? You'd think they'd know, all these movie people who were in the business of manipulating other people's emotions. Yeah, well, maybe they spent so much time dealing with fantasy, they'd forgotten how to recognize the real thing.

Except Stevie Kean.

Her voice pulled him back.

"Carla, tell Mrs. Gill I'll call her later." To the three men in the room Stevie said, "I'm the Society's guest of honor, and I can't let them down. I may not be able to help my own son just now, but at least I can help other children—"

The doorbell interrupted, and Carla hurried to answer it. Stevie and Ansel followed her into the foyer. Lyle and Madden stayed behind in the study.

They were joined a few moments later by Detective Lt. Mike Galvin.

Madden wasn't sure who was the more surprised.

"Well, Joe," said Galvin, coming all the way into the room, "I thought you weren't going to do my job for me. Change of heart?"

"Not at all, Galvin. Change of status. I'm on the case."

Twenty

Lyle was seated alone in his office. The production storyboards, cast breakdowns, shooting script, and day-to-day schedules were spread out in front of him.

He took a long drag on the joint he was smoking. It was a luxury he couldn't afford when Ansel was around. But it was Saturday and the place was deserted, so it was safe.

His free hand tapped the desk, but he stopped almost as soon as he began. There were times when the habit annoyed him as much as it annoyed his business partner.

He unlocked the top drawer, opened it, and pulled out the file folder that contained the insurance papers. Since Wednesday he'd gone over and over the specifics. He'd studied and reread the terms of the completion bond, cast insurance, checked the liability clauses, and the answers were the same each time: *If* he could guarantee completion of the picture and delivery of the negative on schedule, Kline-Hemmings would still be sailing in smooth waters. Cast insurance would cover

Stevie, whether or not she returned to work. There'd be no need to shut down the picture.

And no need for anyone to call an audit.

He took another drag just as the phone rang. The switchboard was closed today, and Lyle's private number was known only to a few people. This had to be important.

"Hey, babe, I figured you'd be at your office."

"Manny!" Lyle hissed. "I told you never to call me here!"

Twenty-one

Todd wasn't having fun anymore. Oh, the clowns had tried to keep him from feeling homesick. They'd brought him toys and books and candy. And two orders of french fries with his Big Mac and chocolate milkshake every day. One of the clowns had even taught him how to use the remote control for the magic monsters—except that Todd was smart. He knew it wasn't really magic, it was some kind of computer. And the animals weren't really monsters, they were computer robots in Halloween costumes. Otherwise they wouldn't just stand there, like dummies, unless Todd pressed one of the numbers on the remote.

At first he'd had a good time, but that was just until the clown who'd brought him here had locked him in. That clown wasn't as nice as the other one who'd given him picture books to look at and told him a bedtime story so he wouldn't be scared.

There were no windows in the place, so Todd couldn't tell if it was day or night. But he could count to twenty. The bedtime-story clown had tucked him in three times in a row, so Todd knew three nights had passed. And he could recite the days of the week by heart. Wednesday, Thursday, Friday. So today must be Saturday. Maybe Mommy would come for him tomorrow night, the way she did on Sundays when he went to visit Daddy.

He tried not to think about that. He didn't want to cry the way he had when Daddy went to stay away from the house. He was bigger now. And maybe if he was good and did everything the clowns told him to—even brush his teeth before bed—Mommy and Daddy would take him home and they could all be together again.

He'd been sitting on the floor leafing through the pages of a baby book. It had pretty pictures in it, but not enough words. Todd couldn't read yet, but he'd memorized his alphabet and could spell out words, even if he didn't know what they meant.

He put the picture book aside and went to the bookshelf. There were lots of grown-up-looking books, but they were higher than his arms could reach. Maybe he could bring a chair over and climb up to the shelf.

He started to drag the chair when he saw another book. This one wasn't on a shelf but on a table, with some other books. Maybe that was better. If he climbed up on the chair, he might fall and hurt himself.

He abandoned the chair and picked up the black book. He had to hold it with both hands, it was so big.

He sat back down on the floor and opened the

cover. What a long name! It had to be a very grown-up book. He began to spell aloud:

"E-n-c-y-c-l-o-p-e-d-i-a." What could that be? he wondered. He went on to the next word. "S-a-t-a-n-i-c." And the next, which was a small word. "C-u-l-t-s."

He was about to start the fourth word when he heard the sound of a key turning in the lock.

The door opened and one of the clowns—the big one—stood looking down at him.

"What're you doing, Todd?"

"Reading."

The clown put down the tray with the good-smelling food and went straight to the book lying open on the floor.

Slamming the cover, the clown asked, "Where did you find this?"

Todd thought the clown sounded angry. "It's okay," he said, "it was over there"—he pointed to the table—"I didn't climb up to get it."

"Never mind. Here's your dinner. And stick to the books we gave you."

"I already read them."

"Then play with the monsters!" The clown grabbed the remote control and tossed it in Todd's lap.

"There's something wrong with it," said Todd.

The clown came closer. "What?"

Todd picked up the remote. "It doesn't work."

"Of course it works. You have to point it at the monster and press the number, the way I showed you. Watch." The clown pressed number 3, and sure enough, a four-foot-high extraterrestrial began waving its arms.

Todd was shaking his head. "It's not the right one! It's the big one, over there!" He nodded toward the huge grizzly bear in the corner, pointed the remote, and pressed the number 5.

Nothing happened.

"See? It doesn't work!"

The clown crouched down beside Todd and hit the same number several times.

"See?" Todd clapped his hands. "I told you, I told you!"

"Shut up! Try another number!"

The clown's anger frightened Todd, especially when the painted rubber face leaned in so close that Todd could smell the horrible breath.

"I want my mommy!" Todd yelled. "I don't want to stay here! I don't want to play! I want to go home!"

The clown's eyes were glaring through cutout holes in the silly mask. Todd leaned as far back and away as he could, but the bulbous red nose was getting nearer, and Todd was scared—so scared that before he could think, he'd yanked the red nose clean off the clown's mask.

And before he knew it, the clown had smacked him. Hard.

Todd tried not to cry.

The clown said nothing, but rose and moved to the door.

"Don't ever do that again, Todd. And I mean *ever!* Do you understand?"

Todd nodded. And then, even though he didn't

want to, he burst into tears. He was sobbing so loudly, he didn't hear the door closing or the key turning in the lock.

Twenty-two

The rainclouds and dampness made the heat more unbearable and thwarted Eppie's plans for a quiet morning sunning herself at poolside. She closed the French doors to shut out the humidity and surveyed her library-office in search of inspiration. As always, her eyes settled on the pink telephone on her matching lacquered pink desk.

She stared at the instrument. Ring, goddammit!

And it did.

At first she heard only breathing. Then a low whisper.

"She drives a blue '87 Honda. Her last name is Reynolds and she lives on Cahuenga. In Hollywood."

A click, and then silence.

Eppie eased herself onto the cabbage-rose tapestry seat of her desk chair.

She wasn't sure if this voice belonged to the same woman who had called the first time.

She didn't care. The info wasn't costing a dime.

Eppie put on her rhinestone-studded reading glasses, cleared space on her cluttered desk, and opened the telephone directory to the letter *R*.

Bingo. Reynolds, T., right there on Cahuenga where the whisperer said she'd be. The excitement made Eppie's palms clammy as she picked up the receiver to make the call.

The line was busy. Just as well; she could use a minute or two to prepare her strategy. She grabbed a long pink pad and began jotting down notes.

Todd's safety should be stressed above all else. "Tammi," she'd say, "together we can help find him." And flattery. "You're the key link in the case, Tammi. The star." Well, that might be too much.

Then what? Money, of course. Maybe start by offering a grand, work slowly to ten; Hubie would okay that. Five up front, five when the interview—the *exclusive* interview—saw print.

Eppie tried the number again. After four rings, a woman answered.

"Hello, I'd like to speak with Miss Tammi Reynolds."

"You and halfa LA. Miss Tammi Reynolds don't live here no more."

Shit! "Well, I'm an old friend, and I saw her picture in the paper, so . . ."

"Everybody seen it, lady. Tammi probably never knew she was so popular. This phone been ringin' off the hook. People she ain't spoke to in years. All because of that trashy, Godless *Scoop* rag what printed her picture. They all after her now."

"It's very important that I find her, Miss, uh . . ."

"Eulaliah."

"Excuse me?"

"That's my name. Eulaliah. E-u-l—"

"I've got it, thanks. Where did Tammi go?"

"You ain't said who *you* are."

"Iphigenia." *So there.*

"Hold on, I'm writin' it down. Okay now, Iffy, I don't know where Tammi's got to. She split from here 'bout five months ago. Real upset over that Stevie Kean divorce."

"You must have some idea where she is."

"Iffy, ole Tammi's sweet, but she crazy as a bed-bug when it come to her movie stars. She already been locked up once."

"Poor thing. You don't think she left town, though?"

"Nah. She around. She always around. Try the bars."

"Which ones?"

"I wouldn't know. I don't go to bars."

"Of course you don't. Where did she work?"

"She didn't, far as I know. Not regular, anyhow. Used to do some of that extra stuff in pictures now and again, but it ain't steady. She also do dog-walkin'. Like I say, nothin' regular."

"I see. Well, thank you, Eulaliah. You've been very helpful. And kind."

"It's why we're here, Iffy. God bless."

Eppie hung up. Great. Her anonymous tipster's info was stale.

She glanced down at her notes. *Tammi—locked up?* Dammit, she hadn't asked where. Well, it wouldn't matter, if her next call panned out. It was a long shot, but Screen Actors Guild might have a more recent address on Tammi Reynolds.

The union offices were closed till tomorrow, and Eppie's story angle was crying to be written *now*. If she didn't want to spend the entire day combing the Hollywood-area bars and scouting pooch-sitters all over town, she'd better find a way to get into the SAG membership files.

Or have someone do it for her.

With Tammi's picture plastered on the front page of *Scoop*, Eppie couldn't trust her usual cadre of informants not to sell whatever they had, including their souls, to a rival paper. So she'd been doing much of her own digging on this one.

But not all of it. Thank God there were a few semiloyal "scouts" listed in her pink crocodile Filofax. One of them was Busby.

Eppie's paid snoop at SAG, however, could find no record of recent employment for a member named Tammi Reynolds.

"Christ on a crutch," she muttered. It wasn't Busby's fault, but Eppie would probably have to visit the bars, after all.

Eppie tried cheering herself with the thought that at least she'd have more material for her best-seller autobiography one day. This chapter would be titled "Sacrifices."

She was on her way out when the telephone rang again.

"Busby here, Eppie!"

"I hope you're not calling to disappoint me a second time, darling," she said.

"*Au contraire.* I've been putting in a little overtime for my favorite columnist."

"*Journalist.* What have you got?"

"Something that you and a private dick, if you'll pardon the expression, and a certain LAPD cop are all very interested in, m'dear."

"Cop? Is his name Galvin? What did you tell him?"

"Nothing. Not even that you got to me first. Ditto Mr. Joe Madden."

"Madden. That sounds familiar. Wait. I'm writing."

"I figured what I've turned up could be worth a bonus . . ."

"Busby, don't jerk me off."

"Okay, okay. Turns out there's a T. Reynolds on the SAG report for yesterday. Scheduled to work today, too, over at Fox. Soundstage C. Big call. Crowd scene, a few hundred extras. Probably why they're using her—from desperation."

"I could kiss you, Busby!"

"Money will do, dear. I'm impeding justice for you."

"Just impede it until four o'clock, then repeat all of this to Lieutenant Galvin."

"What about Mr. Madden?"

"Fuck him."

"Doesn't sound like my type, thanks. Now, about the money . . ."

"I'll make out the check as soon as we hang up!"

Well, that was a reprieve. A film set. Familiar turf. And she wouldn't even have to dress down.

Eppie waited at the door to Soundstage C until the red light went off. Then she pulled open the door to the sounds of ringing bells and the voice of Marty Wollner, the world's oldest assistant director, bellowing, "Clear the set!"

Eppie watched as his Moses-like authority parted the sea of extras. Hordes fled to the coffee urns and Danish pastries on the tables along the wall. At the center of the mob, thanks to Eppie, was an easily identifiable face.

Tammi Reynolds stood surrounded by a dozen other extras, most of them women, all of them her junior by a good ten years. A few held copies of Friday's *Scoop*.

Even from a distance of ten feet or so, Eppie could see that Tammi had changed since the baby-shower tape. Her face was fuller, her hair shorter and grayer. Her body still resembled a lumpy sack of potatoes, but now the sack held more tubers.

Eppie edged her way over to Marty Wollner. She'd need a few minutes with Tammi Reynolds, far and away from her newfound fans.

"Yeah, I can spare her," Marty said. "Now and forever. We'll be shooting the opposite angle after the break. That'll put her out of camera range."

"What's she like?"

Marty glanced around. "Don't quote me, Eppie,

but she's zooey. She was booked before we ever saw her mug in the paper, or I would've nixed her. She elbowed her way into the foreground and got established in the first shot. We're behind schedule as it is, and a weekend of double pay is pricey enough for a crowd this size. I don't need a wacko who can't take direction. I had to keep her for matching, otherwise I'd have dumped her yesterday." Marty looked over toward Tammi and her entourage, then brought the bullhorn to his lips. *Please* clear the set!"

Tammi and her fan club moved to the side.

Marty turned back to Eppie. "She loves the attention, and at least she's leaving the principals alone. Two years ago I threw her off a set 'cause she kept bugging the star."

"You don't mean Stevie Kean, do you?"

"No. The casting people have been clued in about keeping her off Stevie's pictures. Listen, stay here a sec. I'll tell Tammi her press has arrived."

The rainclouds had gone and the sun outside the soundstage was bright. It made Tammi squint, which in turn made her eyes even smaller. She tilted her tattered straw hat against the glare and leaned against the wall.

"I'm sorry there's nowhere else we can talk," Eppie said.

"We do what's necessary," Tammi answered with a grand gesture. "You know, this is my first picture in a while. It's thrilling to be back among the lights and the cameras."

And all those wonderful people out there in the dark. Eppie recognized the lines from Norma Desmond's final speech in *Sunset Boulevard,* but she marveled that Tammi Reynolds had just used it.

"Then I'm happy for you, dear," she said. "Now, about the Klines . . ."

Tammi's face flushed with color. "I don't blame Stevie for that headline, Miss Goldwyn! A star's life is certainly not an easy one, despite what the public thinks."

Tammi's voice was soft. Eppie moved in and angled her purse closer, hoping the tape recorder inside was getting every word.

"Of course it isn't easy, Tammi. Especially for poor Stevie. I mean, when you consider the strain of her separation, and now with little Todd missing . . ."

Eppie wanted to recoil when Tammi touched her arm, but she didn't dare.

"Ansel's mother should just butt out of that marriage!" Tammi exclaimed. "All she's done is interfere!"

A quote! Good girl, Tammi! "And we want to help Stevie and Ansel bring Todd home. Isn't that true?"

"Yes! Yes!" Tammi's eyes filled with tears. "A woman's baby is everything to her. And then God takes him away and there's nothing to fill the void. Except another baby."

"What?"

"If I could just tell Stevie! That's why she and Ansel *must* get back together!"

"To . . . make another baby?"

"Yes! But I try not to meddle in Stevie's business, Miss Goldwyn. I stay out of sight while I watch over her. You might say I'm an extra in the story of her life."

"Like a guardian angel?"

"Exactly! And it's so hard, now that people know me! All we really want is to be left alone."

Garbo talks. "Unless going public can bring Todd home."

"Yes! But I'm on guard, Miss Goldwyn. I see a lot. And I'll see more."

"More, dear?"

"Who comes, who goes. Like the chauffeur, and—never mind. It's just, well, there are certain people who should watch their step, that's all."

"Tammi, do you know who took the baby?"

"God."

"God? He's taken Todd?"

"Not Todd. The *baby*."

"Uh, dear, are we talking about the same child?"

"No," Tammi answered. "I really have to get back to the set. I've already said too much." She turned to go.

"Wait!" This time it was Eppie who touched Tammi's arm. "What you just said. You meant *your* baby?"

Tammi's expression drifted off, as though she were on another movie lot. Or another planet.

"Todd is like a replacement," she said in a dreamy voice. But she snapped back as suddenly as she'd left. "I'm going now. Just remember, we have to help Stevie through this terrible ordeal! Write that down and print it, exactly what I said. Everything."

"I will, Tammi."

"You ought to know, Miss Goldwyn, I don't give many interviews. But this was nice."

Eppie opened her bag, careful to keep the recorder well out of sight. She withdrew a single hundred-dollar bill and handed it to Tammi.

"Here. For your trouble."

Tammi stared at the bill. The color drained from her face and the acne scars seemed to deepen.

"What is this?" she demanded.

"Well, if it's not enough . . ." Eppie pulled out another hundred.

"I don't want money! I *never* wanted money! Stevie mustn't think that!"

"I'm sure she doesn't, Tammi. This is just—"

"People always get in the way! Everything I say gets twisted!"

"I'm sorry if I—"

"How did you find me?"

"Tammi, dear—"

"No! I won't say any more about this! Ever! I thought you wanted to help Stevie!"

"I do."

"You *don't!* I can see now that I'm going to have to take care of everything by myself!" Tammi spun on her heels and ran back to the soundstage entrance.

The overhead red light was blinking as she yanked the door open and let it slam behind her.

Eppie's hands were still shaking as she returned the two hundred-dollar bills to her purse. At the same time, she switched off the tape recorder.

Well, one thing was certain: she'd gotten an exclusive. And then some.

She checked her watch.

It wasn't too early for a drink. Not after this.

Twenty-three

Ansel hadn't wanted to leave Stevie alone at the house, but she was right when she'd said to Joe Madden and Ansel that she wasn't alone. "Just take a peek out the window. I'm surrounded by the fourth estate." She'd almost managed a laugh.

She was also right about Ansel's spine. Another night on the sofabed and he could wind up in traction.

He wasn't nuts about the obvious relief on Madden's face when the detective realized that the matching bathrobes were nothing more than coincidence. Or that Ansel hadn't slept in the master bedroom.

Master. Yeah, of all he surveyed.

At the moment he was surveying his antiseptic-clean luxury rental unit in Westwood. The realtor had referred to it as a bachelor apartment. "With every accoutrement a man in your position could possibly want or need," she'd said. Her voice and manner had suggested that the lease came with an unwritten rider. In short, the lady was available.

Sure, like two-thirds of Hollywood's wannabe's.

All of them gorgeous and willing. Some even had brains. All a guy had to do—especially in Ansel's position, as the lady had said—was ask.

But Ansel wasn't asking, because he wasn't interested.

In the beginning he hadn't understood why. Oh, he'd expected the inevitable comparisons; Stevie was a hard act to follow. But it intrigued him, even puzzled him, that while he and Stevie were splitting up because of irreconcilable differences," a mere ten minutes in the company of another woman made him eager to run, eager to not have to explain himself. The line from *Peggy Sue Got Married*, "I got tired of translating," said it all.

An evening at home. Except that he felt anywhere but home. Seven rooms, six too many. Ansel was the one who had balked at Stevie's instant infatuation with the house in Beachwood Canyon. "We'll need more space," he'd argued. He'd grown up in a three-story hacienda-style mansion, the ultimate in elegance, and Stevie had taken one look, described it in one word: ostentatious.

"We're not into formal receptions," she'd said. "And the Canyon is far less snobby than the Hills." Right on that count, too. Most of their entertaining was casual. Barbecues or buffets. Ansel had even begun to enjoy parties once they'd moved into the rustic wood-and-glass split-level. His mother had hated it on sight, an unanticipated bonus; Carolyn limited her visits to one per week, on Sunday.

Today was Sunday, July 21. But Ansel's preoccupation with the date had nothing to do with his

147

mother. There were eleven days left before the cult was expected to strike again.

The same overwhelming sense of helplessness he'd experienced before was taking hold of him once more, an impotence no less paralyzing for his ability to move. What good was mobility when he felt incapable of action?

He wasn't unfamiliar with this feeling of uselessness. He'd understood it, without ever having considered it, from the moment he learned that Stevie was pregnant.

He'd often ruminated on it since then, usually after Stevie was asleep. He'd been unable to talk to her about it. How did you tell your best friend—when that best friend was also your wife—that you felt left out? Stevie was the one carrying the baby all those months, the one who would suffer the pain of childbirth; Daddy's "job" was finished. Nine months of impending fatherhood, during which the phrase, *stud service*, was seldom far from his mind.

He'd tried to solve that problem the way he'd solved others in the past—by *not* thinking, by just getting on with the everyday details of his busy life. But he'd envied the easy way Stevie could examine her feelings without falling prey to self-pity or doubt.

And sometimes he'd resented her for it. She didn't play emotional games, didn't take his mother's self-righteous attitude or tone. Ansel had wanted the very antithesis of Carolyn Kline, and he'd found her in Stevie.

So where had they gone wrong?

The telephone rang, which surprised Ansel. He'd been at the apartment for the better part of the evening and no one had called until now. Everyone seemed to assume that he could be reached at the house in the canyon instead of here. Except Joe Madden, who had left with him.

Madden had promised to call the moment he had news. Ansel raced to the phone.

It wasn't news, and it wasn't Madden.

"Did I wake you?" Stevie asked.

"Hardly. I haven't even eaten dinner. You?"

"I wasn't hungry. I just thought maybe you'd . . . heard from Joe."

"I'd have called you. Probably after he did. Anybody else call?"

"Just Lyle. He's meeting with the insurance people tomorrow morning."

Ansel wasn't going to discuss Stevie's shooting schedule; that would only lead to speculation about Todd.

"How did Lyle sound?" he asked.

"How does he usually sound these days? You know, 'I am Oz, the great and powerful.'"

"Shit."

"No, coke."

Neither of them laughed.

Ansel wasn't sure what was the best way, if there was indeed a best way, to tell her that he was going back to work in the morning. She might not understand that Ansel's old adversary, Uselessness, was waging his familiar battle again.

149

"Listen, Stevie, I told Barbara to schedule a six-thirty A.M. call tomorrow. We're going with the interiors of the governor's reception."

He waited. They both knew that Stevie had an important scene at the governor's reception. It would require close-ups, reaction shots, and pans of the entire ballroom.

She didn't let him down. "Then you've found a double. Good. Maybe I can loop the dialogue when . . . when all this is over."

"I can't just sit here, Stevie. It doesn't help things, it only makes them worse."

"You're right, Ansel. I'd come to work, too, if . . ." Her voice caught and she didn't finish.

She didn't have to.

"Look, Stevie, I don't know what to say."

"I do. You should have something to eat. There's got to be Chinese takeout in your neighborhood." In the old days, they'd opted for Chinese food on Sundays. "And try to get some sleep. You'll probably have to get up around four."

"Will you be all right?"

There was a long pause, after which she said, "I'll be all right when I know Todd is all right. But with Joe Madden working on it, I guess I'll make it through the night."

"I'll call you from the set tomorrow," he said.

"Please . . . I'd appreciate it."

Ansel knew the words that filled Stevie's pause were the same as his own: *Unless there's news before tomorrow.*

* * *

He didn't send out for Chinese food. And he didn't touch the salad he prepared from leftovers in the refrigerator. He dressed it and tossed it and forgot all about it, leaving the round wooden bowl at the center of the kitchen table.

He wandered aimlessly from room to room, turning out lights, picking up magazines or socks or whatever lay strewn about.

Funny, he hadn't paid much attention to the place until now, hadn't realized that it seemed as though the set decorator from one of his films had gone overbudget at Bloomingdale's and come up with a look that said: "I don't know a thing about the guy who lives here."

Well, at the moment, that made two of them. Ansel felt like a stranger in his own home.

No, this wasn't his home. He didn't really *live* here. No wonder it resembled a movie set. Ansel spent more time there than he did here. And felt more alive there.

When had that begun? Months ago, even before the separation. He and Stevie had become more like roommates. Business partners. The pressure coming from all sides, the gossip timed to publicize their films. Maybe it was a case of too much working together that had brought them to an impasse.

Then again, the only time they'd had together during the months leading to their split-up had been at the studio or on location. They'd been caught up in the Hollywood whirlwind they'd sworn would never come between them.

And before they'd known it, they'd been swallowed up.

Why had it taken their son's kidnapping to bring it into focus?

Ansel was in the den with its fully stocked wet bar. He poured himself a brandy and walked to the window. No press corps on the grounds in Westwood tonight. Of course not. They were stationed in Beachwood Canyon, thanks to Friday's edition of *Scoop* and that goddammed Eppie Goldwyn. He'd given Joe Madden her home telephone number and address, but Joe had hinted that he had a few of his own leads to follow up first.

Ansel finished his brandy and turned out the light. He remained standing at the window, gazing off into the dark and remembering that first night with Stevie, at Malibu, after the Oscars.

She'd been right about not asking for the moon.

Ansel felt a tear trickling down his cheek. They'd had the stars, and lost them.

Ansel hadn't prayed since childhood. He didn't believe in the Standard Edition of God. But just now he felt the need to connect with Something Out There.

Please, don't let us lose Todd, too, he whispered, realizing that his silent words were directed to that part of himself and the Universe that were one with God, whatever, wherever God was.

Twenty-four

Monday, July 22

Dammit, the schmucks were ready to leave and Lyle hadn't had his say. The short, bald "suit," Olson, rose and offered a handshake. Vale, the suit with hair, took the cue and did the same.

"This shouldn't be a major problem," Olson said.

Cigarette smoke curled over Vale's nodding head and he kept trying to wave it away. He hadn't said much during the meeting, but his head was in constant motion.

"Tragic, of course," Olson continued, "but there's no need to think the worst yet."

Lyle made another attempt. "It could be months, and we've shot too much film to replace Miss Kean. Without her, the picture is ruined!"

"We sympathize, Mr. Hemmings. However, our position is to explore every possible alternative of completion, whether that is with or without Miss Kean's participation."

"Mr. Olson, what if it just can't be done?" Lyle asked, lighting another cigarette.

"We will address payment of cast insurance when the Kline child's fate has been determined, and only in the event that Miss Kean is classified as unable to work."

"She's already unable to work!"

Vale, his head still shaking, spoke at last. "It's too soon to tell, Mr. Hemmings. Todd Kline may be found alive and well tomorrow, and Miss Kean could be back in front of the cameras within days."

"What if the worst happens, and she isn't?" asked Lyle.

"We would then consider settlement of the losses incurred for the final four weeks of scheduled shooting in which Miss Kean would be unable to appear." Olson glanced down at the notes and papers in front of him. "Roughly four million, I'd say."

"But you still want a finished negative, and I can't deliver that without my leading lady!"

"Mr. Hemmings, a settlement, should that become necessary, would occur only because the bond you signed guarantees us a completed product."

"So you don't care if the 'completed product' stars King Kong, as long as it's all in the can!"

"You might consider shooting around Miss Kean."

"But everything we've shot so far will go right down the tubes—the *product* will stink!"

Olson shrugged. "We don't guarantee success, Mr. Hemmings."

Lyle wanted to throttle them both.

Instead, he escorted them to the parking lot. They'd already been given the requisite tour of the set and met Ansel. The director at work. Lyle knew that work had nothing to do with Ansel's being here, but it looked good to these jerks.

Olson and Vale climbed into their car, and Lyle allowed himself a smile. The suits were always trying to hide their bug eyes about movies, but it was clear they were reluctant to leave.

They even waved.

Lyle waved back, then rushed to his office, where he locked the door and tried to control a sudden shortness of breath.

He threw off his linen jacket and went to his desk. The air-conditioner was on high-cool, but sweat had turned his gray silk shirt to black. His complexion was gray, too, and the whites of his eyes were bloodshot.

He shoved the storyboards aside to clear space for the blow. He snorted only two lines; if he didn't conserve, by tomorrow he'd be out. Or dead.

Funny that Manny should be the one calling the shots. Some little Spic with a hack license, bullying people at the top. A real scream.

Lyle rubbed the rest of the dust over his gums as he checked his desk calendar. How much longer could he stall Manny and his "associates"?

Long enough. He'd get it under control. There. That felt more like the old Lyle. Or the old toot. Same thing. Now he'd visit the set. A soundstage was the one place where he still knew who Lyle Hemmings was—or was supposed to be. "The nose knows," he muttered, laughing as he returned his remaining stash to the drawer, locked it, and pocketed the key.

The minute he stepped through the door, they called a break. He'd known they would. Goddammed right.

"Geez, how high are you?" Ansel whispered between Lyle's sniffs.

"A little pick-me-up, partner. I just spent an hour with straights."

"And so now you've come down here to throw your weight around?"

"Ansel, baby, you're under a lot of stress, too."

"Yeah, yeah. How'd it go?"

"Four million into Kline-Hemmings Productions. That's net ascertained loss for us being minus our star for the duration of the shoot. Two mil apiece."

"Am I supposed to be happy?"

"You asked."

"Lyle, I'm spinning my wheels here. There isn't that much footage to shoot without Stevie or a major rewrite."

"It won't take that long for an answer."

Ansel stared into Lyle's wild eyes. "You mean ten days, if we don't find Todd?"

"I didn't say that."

"You did, Lyle!"

"Now, look!" Lyle lowered his voice. "We *all* want Stevie to come back to work, because that'll mean Todd is okay. But Ansel, these insurance guys don't *care!* The bottom line is, this flick's gotta get finished, otherwise the cast insurance doesn't mean borscht!"

"All right, all right," Ansel said, running his hands through his hair. "I just don't give a shit about the picture anymore, Lyle." He moved away, past the cameras, the crew, and into the middle of a group of actors wearing forties' evening dress. The set, the interior of a Bahamian governor's palace, evoked a more glamorous version of Rick's Place in *Casablanca*. Two hundred grand a day, including salaries, for seven minutes of film, and he didn't give a shit.

Neither did Lyle. Not about the picture. It was the cash. It had been so different in the beginning—both of them getting high on movies, not on drugs. Lyle had said an occasional snort gave him extra energy for long hours on the set. "You ought to try it," he'd advised. But Ansel hadn't tried it, and now he was glad. Drugs had turned his partner into someone Ansel hardly knew anymore. Something needed to change, and fast.

Ansel cupped his hands at his mouth and called, "Action!"

Lyle nodded. Yeah. Action. Just what the doctor ordered. There was a tap on his shoulder.

"What now, for Chrissake?" he hissed.

"Your ex-chauffeur is waiting for you in your office," whispered Barbara Halsey, not hiding her disgust. "He won't leave until he talks to you."

"Who let him in?"

"Ask. He *ordered* me to get you." Barbara noticed that Lyle's face suddenly paled beneath his tan. "Want me to call Security?"

"No!" He placed a hand on her arm. "No, it's okay. I'll handle it."

"Lyle, what's all this about?"

"Uh . . . just some back salary he thinks I owe him. Forget it."

He knew she wouldn't.

Lyle ruined the shot when he let the huge metal door slam behind him, and Barbara hurried to Ansel, who was shouting at the top of his lungs.

Manny was seated with his hands folded behind his head and his feet on Lyle's desk.

"What the fuck are you doing here?" Lyle yelled.

Manny was up and across the room in a single move. He fell on Lyle with all his weight. Lyle's head struck the door on impact, while Manny's forearm pressed against his throat.

"Who the fuck do you think you're talkin' to, Paco?" Manny's face was so close that Lyle could smell his foul tobacco breath. "And who d'you think we're playin' with here?"

"How'd you get on the lot?" Lyle was gasping.

"Connections." The chauffeur-turned-supplier held up the blade of a knife for Lyle to see, then touched its point against his throat. "My people are puttin' the screws to me, Mr. Movie!"

"I need more time!"

"Right. And then you'll need more blow." Manny moved the blade to Lyle's nostril. "How about I cut your fuckin' nose off, my man? That'd take care of your problem for good. You want that?"

"Stop it!"

Manny increased the pressure against Lyle's throat. "What? I can hardly hear you, babe!"

"I—can't—breathe!"

"Oh. Well, maybe you'd like for me to mess up your little friend Carla instead?"

"No!"

"Good. Now listen, babe, and listen good. I don't die for no junkie! My people ain't waitin' for me no more, and I ain't waitin' for you!"

"I'll get it!"

"When?" Manny touched the edge of the blade to the tip of Lyle's nose. "When? I want a date, and a time. And it better be soon, motherfucker!"

Twenty-five

Stevie hadn't slept Sunday night, even before the unsettling dream woke her. She sensed that something in her subconscious mind was reaching out to her, but once she'd fully awakened, only the feeling remained, a feeling not unlike an all-over muscle ache after too much exercise or an attack of the flu.

She'd considered calling Ansel, but at half past five he'd already have left for the studio. Why bother him on the car phone unless there was news? Besides, he'd promised to call her later from the set. So she'd gone through the motions of trying to fall back to sleep. And hadn't.

At seven she made a pot of coffee and picked up the script she already knew by heart. She opened it to the scene that Ansel would be shooting—around her—today.

The dialogue could have been printed in Chinese for all the sense it made this morning. Stevie's thoughts defiantly refused to stay with the page. Finally, after staring blankly at the same lines for ten minutes without absorbing a single word, she closed the script.

Only when she noticed Friday's copy of *Scoop* on the kitchen banquette—and saw her photograph alongside Tammi-the-fan's on page 1—did Stevie's dream from her sleepless night break through to logic.

And logic told her that despite Lt. Galvin and his task force's conviction—or obsession—that a satanic cult was behind Todd's disappearance, the answer lay elsewhere.

For the moment it was only a nagging suspicion, but Stevie was beginning to feel the familiar twinge. It was the same, visceral response that came whenever she was studying a new role. She would immerse herself totally in a character until she reached a point at which she knew the character as well or better than she knew herself: what the fictive woman felt, the way she thought, spoke, dressed, moved, right on down to her favorite foods, perfume, colors. Then, after days and nights of mental homework, she would at last feel the physical sensation, the sudden rush that told her she'd found her "hook." Or that the hook had found her.

She'd never consciously applied the technique to life, but she recognized the feeling. Stevie was on to something.

By 7:30 A.M., Stevie had showered and dressed, made notes, and realized that she needed much more information than *Scoop* or the weekend edition of the *LA Times* could provide.

She telephoned LAPD. Lt. Galvin wasn't on duty yet. She wasn't surprised that the desk sergeant couldn't give her Galvin's home number, but she asked.

She also asked for the case files—those of the children previously kidnapped and the file on Todd.

"I'm sorry, ma'am," said the sergeant, "that's confidential information."

"But I'm the mother of one of the children!"

"I understand, ma'am, but it's against department regulations."

After three impassioned appeals, she hung up and called Barbara Halsey at the studio.

"Barb, I know you're busy, but I need your help."

"If it's humanly possible, name it. If it's not, I'll send Fran."

"I want to read up on the kidnappings. All of them, since the very first one."

Barbara didn't answer immediately. After a pause: "Stevie, are you sure? I mean, some of it's pretty awful."

"I've got to see all of it, Barb. I don't know how you go about it, whether the newspapers keep a backlog in their morgue, or whether it's on microfilm at the library, but it can't take that long. The first case"—Stevie couldn't bring herself to use the word *killing*—"was in January, from what Lieutenant Galvin told me last Thursday."

Thursday. Five days ago. Had Todd been missing for so short a time?

Stevie heard shouting in the background, and when Barbara next spoke, she sounded rushed. "Listen, Ansel's screaming for me on the set—for a change. I'll see what I can find and get back to you. It may be a few hours. Will you be at the house?"

Stevie started to say yes, then had an idea. "Try me here. If I'm out, I'll have the call forwarded."

"Fine. And Stevie . . . ?"

"Don't worry, Barb. I'm okay."

She remembered, as they hung up, that only last night she'd told Ansel she wouldn't be okay until they found Todd and *he* was okay. Nothing had happened to change that, yet in a way she couldn't explain, something in *Stevie* was changing.

After five days of fighting her worst fears, Stevie had rediscovered hope.

"Joe! I'm glad you're at your office."

"Stevie?" He'd recognized her voice immediately, but she was calling so early in the day. Of course, she probably wasn't sleeping much these nights. "What can I do for you?"

She hesitated, knowing she was asking him to snoop. But he was a detective, that was part of his job, wasn't it? "Frankly, Joe," she said, "I was wondering if you might have access to certain police files."

She didn't have to tell him which files.

"Look, Stevie, even if Mike Galvin and I were

bosom buddies, I doubt he'd hand over the details of his investigation to me or to anyone else. Mike's not the type to share top billing." He reached for a cigarette and lit it, then added, "If it's any consolation, he's a thorough cop. Meaning, he'll follow up every lead, even when it's a wild-goose chase."

That wasn't good enough for Stevie. "Joe, do you have a computer?" If he didn't, she'd offer the use of the one in Ansel's study.

Her study. Ansel had forgotten to move the PC to his apartment.

"I've got a dinosaur-age Kaypro," said Joe. "But even with a state-of-the-art system, you don't get into LAPD's files by just pressing a function key, and as far as I know, USC doesn't offer courses in computer break-in. But the mind is still the best computer there is, so why don't you tell me what's on yours?"

She did, and was relieved that he agreed with her theory, especially since she had no hard evidence to back up what was, for now, wholly based on instinct.

"I'm a great believer in instinct," said Madden. Then he decided to follow his own. "Maybe we could talk about it over lunch."

He suggested Mortons because he knew the studio mucky-mucks spent more time there than they did at home. She explained, without making him feel like an outsider, that Mortons wasn't open for lunch. She suggested Le Dôme, but by then he'd realized they'd be sitting ducks for every paparazzo in town.

"On second thought, maybe you'd prefer someplace a bit more out of the way, off the beaten track." He'd spent years in such places.

Her answer surprised him because it wasn't a cover-up for the usual I-want-to-avoid-publicitybut-I'll-die-without-it practiced by other stars he'd met.

"Actually," she said, "there'll be less of a hassle if we're seen out in the open. High visibility means we'll be among our own, not so much of a novelty."

Nice of her to include him.

Of course he'd be included—like the entrée special—no matter where they went. The paparazzi attached themselves like barnacles to the Hollywood ladies who lunched—particularly when those ladies weren't lunching alone. He could picture tomorrow's edition of *Scoop*. Eyes, hands, gestures, even the way he held his knife and fork, were all grist for Eppie Goldwyn and her cronies' mills. He'd have to keep this afternoon strictly business.

They chose Musso and Frank's. One o'clock. That would give Madden a chance to follow up on the lead he hadn't mentioned to Stevie, and he'd still have time to stop home and change clothes. Yeah, for Stevie Kean, he was willing to dress like a mensch.

Barbara Halsey felt like a gerbil in a cage—running on a treadmill and getting nowhere fast.

At least her assistant was getting somewhere.

Fran had spent the better part of the morning tracking down and photocopying every piece of news that had been printed locally about the cult kidnappings and murders.

And Barbara had spent the last two hours combing through the results of Fran's eyestrain. Whatever it was that Stevie hoped to find continued to elude Barbara until she'd read and reread the same news items four times. There was a single fact that didn't fit what the police called a recognizable pattern. It didn't connect the previous cases to Todd, and Barbara wanted to figure out why before calling Stevie.

But after her fifth fruitless read-through, she gave up and reached for the phone.

Madden appreciated that Stevie hadn't given him the address. He liked to think she considered him one of the cognoscenti who frequented the popular celebrity spot, even if the truth was probably simpler—that everyone in town except Madden knew where to find the place.

He'd offered to make the reservation, and she'd agreed, with the very tactful suggestion that he mention her name. Good thing, too. After he checked the phone directory for the exact number on Hollywood Boulevard, he called the restaurant. They were booked solid for days—until Madden said the table was for Stephanie Kean.

* * *

He made sure to get there five minutes to one, so he was waiting for her when she arrived.

She was wearing navy-blue. Pants and a matching safari-style shirt. Hair swept up off her neck the way it had been at the house on Saturday morning. Very little makeup, very dark glasses. She looked fabulous.

There was a lot of vocal gushing inside as she was greeted like returning royalty. Madden didn't mind; he was treated like her prince consort, or whatever it was called when the queen's prime squeeze walked not beside her but six paces behind.

He'd hoped to learn more about her personal life aside from the case. So far, though, she wasn't giving any signals. He also had to remember that just because no flashbulbs were popping, they were still candidates for *Candid Camera*.

And he had news.

"I spoke with Tammi Reynolds this morning," he said, taking a sip of his Evian water. Stevie had ordered the same, although he was certain she would have preferred wine.

She had removed the dark glasses as soon as they were seated, and hearing Tammi's name seemed to deepen the violet of her eyes.

"Does she . . . did she . . ." Stevie's voice was pinched. "Is there a link between Tammi and Todd?"

Madden shrugged. "She wouldn't tell me much, except that she doesn't trust anyone, that people have exploited her, et cetera."

"But did she give you the impression, was there

anything that . . ." Stevie couldn't finish the sentence. If there was no connection, she'd have to accept Galvin's cult theory, and that was too terrifying to contemplate.

"I get the feeling Tammi knows more than she's willing to tell me," said Madden. "Apparently, Eppie Goldwyn led Tammi down the garden path, then tricked her. And Galvin intimidated her. So now she won't open up to anyone except her idol."

"Her idol?"

He nodded. "You."

His "you" coincided with the waiter's arrival at tableside with a cellular phone. Madden had noticed earlier that instead of BYOB, Musso and Frank's seemed to be a BYOP—Bring Your Own Phone. Stevie was one of the few lunch guests who had arrived without one. The food courses were akin to sorbets between calls. Hollywood was unique.

"Sorry to interrupt your lunch, Miss Kean," said the waiter with practiced obsequiousness and a phony British accent in need of more practice, "but the caller said it's urgent."

Stevie's adrenaline started pumping, and her visible reaction matched Madden's. *Don't let it be the cops with bad news,* he silently commanded the phone as Stevie lifted it to her ear. *Don't let it be Galvin or anyone from LAPD.*

It wasn't.

"Stevie, it's Barbara, and I didn't mean to—"

"No, no, it's okay." Stevie paused. "*Is* everything okay?"

"It's the newspaper homework you assigned me

this morning." There was commotion at Barbara's end of the line. "Listen, I'll make this fast. The setup's ready and I've got to get back."

"You found something!" Stevie was breathing hard, and Madden leaned across the table. Screw the tabloids. He offered his hand and Stevie took it.

"Well, yes," said Barbara, "I did find something, although I'm not sure what. All four cases read like carbon copies, but there's a glitch and I don't know what it means."

Madden felt the pressure of Stevie's fingers tightening around his hand. And even from across the table he could hear Barbara covering the phone and yelling, "I'm coming!" Then, to Stevie: "The first three babies kidnapped were—"

"Babies?" Stevie cut in.

"Infants."

"But Todd is four." Stevie broke into a sudden, cold sweat. "Barb! That's it—the glitch! It doesn't fit the pattern!"

Stevie had laid the phone aside and loosened her grip on Madden's hand. Now she released it altogether. He waited for her to speak.

When she did, her words confirmed his earlier suspicions.

"It isn't the cult," she said slowly but with new conviction. "It's a copycat kidnapping to make everyone think it *is* the cult."

And then a different fear engulfed her. If it wasn't the cult, who had taken Todd? And why?

"Joe," asked Stevie, her eyes welling with tears, "where does that leave us? Where do we go from here?"

Twenty-six

Galvin had stopped feeling grateful for the tip from Busby after spending only a few minutes with Tammi Reynolds. That she was Looney Tunes was bad enough; that she refused to talk after her interview with Eppie Goldwyn was worse. Time was running out on Todd Kline, and too few people were cooperating. Maybe Rover Jarvis would.

A quarter hour's search yielded Galvin a parking space two blocks from the address he'd gotten from the parole board. He was soaked in sweat when he trudged across the burnt lawn of the run-down courtyard. The deafening sound of electric guitars and human screeching was blaring from one of the bungalows. It grew louder as he drew closer to number 9.

Ringing the bell was useless, so he banged on the door with his fist.

The noise—it could hardly be called music—stopped abruptly. It was instantly replaced by a male voice shouting, "It's only one o'clock! If it's too loud, you're too old!"

The door flew open. A post-thirty, six-foot-tall,

half-naked man covered in hair and tattoos stood glaring at Galvin.

"Why aren't you at work?" Galvin asked.

"I'm on vacation!" He stared at the shield in Galvin's hand. "I thought you were my next-door neighbor."

Rover Jarvis stepped aside to let Galvin enter the darkened living room. The air smelled of stale beer and body odor. Posters for Iron Maiden, Guns 'n' Roses, and Megadeath were taped to the walls.

"Sit down," Jarvis said, throwing soiled shirts onto the floor to clear space on a tattered armchair. "You want a brew?"

"No," Galvin said, sitting. "But you go ahead."

"I will." Jarvis went into the kitchen. "I was scared when you phoned," he called from down the hall, "but I haven't knocked over any more gas stations, so I figured I shouldn't be. Right?"

He returned to the room with an opened bottle of beer and emptied a bag of potato chips onto the Formica coffee table. "Help yourself."

Galvin pulled out his notepad and pen. "You belong to a club named Forfar?"

"*Belonged.* Unofficially. And it's a cult, not a club." Jarvis sat on the sofa and put his bare feet on the table amid the potato chips. "You wanna know about Forfar, you should question Lucas Cabot. He's their high priest."

"We did, with his lawyers right beside him. We got nowhere."

"But you can badger me all you want or you'll screw up my parole, is that it?"

"Something like that."

172

The truth seemed to stun Jarvis, who offered a blank "Oh."

"Why'd you leave the cult?"

"I'm a head banger—like you couldn't tell. The sound got me itchy about satanism. I was never a full-fledged member, but I went to a couple of black masses with a guy who was. 'Course, I was drunk, but even so, it just got too weird with their big Grand Sabbat last August." Jarvis took a guzzle of beer. "Y'know, the cops already asked me all this, man. Why don'tcha read what I told them?"

"I did. I want to hear it from you."

"Well, it don't get any better."

"Tell me anyway." Galvin withdrew his lighter and flipped the top.

"They seemed like a bunch of old hippies pretending to have some class. It boiled down to 'kill the pigs' and all that tired sixties' stuff."

"Drugs?"

"Not that I ever saw. And I don't touch 'em, man! Booze and butts do me fine." Jarvis eyed Galvin's lighter. "You got a smoke? I'm out."

"So am I. Talk to me."

"Okay, let's see. I left in the middle of one of their annual gigs. A summer convention, sort of, up in the hills. About forty of 'em. Cabot, the leader, spoke real strange shit. Really spooked me. The guy I was with wouldn't leave, so I said fuck it, it was my car. I split, and a couple of 'em chased me. Jesus, I thought *I* was gonna get sacrificed!"

"Did you ever witness one?"

"A sacrifice? Nah. But they'd already done, like, chickens and puppies, in the past. I heard they just tore 'em apart and ate some of 'em. I guess that's what they were gonna do later. Cabot was screaming stuff about punishing the rich, appeasing Satan by switching to humans instead."

"Didn't any of the cult members object?"

"A few, but they were too scared to speak up. I guess Cabot must have convinced them eventually, 'cause the baby kidnappings started about six months later."

"And you think the Forfars are responsible for the killings?"

"I wouldn't put it past them. Y'know, I was almost glad I had to spend those three months in the slammer. They couldn't find me, even if they were lookin'. When I got out, I shaved my beard and did this." Jarvis pointed to his palm-tree hair. "Then I moved here."

"Would you recognize any of them?"

Jarvis shook his head. "It's like the Klan. Capes and cowls and masks. And it was dark. They all carried black candles. And there was this cross standing upside-down in the dirt."

"What about your friend?"

"He wasn't a friend. He was hired for a couple days on a construction site I was workin'. That's what I do. I haven't seen or heard from him since that night."

"His name?"

"Called himself Perry Fang."

Galvin looked up from his notepad. "Perry . . . Fang?"

"Hey"—Jarvis made a helpless gesture—"a lot of

metal heads change their names. It's the voltage, man. Makes their ears bleed."

"Where did this Fang hang out?"

"We used to go to FM Station or The Bordello. Gazzari's, once in a while. But he was an up-all-night, sleep-all-day dude. I had a steady job and couldn't party 'cept weekends. Besides, I never got laid with Perry around."

"Cocksman?"

"Tried passin' himself off as a bass player for a thrash band."

"It used to be the drummer," Galvin muttered.

"What?"

"Nothing. What else?"

Jarvis scratched a hairy shoulder and thought. "I don't do the clubs like I did, but I still kinda keep my finger on the pulse. I heard Perry got thrown outta Forfar."

"Did you hear why?"

"Fucked if I know, man, but it musta been serious."

"How long ago?"

"April, I think. And no one's seen him since." Jarvis put his feet on the floor and leaned in. "You think they iced him?"

"I hope not. You wouldn't have a picture of him?"

"Nah. I could tell you what he looks like, but the dudes change the look more often than the names."

"Just the same, Jarvis, I'd like you to drop by headquarters and describe him to a department artist."

"I don't go back to work till next Monday."

Galvin grinned. "You really *are* on vacation."

"Yeah! What'd you think, I was shittin' you? That's too easy to check."

"I'll have someone call to set up a time." Galvin rose to leave. "Thanks, Jarvis. This might help."

"You'll tell that to my parole officer?"

"Yeah. I'll tell him."

Galvin was at the sidewalk when the noise started again from number 9. He remembered back to when rock was fun. This was work. And loud enough to wake the dead.

Maybe that was the point.

Twenty-seven

Stevie drove. Madden's own car was still parked where he'd abandoned it before lunch, down the street from the restaurant. He didn't know if Musso and Frank's had valet parking—and he didn't care. He wasn't going to embarrass Stevie Kean by posing his heap for the paparazzi. With any luck, someone would steal the rattletrap. Otherwise, he'd spend some of his daily expense money on a taxi and double back later to retrieve the clunk.

Madden and Stevie rode in silence. He didn't have to ask what she was thinking. She was right, and he knew she knew it. For all the circumstantial evidence surrounding the Forfars, they'd reached the same conclusion: Todd was simply too old for the cult.

So where was the ransom demand? The Landaus had received and paid theirs four days after the snatch. There'd been no ransom for the other two boys, and they were both dead. And both babies. But so was Andy Landau.

So what was wrong with this picture? Stevie's

words that had ended lunch before it began—
"Where does that leave us?"—were what was wrong.

He'd interrogated Todd's nanny, Jill Densen, although most of their interview had consisted of
his trying to convince the nanny that Todd's abduction wasn't her fault. He hoped he'd succeeded,
because Madden himself wasn't so sure. If not for
Jill Densen's dyslexia, the alarm system at the
house would have been functioning and the perp
might have looked elsewhere, might have grabbed
some other star's kid.

So just how many people knew about the nanny's
disability? Carla, for one, although it beat Madden
how Carla could keep track of her own name and
address.

Tammi Reynolds probably knew; she had info
on everything, from the love lives of her favorite
stars to their preferences—literary, dietary, or sex-
ual. Tammi had begun blabbering about Lyle
Hemmings's drug habits, and something had
made her stop.

Madden, unwittingly, had made her stop. By telling her that Lyle's *affaire du coke* wasn't news.
Tammi's ego needed stroking, and his impatience
had gotten in the way.

Back to the nanny's dyslexia. When he thought
about it, was there anyone really close to Stevie or
Ansel who *didn't* know about the alarm system, not
to mention every other aspect of their personal
lives? Madden wondered how Eppie Goldwyn and
people like her continued to escape libel suits. Or
murder.

His mind returned to Ansel. Stevie claimed never

to have told him about Jill. "Ansel would have fired her on the spot." Could he have lived in this house and not known? And how had that aspect of the story escaped the media?

Madden wondered what the columns would say tomorrow about his lunchtime rendezvous with the glamorous but distraught Stephanie Kean. He didn't think Stevie had noticed the cameras snapping away as they'd hurried from the restaurant— her mind had been wholly occupied with Barbara Halsey's call—but Madden had seen them. And heard the whispers of "who's the guy?" He had no doubt they'd find out in time to make their papers' deadlines.

He glanced over at Stevie in the seat beside him and had to admit he wouldn't mind if they were labeled "an item." As long as it didn't get in the way of solving the case.

The case. They weren't any closer to finding Todd Kline, and it was already July 22. August 1 was ten days away.

Then again, if they were right and the kidnapping *wasn't* cult-related, the date for the next black sabbat or whatever the hell it was called no longer held any relevance.

On the other hand, the perp, or perps, had gone to a lot of trouble to make it *look* like the work of the cult Galvin was investigating.

Why?

And what, Madden asked himself, was he doing to earn his four hundred bucks a day? Courting Stevie Kean was a fantasy come true, but it wasn't enough.

By the time they reached the house, Stevie had checked twice for phone messages. Madden could see both disappointment and relief in her eyes. She'd probably have checked a dozen times if he hadn't been with her in the car.

They'd stopped to pick up groceries; she'd waited outside and he'd been happy to play the domestic role. Hard to picture her in the kitchen, though. Even harder to picture himself sitting still long enough for a meal.

Right. And wasn't that what had helped screw up his own marriage plans? "I'm a busy cop," he'd said each time a weekend had to be canceled or postponed. "I'll make it up to you," he'd said. But he never had. The job had taken over, he'd allowed it, and the booze—"to unwind, that's all"—had only made it worse. Finally, she'd walked.

Madden was smarter now. At least he'd found out what really mattered, and maybe not too late.

Sure. For some of us, the simplest lessons were the hardest to learn.

Ask Ansel Kline.

Ansel had tried to call the house several times during breaks in shooting. He'd received Stevie's messages saying she had no news. He'd spoken with Galvin, who had information he couldn't, or wouldn't, divulge just yet. That had frustrated Ansel while giving him hope.

They'd wrapped for the day, and without consciously planning his evening, Ansel found himself stopping at Stevie's favorite Chinese restaurant for takeout and then heading toward Beachwood Canyon.

He spotted reporters and photographers lurking among the shrubs at the foot of the road. Well, *lurking* was somewhat extreme for a few guys who were leaning against fences or cars and were probably as bored and tired as he was. Why didn't they just give it a rest and go home?

He hadn't considered that Stevie might be out. During the marriage she'd accused Ansel of taking her for granted. Well, maybe he had. Not intentionally; sometimes habits formed from routine, like the way he'd just turned off the ignition a moment ago without thinking about it. Okay, it was true, he'd done a lot of things without thinking.

A mood was beginning to settle over Ansel, but he shook it off and reached over to the package beside him.

The smells of aromatic eggplant, beef in oyster sauce, and pecan chicken wafted up to intoxicate him as he lifted the bag from the seat. It was quiet, and his footfalls echoed on the flagstone steps leading to the front entrance.

From outside he could see only the foyer lights shining through the frosted glass brick panels that flanked the door. The lights were timed to go on automatically at dusk whether Stevie was there or not. But her Lexus was in the driveway; she *was* home.

He decided to ring the bell—and damn the reporters. But he immediately changed his mind; he didn't want to frighten her if she was taking a nap.

Carefully he cradled the bag of food in his left arm and with his right hand fished the housekeys from his pocket.

He heard a voice, Stevie's, coming from the deck out back. At first he thought she was on the telephone, so he deposited the shopping bag on a console table and hurried toward the garden.

He stopped short when he saw her—and before she could see him.

She was reclining on a chaise longue and yes, she was talking, but not into a phone. It took Ansel a moment to discern a figure almost completely hidden in shadow. A neighbor? There was only Stevie's Lexus in the driveway.

". . . I can't really pinpoint when things started to change," she was saying. "Or whose fault it was. I guess both of us were so busy playing the roles of the perfect Hollywood couple that the reality couldn't possibly live up to the image."

"Marriage isn't easy even when you're not in the public eye."

It was Joe Madden's voice.

"You say that as though you've been there," Stevie replied.

"I'm not a has-been. More like an almost-was."

"She didn't want to marry a detective?"

"I was a cop then. If I were a woman, I wouldn't

182

want to marry a cop, even a sober one, which I wasn't."

From behind the French doors that opened onto the deck, Ansel heard the clink of ice cubes.

"More tonic water?" asked Stevie.

"Not without gin, so I'll pass, thanks."

"Joe . . ." Stevie hesitated. "This may be none of my business, but—"

"Four years dry," he answered.

"You should be proud."

"I am. Except for a slip last Christmas."

"Yes. Christmas was hard." She sipped the drink. "What was her name?"

"Nina," he said. Then, "Why are you smiling?"

"It's a lovely name. The young actress in *The Seagull* is called Nina. I've always wanted to play her. Now *you're* smiling."

"I know the play and never made the connection. My Nina was nothing like Mr. Chekhov's seagull."

"Just as well. Her genius-lover leaves, she loses her child—" Stevie stopped in mid-sentence.

"She's also very beautiful and kind," Madden said.

They both fell silent. Dusk was turning to night as Ansel stood listening. At last, Madden spoke again. "Mind if I ask *you* a very personal question?"

"Go ahead," said Stevie.

Ansel leaned in closer.

"You still love him, don't you?" said Madden.

There was a pause before Stevie answered. "Loving someone and living with someone are two different matters."

"Did you and he ever talk about it?"

Ansel heard Stevie's familiar laugh to the familiar question.

"Oh, Joe," she said on the breath of a long sigh that followed the laugh, "I get to wear the most glamorous clothes, speak the most romantic dialogue, and ride off into the sunset with the most loving, wonderful, understanding man who ever existed—and he *doesn't* exist! You wrap for the day and come home to the reality of a leaky roof and the hot water heater that isn't working."

Ansel was remembering, too.

Stevie continued. "The business places demands on those of us blessed with stardom, and God help those who break the rules. You can't do a serious play by Chekhov or Shaw because it means working for minimum, word spreads that your cachet has dropped, and you lose your table at Mortons. Did you ever hear anything so ludicrous?"

"Did you try sharing your thoughts with Ansel?"

From behind the draperies Ansel nodded. Yes, she'd tried. And he'd told her not to bite the hand that fed her.

The mood that had threatened now descended with force, and Ansel realized that he had no legitimate reason to be there. Without giving away his presence, he tiptoed back through the living room and into the foyer, opened the door, and crept out.

Flashbulbs began popping all around him. Instinctively he shielded his eyes, but it was too late. He was momentarily blinded.

Ansel lashed out with his arms and apparently made contact. A camera fell to the ground and landed with a loud crash. He heard expletives, some of them his. They were followed by a hard punch.

The next thing Ansel saw was a blurry Joe Madden standing over him and an out-of-focus Stevie on her knees as she pressed an ice pack to his hurting right eye.

More flashbulbs popped. The odds were that they hadn't stopped, even while Ansel was "out."

He looked up at Stevie, whose expression was a combination of concern, anger, and mild amusement.

Madden helped Ansel to his feet and regarded him quizzically as Stevie brushed dirt off the sleeve of his jacket.

"They won't use this for the caption in tomorrow's paper," Ansel said, "but there's Chinese takeout in the foyer."

Twenty-eight

Ansel looked as though he'd gone ten rounds in a prize fight—and lost. It felt worse the morning after than it had the night before.

He laughed—his first genuine laugh in almost a week—when he saw the newspapers. The tabloids had plastered their front pages with grainy telephoto close-ups of Ansel taking the punch, Stevie ministering to him, and Joe Madden with a menacing expression on his face. The headline of one paper was typical. It read: STAR, PI, AND BLACK EYE. IS TRIANGLE NEW ANGLE? Ansel swore under his breath. Someday he'd do a movie about this brand of Freedom of the Press.

Well, no one snapped his picture when he rang Stevie's bell this morning.

She was expecting him—and the papers. She found the whole situation ridiculous. Not quite as ridiculous, though, as Ansel's souvenir from last night. His eyes were hidden behind mirrored aviator glasses, but the lenses drew more attention to

186

the shiner, especially on an overcast day that promised no sun. It stirred feelings of sympathy in her.

She poured coffee and slid onto the banquette beside him. *Scoop*, with Eppie Goldwyn's exclusive Tammi Reynolds interview, lay open on the table. Stevie moved it closer to Ansel.

"I've read it," he said, downing his coffee in quick gulps as he checked his watch. "Eppie didn't leave much out, although she, for one, gave more space to Tammi than she did to our threesome."

"Our what?" said Stevie.

"Our ménage à Chinois," he said, sorry that he'd brought Madden into the conversation. But he couldn't stop himself. "I don't know which is worse, my shiner or the company you're keeping."

"You're jealous of Joe Madden?"

"*I'm* not, but the newspapers seem to think otherwise."

"Well, he's attractive. And attentive."

"You like him?"

"What's not to like?"

"You know he's interested," said Ansel, studying the paper he'd already read.

"You can see that after sharing Chinese take-out?"

I can see that because I'm not blind, Ansel thought but didn't say. Instead, he checked his watch again and rose. "I'm running late. You know where to reach me."

He bent to kiss her cheek. Habit again. He'd always kissed her when he left for the studio, even when he was in a rush.

Stevie was so engrossed in reading that Ansel

187

thought she hadn't noticed. But when she glanced up, her face was flushed.

"She may try to contact you," he said.

"Eppie?"

"Tammi. Madden's right. She'll be livid when she sees how Eppie has painted her, no matter how publicity-hungry she is."

"The opening alone is enough to make her want to kill Eppie."

"She'll have to get in line," said Ansel.

An hour and three cups of coffee later, Stevie was on her second read-through of the papers. A devastating cyclone in Asia, with sixty thousand people reported dead or missing, had been relegated to page 5 in order to make room for Eppie's "scoop."

TAMMI TALKS! proclaimed the banner headline. Below, the boldfaced—barefaced!—teaser: "Eppie Digs Deep—and Digs Tammi! What does the mysterious fan know? More than you think! Full story on page 2." Stevie downed the tepid remains of her coffee and turned to the article once more. Eppie had covered all the bases; she'd even managed to stab Carolyn Kline and put Tammi's quotes around it. Only Tammi's allusion to the chauffeur made no sense. Stevie and Ansel had never employed a chauffeur.

"I'm an extra in the story of her life," the interview began.

Stevie jumped when the telephone rang. The deluge of calls didn't usually start this early.

"Don't get nervous," said Madden when she answered, "it's Joe. Seen the papers?"

"I have. You're better-looking in person, if that helps."

"It doesn't, but I'm glad you haven't lost your sense of humor. Did you read the *Scoop* piece yet?"

"Three times."

"So has Tammi Reynolds. She just phoned. She's *very* upset."

"I can't blame her. But why call you? Why not Eppie Goldwyn?"

"Tammi wants a meeting. With you, face-to-face. Today. Says she has to set the record straight."

For a moment Stevie was speechless.

"Stevie? You still on the line?"

"I'm thinking. Will you be there?"

"Tammi insisted. But no one else."

"It's probably better that way."

"Will Ansel buy that?"

"I'll tell him afterward. Did she say what time and where?"

"Six-thirty, outside the box office at the Hollywood Bowl. I'll meet you there at six-fifteen."

"I'd feel better if we arrive together, Joe."

"Likewise, but I've got some people to talk to first. They may give us a lead on what we should ask Tammi."

Stevie agreed, but her stomach had already begun to churn.

Tammi Reynolds flopped down on the edge of her Murphy bed and breathed slowly in and out as she tried to calm her racing heart. She'd long feared that her single previous meeting with Stevie would be their only meeting ever. She'd purposely not thought about the baby shower too often; too-frequent recollection might use up the cherished moment, which had become a favorite dream. Now, though, there would be another, better dream.

She looked at her Stephanie Kean wall. Eight-by-ten glossies, scenes from every film Stevie had made to date, were arranged in a circle around a full-color studio portrait Tammi had cut from a Sunday magazine section of the *Times*. On the mantel below were more pictures: a ten-year-old Stevie posed alongside other children at the orphanage; Stevie with Ansel on their wedding day; one of the first published photos of Stevie with her baby. The matching silver-plated frames had been Tammi's gift to herself upon release from the hospital. The frames were symbolic; they'd cost Tammi what she'd previously spent on drugs in a week. Even though Stevie Kean didn't know it, she, as much as the hospital, had helped Tammi kick her habit.

Her hands finally stopped trembling. It was safe now to pick up, carefully and by the stem, the champagne flute from which Stevie had sipped ginger ale on the set of *The End of Eden* five years before. Stealing the glass had been no easy trick for an extra. Tammi recalled worrying that the lipstick on the rim of the glass would rub off. But it hadn't. It was still the same deep shade of pink. Not the color Stevie would have picked for herself, Tammi knew.

Love and pride brought tears to Tammi's eyes. She'd succeeded in becoming a part of Stevie's life, and after today, in however small a way, she'd even be a part of film history. Perhaps more than just a footnote in Stephanie Kean's autobiography.

She cradled the crystal goblet on her pillow so it wouldn't roll off and fall to the floor. Then she looked down at the newspapers she'd spread across her unmade bed.

First, I'll have to explain to her about the interview.

Eppie Goldwyn had portrayed Tammi as a dangerous lunatic, all the while quoting her exactly. And she'd mentioned the chauffeur.

Stupid! thought Tammi, slapping her thigh. Stupid of me to bring him up!

She went to the kitchenette counter and withdrew the carving knife from the crammed utensil drawer. It was so sharp, she'd never used it, not even once.

She wrapped the blade part in a towel, then put it at the bottom of her oversize canvas bag. Just knowing it was there made her feel safe.

Then she turned her attention to the clothes rack behind the sheet that doubled as a closet door.

What should she wear to a memory?

Twenty-nine

Stanley and Blanche gave a brief, welcoming chirp and went silent. Madden leaned against the sink to sip his coffee. He yawned and dug the last cigarette from the pack in his shirt pocket. His hands were tired, and his calloused fingers ached, but it was a good hurt.

Tobacco smoke filled the beam of morning sun coming through the kitchen window. It cast a natural spotlight on the center of the table. He squinted through the glare and nodded, satisfied with his work. He'd only slept four hours, but it was worth it.

The paperback copy of Chekhov's play, with its cover photo of the bird in flight, was still propped against the ketchup bottle on the table. From the partially carved block of wood, a seagull, its wings spread wide, had begun to emerge. Madden knew already that it was the best work he'd ever done. And it wouldn't be for sale. He'd give it to Stevie, once this was over and Todd was returned safe.

If Todd was returned safe.

* * *

It was impossible for Madden to think straight and drive at the same time in the staggering heat. So he endured the wait and the haggling, and ended up accepting the shop's estimate. He'd used up most of the morning, but the shop threw in a loaner—an '86 Toyota with 75,000 miles on it, a wreck almost as decrepit as his own heap, but at least the air-conditioning worked. He could live with anything for two days, as long as it was cool.

Even without a radio, he enjoyed the drive to Beverly Hills. He couldn't say the same for his lunch date with Barbara Halsey. They'd agreed on Maple Drive—her choice—and once there, she made it no secret that she disliked being questioned about her employers. Aside from a terrific meal, the hour was a waste of time. And a waste of Ansel Kline's expense money. Seventy bucks and he hadn't learned a damn thing, except that Barbara Halsey was lousy company, and that her tight-lipped attitude stemmed more from job loyalty than from a need to protect Ansel Kline or Lyle Hemmings.

What the hell. Hemmings was his next stop, anyway.

Madden stopped in front of a massive gate with *LH* wrought into the iron. The main house far beyond was a sprawling, multi-tiered monstrosity with castlelike turrets and walkways right out of the gothic quickies that had made Lyle a millionaire producer in half the time it had taken Roger Corman. Madden wouldn't be surprised if Vincent Price appeared to greet him.

He rolled down the window and pressed the intercom. After a full minute, a squawk asked who was there. Even distorted, the voice was recognizable. "Carla? It's Joe Madden!"

"Hya, Joe! But we, like, talked yesterday. Right?"

"Right. I thought I'd buzz by and speak with Mr. Hemmings."

"Well, Lyle—I mean, Mr. Hemmings—won't be back till three."

"It's almost that now."

"Is it? Oh. Yeah. It is."

"I can wait, can't I?"

"I guess so." There was a loud *click!* and the gates opened. A winding, palm tree-lined road led to a circular drive before the pillared entrance. Carla, standing in the doorway and dwarfed by all the stone and shrubbery, looked like a toy doll. Yeah, a space-age, spaced-out Barbie.

"Very cozy," Madden said, walking up the steps.

Carla laughed. "It's not much, but it's home. To Lyle—Mr. Hemmings—I mean."

She led him through a vast stone foyer from which a wide, curving staircase rose to a distant landing. The place was freezing; Madden figured the electricity bill alone came to more than he made in a good week.

"It's warmer in the Casino," Carla said, beckoning him into a room at the end of a tapestry-lined corridor.

The Casino boasted two-story-high vaulted ceilings and a fireplace that was big enough to walk into. Above its green marble mantel hung a larger-than-lifesize, ersatz modern rendering of Lyle Hemmings in oil. It was framed in ornately carved and gilded redwood. Madden found the painting and the frame hideous.

"How many rooms in the castle?" asked Madden.

Carla giggled. "Y'know, I'm not real sure. I still haven't cleaned all of them yet." The giggle echoed. Madden felt as if he were surrounded by a dozen Goldie Hawns.

"Name your poison, Joe," said Carla from behind the fully stocked, mirrored wet bar.

Madden surveyed more gilded, carved wood. Everything was probably museum quality, but the word *mausoleum* came to mind.

"Got any iced tea?" he said.

Carla sneezed and said, "Sure. Sugar?"

"No, thanks," Madden answered, taking in the rest of the room through the reflection in the bar's mirror.

The far wall explained how the Casino had gotten its name. A series of antique one-armed bandits, nickelodeons, and peep-show machines, all made of polished brass, stood in an impressive row. A wheel-of-fortune, four feet in circumference, blocked a window.

"Amazing!" he said.

"Isn't it?" Carla handed him a sweating Baccarat tumbler of iced tea and sneezed again. "Lyle loves games and toys. There's stuff like this all over the house. You should see upstairs!"

"That would bore Joe!"

Lyle Hemmings made a grand entrance, throwing his jacket over a chair as though it were Dracula's cape and extending his arms in greeting. But Madden caught the look that passed from the Ken doll to Barbie. The Ken doll was pissed off.

"Uh, like, you'll excuse me?" Carla's face had turned scarlet.

"We'll both excuse you," said Hemmings, dismissing her with a princely wave.

"Thanks for the tea, Carla!" Madden called after her, but she was already gone.

"Freshen your drink?" Hemmings asked. Madden noticed a tiny cut-scratch on the tip of his host's nose. *Must've missed with the straw.*

"I'm fine, thanks," said Madden.

"Good. All I have time for is a quick scotch, myself. Then I have to dress for a preview. Not that I'm rushing you, of course."

Of course. "This place of yours is great. I'm surprised you don't have more help, though."

Hemmings dropped two ice cubes into shorter Baccarat, and sneezed. "Summer colds are the worst, aren't they, Joe?" He made a show of blowing his nose into a handkerchief, then said, "About the help. I hire extra people when I entertain. Otherwise, I don't like having strangers in my home."

Point taken. "Understandable. I just came by to ask you a question."

"Ask." Hemmings poured a finger of Chivas and took a sip.

"You weren't on the set for the entire morning last Wednesday."

"That's not a question."

"And that's not an answer."

"No. I wasn't. I was in my office. I heard about Todd Kline from Barbara Halsey. Ask her."

"I already have."

"Then why ask me?"

"Just thought someone might have seen you *in* the office around the time of the kidnapping."

"No one did, I'm afraid. Why, you don't think I had anything to do with it, do you?"

"I'm only trying to help the Klines," said Madden.

"So am I! Ansel Kline is my best friend as well as my partner. And Stevie, well, she's special."

"Yes, she is."

"She's so genuinely nice, sometimes it's hard to believe she's in the business—and successful, too." Hemmings put the glass down and came to Madden. "She doesn't deserve this, Joe. I'm damned upset about the whole thing." There were tears in his eyes.

"I can see that," Madden reassured him.

"But"—Hemmings looked at his watch—"I promised I'd make a little speech tonight, and I can't be late, so . . . ?"

"So, I can find my own way out," Madden offered. "Thank Carla for the tea. And the tour."

"Tour?"

"Oh, just through the hall and here. But it gave me the general idea." Madden thought a vein in

Hemmings's neck had twitched, but if it had happened, it was too fast for Madden to be sure.

Madden had been driving for half an hour before he realized how close he was to headquarters. It was the next left. He hadn't been back for a visit in a couple of years.

And he hadn't seen Galvin's new office. He knew Mike would be dying to hear about the inside of Hemmings's mansion—even if he'd never admit to it. They might be able to trade information. Galvin was a good cop. Maybe he had dug up something by now.

The trick would be prying it out of him.

Thirty

Stevie was seated in the upstairs den with the stack of photocopied material on her lap. She'd been reading since the messengered delivery hours ago.

Barbara and Fran had done a thorough job. Every detail about the kidnap-murders published in LA over the last six months was here. Stevie had spent the better part of the afternoon poring over them. In some ways, the factual reports in the more respected papers disturbed her more than the sensational aspects played up in the tabloids. Together they created a grisly scrapbook, ending with Todd's unfinished story.

Stevie's eyes stung from strain. There had to be more than just the age discrepancy, some clue in the form of a word or phrase on one of the pages just begging to be seen. She hadn't found it yet, but she wouldn't give up looking.

She'd called Ansel that morning about the glitch, and he'd said she was grasping at straws. Maybe he'd agree after seeing it in print.

She hefted the papers, put them into an expanding leather envelope-file, and placed that in the bottom drawer of the desk. The clock on the desk said five-twenty. It was almost time to leave.

The tires sent up a cloud of dust and Stevie was off before any of the reporters could give chase.

She entered the last curve near the bottom of Mulholland. It wasn't much farther now, and she was filled with dread. At least Joe Madden would be there. Tammi would divulge whatever she felt only Stevie should hear, and Stevie would tell Ansel everything tonight.

She hoped he'd understand why she hadn't told him beforehand. She wasn't up for accusations about secrets, even if they were valid. She'd never purposely withheld truths from him—except the truth about Jill Densen and the alarm system. He'd find out eventually, but she'd deal with that when she had to.

Stevie made a right turn on Cahuenga. It was six-ten. She was almost there.

Madden wondered if the Toyota would make it through the last quarter mile up the drive to the parking lot. The engine was beginning to sputter. Come on! he urged. It wasn't much farther.

The sputter stopped. Dusk was settling over the smog and turning the sky a hazy pinkish beige. In another hour, traffic on this road would be bumper to bumper because of tonight's concert. Tammi Reynolds apparently knew that, too. The place would be mobbed then, but it was deserted now.

He'd hoped to get there ahead of Stevie. Just early enough to check things out. But Galvin had been unexpectedly forthcoming, and now it was ten after six.

Galvin hadn't been excited by the possibility that Todd Kline was too old for the cult. He'd been eager to gloat over what he called a *real* lead; some heavy-metal freak with ties to the satanists. Madden's reaction—that the cult *wouldn't* lead to Todd—hadn't dampened Galvin's satisfaction. Neither of them had said a thing to change the other's mind.

But each had conceded that both points of view had merit, certainly worth mentioning to Stevie, and—

BAM!

The car was suddenly out of control. Madden veered into the opposite lane, righted the wheel, and pulled over.

At first he thought he'd been shot at. Easy to do, with so much tree cover lining the road.

He walked around to the back of the car. The right rear tire was punctured. "Shit!" he said aloud.

Madden hadn't passed a single car since the turnoff. No reason to hope for a lift up the rest of the drive.

There was a spare in the trunk. He measured the time it would take to change the tire against hiking. The new tire won.

He rolled up his sleeves and pulled out the jack.

It was six-fifteen. He could be on his way in ten minutes. With a little luck, Stevie would be late.

Stevie eased the Lexus slowly around the empty parking lot and stopped some twenty feet from the box office. It would be seven o'clock before tickets went on sale and members of the orchestra arrived. Right now, the only signs of human life were laughing Japanese tourists being herded aboard a huge bus. A few stragglers appeared from inside the Bowl and scurried across the lot like palm-shirted squirrels with cameras.

From her vantage point, Stevie could survey the entire area. Joe's "heap," as he called it, was nowhere in sight. That momentarily unsettled her nerves.

Maybe her watch was running fast. Maybe Joe was stuck in traffic. And Tammi, too. Stevie didn't see the blue Honda anywhere. *Just take it easy. Lighten up.*

The sun looked as though it were perched on the surrounding treetops. Over and beyond the dark walls of the amphitheater, the moon was already visible in a lavender sky.

Stevie opened the door of the car and stepped out. The temperature had dropped, and a strong, cool breeze rustled the trees. She breathed deeply. It was going to be a beautiful night.

The last of the tourists boarded the bus. They beamed happily. Innocently.

The bus door closed. As it pulled away, Stevie

glanced at her watch. Six-thirty. Tammi should be here any second.

Where's Joe?

When she looked up again, the bus was gone. And there, some fifty feet away, was a blue Honda.

The bus had blocked it—it must have been there all the time!

She heard the sound of her own heart pounding and turned, knowing no one was there yet hoping that Joe might magically appear.

She didn't move. What should she do? Approach the car, or let Tammi come to her? She couldn't just stand there like an idiot.

She didn't see anyone behind the wheel, but she couldn't be sure, because the parking-lot lights hadn't gone on yet and the sky was growing darker.

Stevie, deciding that *not* moving might be the most foolish inaction of all, started toward the Honda.

The click of her heels on the pavement echoed through the cavernous space. A candy wrapper, traveling on the wind, skittered across the concrete and made a scraping sound.

By the time she came within ten feet of the car, Stevie could see that it was empty. She came closer and peered through the dirty rear window. There were old, dog-eared copies of tabloids and magazines strewn across the torn upholstery of the backseat. Maybe this wasn't Tammi's car after all.

The door on the driver's side was unlocked. She opened it, remembering too late about fingerprints. Ridiculous, anyway; *she* wasn't a criminal, for God's sake.

On the floor lay the current issue of *Scoop*. Its screaming headline was circled in black Magic Marker, with the word *LIES!* scrawled along the top. This *was* Tammi's Honda.

Something else lay beside the newspaper on the floor. It looked like a piece of wood. Stevie leaned in.

The parking-lot lights suddenly flashed on, illuminating the blade of a long knife at the end of a wooden handle.

Stevie slammed the door and rested against it, her breath heaving. *Why* would Tammi bring a knife? And since she wasn't in the car—*where was she?*

A stronger wind had come up. The lights transformed the parking lot into an arena. Or a stage in the round. Stevie was a clear target with no place to take cover. Alone.

Stop it, Stevie! Stop overdramatizing!

But crazed fans *had* killed before. And Todd *had* been kidnapped.

Stevie pushed away from the door and began walking, almost running, back to the Lexus.

She heard the squeal of rubber. Headlights in the distance were looming larger, blinding her. She ran, but the car was bearing down on her.

It came to a screeching halt a yard behind the Lexus. Stevie jumped into her driver's seat and started the ignition as she reached out to yank the door closed.

"Wait!" He grabbed her arm.

She screamed, already fighting him off.

"Stevie! It's me! *Joe!*"

She froze as she looked up into Madden's face. "Oh, Joe—my *God!*"

She threw her arms around him with such force, he almost lost his balance. She was laughing and crying, and Madden held her, letting the tears soak the shoulder of his shirt. He could smell her hair as the breeze brushed it past his face.

When she was calmer, and after they'd talked and Madden had checked Tammi's car, he asked, "Are you up to driving?"

"I think so. Yes. Of course I am."

"Go home then. I'll follow you."

Madden called Galvin from Beachwood Canyon. He filled him in on the aborted meeting at the Hollywood Bowl, then said, "I'll let Stevie tell you the rest."

She did, and knew that Galvin was right. She could have been killed. But she didn't like hearing the reprimand from him.

Madden fixed the drinks—vodka on the rocks for her, tonic water with lime for himself. They talked for a while. No insights or revelations, just talk.

When he rose to leave, Stevie accompanied him to the door and hugged him. "Thanks, Joe. And don't you dare say it's all part of the job."

"I won't." But he didn't return the hug. "See you tomorrow."

He left, and Stevie was alone with her thoughts once more. She thought about Todd. And Tammi Reynolds. What was so important that she had to tell Stevie and no one else? Where was she—or, more to the point, what had happened to her?

Stevie dropped another ice cube into the watery remains of her drink and flopped down on a chair.

She was exhausted. She longed for a good long soak in the tub followed by a halfway decent sleep. But first she had to call Ansel. There was no putting it off. And no leaving anything out.

She added a splash of vodka to her drink and took a swallow that emptied the glass. She stalled for another five minutes by washing out the tumblers and rehearsing what to say.

Then, when she realized she couldn't stall any longer, Stevie picked up the phone.

Thirty-one

Ansel stepped from the shower and toweled himself dry, careful not to disturb the makeup magic of Yolanda Eastmore. She'd promised that his waterproofed cheek would withstand even the harsh glare of television lighting—as long as Ansel promised not to disturb the bruise beneath.

He hadn't. In fact, except for tenderness at the slightest touch, his image in the mirrored wall reflected no trace of Monday's boxing match. Just like Bugs Bunny; knock him flat or hurl him from a cliff, and the next frame shows Bugs in fine fettle, as though nothing had happened.

Ansel started at the sudden memory of Todd singing "Kill the Wabbit" from the Bugs Bunny version of Wagner's *Die Walküre*.

Lt. Galvin had reported that his special task force was making headway; all the same, he hadn't explained, and if he wasn't stalling to placate Ansel, why all the secrecy?

Speaking of secrecy, why hadn't Stevie told him—

before the fact—about yesterday's meeting with Tammi Reynolds? Had she shared the information only because Tammi had stood her up?

Ansel was still miffed. Stevie must think that Joe Madden, singlehandedly, could provide some brand of supernatural protection. Didn't Stevie realize that Tammi Reynolds had a screw loose? That Eppie Goldwyn's depiction of her wasn't so far off the mark? What if Tammi wanted to harm Stevie and had stayed away because at the last moment she'd discarded one plan for another, more clever one?

What if Tammi was another John Hinckley, craving the world's attention no matter the means? What better way to capture the spotlight than on live TV?

Ansel would only be a member of the celebrity-packed audience at tonight's charity telecast, but Stevie was one of the star attractions. The gala benefit would be beamed by satellite to countries all over the globe. What if Tammi Reynolds was planning to crash the event the way she'd crashed the baby shower, this time for a violent act?

Ansel quickly finished drying off, then reached for the phone. He tried Stevie at the house, but the assistant stage manager answered. That meant Stevie was already forwarding calls to the Hollywood Roosevelt Hotel, the site of the charity gala.

When it came to formal industry occasions, Ansel was usually a slow and meticulous dresser, knowing the importance of "image."

Today he didn't give a damn about image. When one of the square onyx studs on his tux shirt refused to pass through the buttonhole, he left it undone. He stuffed the black satin bowtie in a pocket of his jacket, grabbed his car keys, and was on his way to downtown Hollywood in record time.

Eppie Goldwyn studied herself in the bulb-framed mirror at her dressing table. She didn't understand how Yolanda Eastmore had accomplished the miracle, but Eppie looked—and felt—years younger.

Yolanda was packing up the tools with which she'd worked the transformation and was preparing to leave when Eppie said, "By the way, darling, I hear you did a little patch-job on Ansel Kline en route to my place. I suppose that's what made you late . . . ?"

Yolanda Eastmore was one of the most valued makeup artists in town. She disliked Eppie—particularly Eppie's pauses, which demanded filling in, and *not* with the latest weather forecast. But it wasn't healthy for business to antagonize *Scoop's* main snoop. So, instead of suggesting that Eppie take her prying nose and shove it—a nose that Yolanda had shortened by means of subtle highlight and shadow—she smiled and said, "You know everything that goes on, don't you, Eppie?"

"If I don't, I make it a point to find out." Eppie smiled back, but her expression said, "I accept your acknowledgment. You are dismissed."

Just as well. Yolanda had promised to check Stevie Kean's makeup and hair before half-hour was called.

* * *

Madden wished he'd rented one of those prefab bowties along with the tux. Instead, he'd spent the last ten minutes fiddling with the strip of black satin around his neck. Not to mention the cummerbund that was cutting off circulation at his midsection. He wondered if headwaiters at the swankier joints around town felt the way he did now—like a fucking penguin—or if time and tips helped them get used to it.

Madden would never get used to the shoes. Little girls, not PIs, wore shiny black patent leather with grosgrain bows. All he needed was a towel draped over his sleeve to complete the picture.

No, all he needed was Galvin to rib him about it. And the SOB was sure to be there tonight. Madden was whistling "What I Did For Love" when the first line of the song sobered him.

"Kiss today goodbye," he said aloud, reaching for the tux jacket. To hell with the goddammed tie.

Galvin wasn't about to pay some hotel parking jock to scratch up his fenders. There were enough uniformed cops on duty tonight to fill Dodgers Stadium. He hoped none of them was working to fill a ticket quota, because the spot where he parked his unmarked car was an illegal zone about a block from the Roosevelt Hotel. He was tempted to leave a police sticker under the windshield, but that would be an open invitation to vandals. This wasn't the downtown Hollywood of his youth, where he'd hung around hoping to catch a glimpse of Bogie or Gable or the rest of the ghosts.

Galvin straightened his jacket in the car-window reflection. He was wearing a gray summer suit—he didn't own a tux and wasn't about to spring for a rental. He hoped he'd get inside without having to flash his badge. Incognito was a plus when you didn't know the face of whomever it was you were looking for.

Except for Tammi Reynolds's face. Either she'd become invisible, or she was dead. He hadn't noticed blood or any signs of violence in the Honda, but he'd know more after forensics finished going over the car and the butcher knife.

If she was alive, maybe she'd moved to Tahiti. He wouldn't blame her, after the hatchet job that stupid bitch at *Scoop* had done on her. He hoped Eppie Goldwyn hadn't lost Tammi for them.

Todd Kline had been missing for a full week. Galvin hadn't told the parents that the longer a case dragged on, the less probability there was of solving it. If—and it was growing chancier by the day—Todd Kline hadn't been murdered, his captors were waiting for an opportunity to make their demands known.

Everything Galvin had put together so far—in addition to a gut feeling that was seldom wrong—pointed to tonight. If the gala went off without a hitch, it meant his original instincts were spot on, no matter what Rover Jarvis had said or what Joe Madden and the Klines believed.

The cult.

Rover Jarvis had told Galvin about a guy named Perry Fang. The task force was still checking out the clubs where Jarvis said the ejected cult member used to hang out. But even with Jarvis's description and a police artist's sketch, they hadn't had any luck.

"The dudes change the look more often than the names." Jarvis's words hit Galvin like a blow as he made his way to the front entrance of the hotel.

All Perry Fang had to do was put on a tux, clean himself up, and show as a guest.

Again Galvin noticed the heavy security surrounding the hotel and wondered who was minding the rest of LA tonight.

Christ, Perry Fang could even come dressed as a cop!

That was particularly unsettling as Galvin pushed his way through a mobbed foyer and was stopped by an arm on his shoulder.

"Excuse me, sir," said a polite voice behind him.

Galvin turned. Even the ushers were wearing tuxes. "Yeah?"

"No one is permitted inside without an invitation, sir."

Grudgingly, and surreptitiously, Galvin pulled out his badge.

Lyle Hemmings was dressed and ready to leave when he started to come down from his earlier high. He glanced at the diamond-studded Piaget at his wrist. Yeah, there was time for one more line. Just to get him through tonight's "festivities."

God, how he hated these charity gigs. The biggest givers were the biggest getters. Kick in a few extra thou and your name was printed in boldface. When you thought about it, a metaphor for life.

Yeah. Boldface and top billing. Over the title as in "Lyle Hemmings Presents." So he'd kicked in another five grand he didn't have.

Yet.

He tossed his tux jacket onto a chair and began searching frantically for the stash he'd left under a corner of the Aubisson carpet. For emergencies.

It wasn't there.

Dammit! Only one person could have taken it!

"Carla!" he bellowed, running from the library.

He found her in a similarly ridiculous position. On her hands and knees in the kitchen, trying to collect the telltale white powder she'd spilled.

"You rotten little thief!" he cried.

She cowered as though she expected him to hit her.

He didn't. Instead, he joined her on the floor and started scooping up the coke. The small hill of what was left soon disappeared, with Lyle managing to snort the larger amount. Goddammed right—it was his stash! And he wasn't too sure there'd be more where that came from.

A moment later it didn't matter.

The phone rang. Lyle took the call in the downstairs pantry, and within seconds was upstairs in his private study on the third floor, scrambling at his desk for pen and paper. Sweat rolled down his face as he wrote, and his pleated white silk shirt was soaked through to his skin despite a temperature of sixty-five degrees in the house.

The near-panic ebbed away as the coke took effect. Calmly Lyle deposited his checkbook and notepad inside the top desk drawer, locked it, and dropped the key into his pants pocket. Then he retrieved his jacket from the library and headed out to the Rolls.

"Evening, Mr. Hemmings," said Ralph, his new chauffeur. "How's it going?"

Lyle gave Ralph a friendly slap on the back. "Hey, buddy, it's going fine, just fine!" He climbed into the backseat of the limo, opened the bar, and poured himself a scotch, then leaned back to enjoy the drive.

Yeah, it was going just fine. And it was gonna go better.

Thirty-two

Stevie instructed the limo driver to let her out at the service entrance to the hotel. She knew she'd be disappointing fans who'd probably been waiting out front since early afternoon, but the only reason she was honoring her commitment was because of a childhood promise to help others if she was ever lucky enough to make it to the top. Amazing the way she'd bought into the Cinderella story, straight on through to the myth of happily-ever-after.

Yolanda Eastmore was waiting for her in the hotel suite assigned to Stevie as a dressing room/ green room.

"Well, you're making it easy on me," said the makeup artist in greeting. "All we'll need to do is powder you down a bit."

"You've got to be kidding," said Stevie, who still hadn't shaken her feelings of general discomfort even though she wasn't ill.

"With any other actress in this town," Yolanda observed, "I'd say that was fishing." She gave Stevie a once-over. "Even the dress works. You look gorgeous."

Stevie was wearing a simple 1920's-inspired sleeveless chemise that fell to her ankles. The gown was a deep burgundy silk, completely covered in iridescent burgundy bugle beads. The neckline was a modest *bateau,* but the back plunged to a deep V. The shoes were simple, matching beaded pumps.

"Bob Mackie?" said Yolanda.

Stevie shrugged. "Could be. I can't see spending seventy-five-hundred dollars on a gown I'll wear once. I found this on sale. The label had been removed."

"Your secret's safe with me as long as you tell me where you got it and how long the sale is on."

Stevie, seating herself in the boudoir chair at the dressing table, felt her throat tightening. "I bought the gown the week before Todd's birthday. I was going to wear it to the Oscars, then changed my mind."

Yolanda didn't miss the catch in Stevie's voice or her sudden pallor.

"Okay, you changed your mind. I'll change the subject. Unless you don't want to. I imagine everyone's been after you about . . . things."

"It's funny," said Stevie, "but talking about Todd—saying his name—actually keeps me thinking that he's all right. In fact, I wish everyone would stop treating me with kid gloves."

"Done." Yolanda took a comb and brush from her voluminous tote bag and contemplated Stevie's hair. "Eppie Goldwyn's here, you know. So's your mother-in-law."

Stevie nodded as Yolanda began brushing. "Carolyn's one of the heads of the organizing committee." She managed a laugh. "The only favor she's ever done for me was getting me involved with Save Our Children." A pause as she remembered, then another laugh. "Of course she manipulated me by reminding me of all the things someone in my position—someone with my *background*"—here she imitated Carolyn perfectly—"could do to help those less fortunate." Stevie's voice caught again, and this time it puzzled her. They weren't talking about Todd, now; why should Carolyn provoke such a reaction?

"Anyway," she concluded, "I'm grateful she did. I'd like to think that my 'fifteen minutes of fame' can make a difference."

"You're one of the few stars I know who means that," said Yolanda. She fanned the sides of Stevie's hair with her fingers and added a touch of gel to help it hold up under the lights. Then she gave Stevie's face a featherweight film of powder to eliminate shine and stepped back.

"Voilà," said Yolanda. "I repeat—gorgeous."

Stevie rose and crossed to the full-length mirror. There was no avoiding the irony. As Yolanda had said, she looked great. Stevie Kean, whose child was missing, whose pictures and history—including blatant lies and speculation—were plastered on front pages across the country, and she looked as though the world was hers for the asking.

Even though Stevie understood that her need of the SOC tonight was as great as the SOC's need for her, she also thought her appearance on the Society's behalf was important. But what if the tele-

vision audience misinterpreted? The FBI had issued a nationwide alert on Todd Kline, yet here
was his mother, confident and gorgeous. What if
they saw Stevie's presence as publicity-seeking, un-
caring, and selfish?

She hoped she wasn't making a colossal mistake.

Below the stage in the grand ballroom, the glittering crowd took their seats at round tables for
ten. The more recognizable luminaries were, of
course, placed down front and closest to the cameras. It didn't matter if some of the guests hadn't
contributed a dime to SOC; what mattered was
clout.

Which put Carolyn Kline, in gold and white sequins that matched her hair, at the head table. At
the same table were Ansel, Lyle, and other industry names: Pia Decameron, head of Three Muses
Studios, and her actor-husband; screenwriter Rachel Allenby and her husband; and Aurora Styles,
the former actress whose orphaned childhood
made her, according to the press, Stevie's sister-
under-the-skin. She, too, was with her husband.

Ansel, Stevie observed, was alone.

The show began. The dancers' number, then a
stand-up comic, followed by a singing group. Stevie
barely paid attention. She was scheduled to speak
after the second commercial break.

She was pacing back and forth in the wings

when the stage manager squeezed her arm and said, "You're next, Miss Kean."

She felt the old, familiar flutter in her stomach.

Pia Decameron was center stage. Stevie heard her say, ". . . and she's a treasured friend."

They'd met twice. Show biz.

A page thrust a note into Stevie's hand and said, "Break a leg, Miss Kean."

Stevie took the folded sheet of paper from its envelope, glanced at the message, and felt her head start to swim.

Just as Pia announced, "Ladies and gentlemen . . . Stephanie Kean!"

Stevie didn't hear the rousing applause. She didn't see the blinding lights. She strode unsteadily to the mike and gripped its base for support. Her voice, when she spoke, sounded like an entity separate and apart from her.

"I had planned . . . had wanted . . ." she stammered. "I mean . . ."

Who are you and why are you doing this?

"I came here tonight . . . to plead the case . . . of children . . . everywhere."

To plead for my child!

"As you know . . . Save Our Children . . ."

Save my child!

". . . was organized to help . . ."

Help me! Help Todd! Oh, God, don't do this to us!

". . . children less fortunate . . ."

Less fortunate than Todd???

Stevie's eyes were glazing over.

"Please," she began again, "whoever you are, out there, please . . . don't hurt . . . my . . . baby!"

The director saw it coming. He cut to the commercial a split-second before Stevie passed out cold.

When she came to, she was lying backstage on a cot and surrounded by a dozen faces, some strangers to her, others familiar.

Ansel was there. So were Joe Madden and Lt. Galvin. And Yolanda, Barbara, and Lyle. Eppie Goldwyn was trying to edge her way closer until Carolyn Kline grabbed her arm.

As Stevie revived, she realized the only face missing from the crowd around her was Tammi Reynolds.

"What does it say?" asked Madden.

She looked up at him questioningly.

"That piece of paper you slid into your pocket when you went onstage."

Incredible. Stevie hadn't remembered that the gown had a pocket, hadn't remembered putting the note there. But Madden had seen it.

She shook her head, and he understood.

"Okay, folks, let's give Miss Kean some breathing space."

Galvin seconded the motion and soon only he, Ansel, and Madden were beside her.

"Stevie . . . ?" Ansel prompted.

She reached into the slit pocket and brought out the folded piece of paper. Without speaking, she handed it to Ansel. He read the contents, then offered it to Madden and Galvin.

"Goddammit!" spat Galvin when he'd read it.

Printed in awkward letters—purposely awkward, to avoid detection—were the words: *$1 million. Unmarked bills. By August 1. Or Todd is dead.*

Thirty-three

Stevie felt as though she were trapped on a carousel whose gears had locked. Everything seemed to be swirling around her. People. Questions. Friends. Strangers. And enough policemen to mistake the backstage area of the Hollywood Roosevelt Hotel for the White House.

For the first time she was grateful for Lt. Galvin's abrasive manner. His "Move it!" had dispersed the crowd and moved everyone who wasn't involved out of the area and out of the way.

He'd anticipated Stevie's reluctance to return to the suite upstairs; after he'd handed the ransom note over to one of his men and questioned the appropriate personnel who'd been in Stevie's general proximity before the note's delivery, Galvin agreed that a quiet, unobtrusive exit through the hotel kitchen was preferable to a visible departure through the front lobby.

In an eerie replay of the week before, Ansel helped her into his car and headed for Beachwood Canyon. Stevie had refused a sedative this time, however, so she hadn't missed Joe Madden's offer to see her home or Ansel's "Thanks, I can handle it." She wondered why her thoughts even included such trivia; none of it mattered. She closed her eyes. Galvin had said perhaps she'd recall something, some seemingly insignificant detail that might hold importance and come to her later when her mind was more rested. So far, all she remembered was the face of the messenger. The police would find him and he'd be exactly that: a messenger. He'd say he'd been hired to deliver a note to Miss Kean. He'd say he hadn't seen the person who gave him the note, and he'd be telling the truth; Stevie had read enough suspense novels to know that much.

She glanced over at Ansel as he made the turn into the drive. They'd hardly spoken all the way there, but it was a shared silence. Stevie suspected that they were thinking similar, if not the same, thoughts.

He parked around back to avoid any paid gawkers with cameras who might still be camped out front. They entered the house through the garage. The only noise was when Ansel tripped over one of Todd's toy trains that hadn't been put away. In the dark he took Stevie's hand and she led him through the obstacle course that was their son's playroom.

When they reached the downstairs study he said, "I'll stay."

She said, "Yes. . . . Thanks."

* * *

Stevie's dreams that night, however, were not like those of the week before. They were worse.

The bedroom was a soundstage, and Detective Lt. Michael Galvin, a bullhorn at his lips, was directing two hundred police-uniformed extras in a chant that Stevie could almost but not quite hear. Bits of paper, scraps of the ransom note torn into fragments of confetti, whirled past her. She tried to grab at them, but they remained just out of reach. Disembodied hands pecked at her—Eppie Goldwyn's fuchsia talons on the left, Carolyn Kline's ten perfectly shaped, frosted-beige ovals on the right. Even in her nightmare, Stevie recognized the surreal scene from *The Birds*.

The sea of blue increased its volume, and now Stevie could make out the words of their chant. *"Where's Tammi?"* taunted the chorus. *"Behind the curtain?"* The scene changed, and before Stevie was a beaded burgundy curtain that matched her gown.

"Don't look, Stevie!" hissed the two hundred voices.

But Stevie ignored the warning. She parted the curtain and, through the magic allowed only in dreams, the policemen were gone. In their place were clowns. Giant clowns, dwarf clowns. All laughing. Stevie was laughing with them. She laughed until her rib cage ached.

And until one of the clowns, with a hideous smile, tossed something to her. His mocking grin made her jump out of the way. The object was already in flight when Stevie recognized Todd's lifesize stuffed Bugs Bunny that Lyle had given Todd for his birthday.

She tried catching the rabbit as it sailed through the air. Too late; it hit a wall and fell in a heap. Gingerly, Stevie tiptoed forward to retrieve it.

The lights dimmed and the soundstage was suddenly a dank basement hole. A horrible stench rose up to choke her. And then, when her eyes had accustomed themselves to the dark, Stevie was able to focus on the image lying beside the stuffed toy.

"Nooo-oooo!" came her whimper-scream. *"Please— nooooo!"* Her arms flailed out violently as she shoved the image away and willed herself awake.

She was drenched with perspiration and her heart was hammering. In her nightmare, lying there beside Bugs Bunny, was the lifeless form of a small boy.

Thirty-four

Ansel's voice, when he knocked on the bedroom door in the morning, was tense. Stevie prayed that her nightmares had not come true. She'd already envisioned the news coverage of her coast-to-coast satellite panic and collapse. She wasn't curious enough to reach for the TV remote.

The door opened, and Ansel, the area around his eye still bruised but less angry-looking, entered with the cordless phone. The antenna was up, which meant there was a caller on the line.

"Lieutenant Galvin wants to know . . . if Todd has a toy rabbit."

Stevie heard him and didn't hear him. Of course Todd had a rabbit. Ansel knew that. "Bugs. Lyle. Birthday." *What's wrong with me? Why can't I form a sentence?*

Ansel repeated her answer into the phone. His speech was almost as staccato as hers. Then, "I can't be sure. Just a moment." He turned toward Stevie, who had hurried from the bed to his side.

226

She watched him trying to find a way to tell her whatever Galvin had just told him.

"Ansel?"

He took her hand.

Oh, God, Todd's rabbit. The dream.

"Ansel!"

Seconds later they were heading down the hall toward the nursery.

Todd's collection of stuffed animals, a Steiff zoo that could rival FAO Schwarz, covered three walls. A lifesize tiger and lion lay at the foot of his bed. There were monkeys and skunks and elephants and bears. On the shelves of a floor-to-ceiling étagère sat his Disney and Warner Bros. menagerie.

The phone connection to Lt. Galvin was still open as Stevie went to the Looney Tunes characters and took a quick mental inventory. "Sylvester, Tweety, Elmer, Porky," she said aloud. She didn't see Bugs Bunny anywhere. The rational part of her knew this from the moment she spotted the rabbitless shelves. But another part of her refused to accept the fact until she had listed every member of the Warner Bros. cartoon family.

Ansel watched, and understood. He wasn't going to rush her. Who was he kidding? Rushing her would be rushing himself. And what would they be rushing to? He hadn't told her yet why Galvin was calling.

Now, though, he'd have to. Stevie had moved from the shelves to Todd's closet. Ansel thought he heard sniffling from inside, and Stevie emerged a moment later visibly holding back tears. She shook her head, bent down to look under Todd's bed, and came up empty-handed.

Ansel said into the receiver, "Okay, we've checked. No rabbit. What now, Lieutenant?"

He listened, nodded, glanced at Stevie, and finally said, "I'll tell her. We'll be there as soon as we can."

Stevie didn't wait until he'd lowered the antenna on the phone. "You'll tell me *what?* We'll be *where?*"

Christ. "Stevie, Galvin says they've found a child's toy. It could be nothing—"

"But Galvin thinks it's Todd's rabbit, doesn't he? That's why he called, isn't it? They didn't find just *any* toy, they found a rabbit—*Bugs Bunny!*" She was starting to hyperventilate, and he had to shake her to stop her.

"Stevie! *Stevie!*"

She broke down in hysterical sobs for the second time in less than twenty-four hours. She was half blinded by tears as she threw on jeans and a shirt, climbed into Ansel's car, and tried to prepare herself for whatever awaited them at police headquarters.

In another situation, Ansel might have been annoyed to find Joe Madden sitting in Lt. Galvin's empty office. Or surprised. Today, nothing was so important.

Madden, however, felt the need to explain. "I tried the house and Stevie's machine answered. I figured she was in a rush because she didn't leave a forwarding number. So I called Mike and he told me. He'll be back in a minute."

He was back before that. "Mr. Kline," he said from the doorway, "Mrs. Kline might want you to handle this alone."

"That's up to *Mrs.* Kline, Lieutenant!" Stevie snapped. "If it's about our child, I'm just as involved as my husb—Ansel!"

Galvin offered a have-it-your-way shrug. "Okay. There's still nothing on the ransom note, but something else has turned up."

One of his men had arrived with a transparent plastic bag. He glanced at Stevie as though reluctant to let her see its contents, until Galvin said, "I'll take it from here, John. Now, Mrs. Kline, Mr. Kline. Does this belong to your son?"

Stevie forced herself to look at the three-foot-high gray-and-white rabbit. Bugs Bunny smiled his buck-toothed grin at her, and Stevie, feeling as if she were being filmed in slow motion, found herself smiling back. The corners of her mouth curved upward until her eyes had regained their sparkle. Then she began to giggle. Softly at first, but gradually the giggle expanded into a laugh. The more she tried to suppress it, the bigger the spasms became.

Galvin glanced at Ansel, who shook his head. Then, gently, he tapped Stevie's arm. He was afraid to call her name. What if the sight of Todd's rabbit had induced some kind of shock?

She turned at his touch, and sobered instantly. "Oh, Ansel, forgive me! I'm so ashamed!"

"Ashamed?" said Madden, coming closer.

She nodded, and this time the tears had returned. "I'm ashamed . . . because . . . I'm so *relieved!* This isn't Todd's rabbit!"

"It *isn't?*" whispered Ansel.

"No."

"How can you be sure, Mrs. Kline?" said Galvin.

Stevie's legs suddenly felt as if they were made of rubber. Madden was close enough to grab a chair, which he slid under her to keep her from falling. She sank into it, accepted a glass of water from Galvin's sergeant, and reached for Ansel's hand.

"Todd's rabbit has purple ears."

"Purple?" echoed Ansel. "How can they be purple?"

"Magic Marker." The image of Todd and his ink-smeared bunny loomed before her. "He painted the ears so his Bugs wouldn't look like anyone else's—and he was right! His Bugs *doesn't* look like that one"—she pointed to the police exhibit in plastic—"because *that* Bugs has *pink* ears! It's *not* Todd's rabbit!"

Ansel was trying to keep his own overwhelming relief from becoming too apparent; after all, this toy rabbit with pink ears belonged to *someone*'s child. He hoped it was no more serious than a stolen or lost toy.

But that made him think. "Todd brought Bugs with him the last time he came to the studio. How could I have missed purple ears?"

"That's easy," Stevie explained. "He only did the paint job a week ago." Her temples throbbed for a split second as she realized her mistake. "I'm wrong, of course. I meant to say *two* weeks ago . . ."

Todd had fallen asleep. He'd grown tired of looking at books with not enough pictures and was bored with the robot animals. All they could do was go forward and back or from side to side. And the biggest one—the grizzly bear that was broken—couldn't do anything. Todd didn't dare mention it to either of the clowns. Not after the last time, when the bigger clown had slapped him.

He still hadn't gotten over that. He was pretty sure the smaller clown wouldn't hurt him, but he wasn't going to take a chance. The tall one hadn't come to Todd's room very often since the slap, and that was okay with Todd. The littler one treated him better. Even dinner was better. A double order of fries, or an extra cupcake.

Still, he was scared. There was nobody to talk to. Well, nobody except for Bugs. And he couldn't answer back.

Todd was clutching Bugs protectively under one arm as he slept.

It made a touching picture. A small boy and a toy rabbit with purple ears.

Thirty-five

Madden could hear Ansel and Lyle's voices in the foyer.

"I'm sorry I can't stay to see Stevie," Hemmings was saying. "Be sure to tell her that I'm there for her. For both of you."

"She already knows that, Lyle, but thanks."

"I'll take care of the press. And Barbara said she'll run interference with your mother. If there's anything else, babe, anything at all, let me know. No matter what time it is. Deal?"

"Deal." He closed the front door, then stopped in the living room and said to Madden, "I'll be right down. I just want to check on Stevie."

"How's she doing?" Madden asked when Ansel joined him less than five minutes later.

"Asleep. Or pretending to be." Ansel poured himself a second scotch.

"Pretending?"

"She's been keeping to herself lately. Around me, anyway. More club soda?"

"No, thanks." Ansel settled himself in the chair facing Madden's. There was a long silence that neither of them seemed eager to fill.

"Well," Madden said at last, "the ransom note's a good sign."

"So I keep hearing. You'll pardon me if I don't get excited."

"I only meant that Todd is still alive," Madden offered.

Ansel took a large swallow of his drink. "Why don't you ask me if I think Todd has his toy rabbit with him? Everyone else has."

"I don't blame you for being tired of all the questions," said Madden.

"You don't know the half of it. The note leads us nowhere. If it's from the cult, my son is a . . . a sacrifice. Otherwise, we have a total stranger to hunt and find in seven days." Ansel rose and crossed to the window. "A total stranger who wants money."

"You're going to pay it, aren't you?"

"That's not a problem. But the Landaus paid, too, and their son hasn't been found, right?"

Madden had no answer. He listened to the tinkling of ice cubes in Ansel's glass and reflected. It was worth another try. "We can pretty much clear Tammi Reynolds as a suspect," he said.

"Thanks for letting me know that much."

"What are you getting at?"

Ansel turned to him. "I'm getting at the fact that you were retained by *both* of us, Madden. Not just by Stevie."

"Meeting her alone was Tammi's stipulation."

"I'm not talking about that! Why wasn't I told anything beforehand?"

Madden shrugged. "I figured that's between you and Stevie."

"Except when it isn't. I'd have been the last one to hear about the ransom note, too, if I hadn't been there when it happened. What's next? I pay the ransom and then read Eppie Goldwyn's column to find out how it went?"

"Look, Mr. Kline, you're strung out right now."

"You're damned right, Madden!" Ansel pointed an accusing finger.

Madden kept his voice and temper in check. "When we get word where to make the drop, you'll be the *first* to know."

"Sure. After Galvin. And Stevie." He paused. "And you."

It could have been the booze talking, but Madden doubted it. "It's part of the job."

"Is it part of the job to keep me in the dark? The police are *still* looking at me cockeyed!"

"That's because they haven't completely ruled either of you out."

"As suspects? Are they nuts? We *love* Todd! And I love *her*, goddammit!" Ansel was fuming. "The divorce isn't final yet, Madden. We're still married!"

"The only thing I've gotten from your wife is her confidence, Mr. Kline. That's all."

"Well, it's more than I have." Ansel poured another drink. "I'm supposed to finish shooting this crappy picture while you're out tracking our son."

"There's not much else you could be doing just now."

"Right! I'd be interfering, while you. . . . Never mind."

"If it's any help, there's more information."

"Something you'd like to share with the distraught father?"

"Take it easy," said Madden. "The police feel it was Tammi Reynolds who made the anonymous phone calls to Eppie Goldwyn."

"What's your opinion?"

"It's possible, even probable, from what Eppie told me."

"When was that?"

"Last night. At the benefit."

"Did you tell Stevie?"

"Yes."

Ansel took another sip of his drink. "See what I mean?"

"Yeah," Madden admitted. "I do."

"Do you think Tammi Reynolds is dead?"

"I hope not."

"I'm getting tired of that word, Madden."

"Okay. I think maybe she got too close."

"To whom?"

Madden shrugged. "Whoever he is, the guy's a chauffeur."

"We've never used chauffeurs. Except for limo rentals. But—" Ansel stopped himself.

"But what?"

"Nothing. I was just going to say that my partner likes to flaunt it."

"I don't mean to steal your thunder, but Galvin's

already checking out Hemmings's current driver. And looking for his ex. Some guy named Manny."

"I remember him."

"Good. It might come in handy."

"What about this character who calls himself Perry Fang?" Ansel offered a wry smile. "I manage to find out *some* things."

"They'll find him. Or I will." Madden put his empty soda tumbler and coaster on the coffee table and rose. "I've got to go."

"A meeting?"

Madden studied Ansel for a moment, then decided there was no malice in the question. "Probably. Watching you swill that hooch doesn't help. Want a lift?"

"I've got my car."

"Then don't have another one of those."

Ansel put his half-empty glass on the desk. "It's not working, anyway."

"You're lucky," said Madden. "It never failed me." He moved toward the entrance foyer. "Hang in there."

Thirty-six

Galvin saw a Toyota pass in the opposite lane. It didn't register that Madden was behind the wheel until Galvin turned into the drive leading to the Kline house.

He picked up his briefcase and sprinted across the lawn, trying to outrun the reporters while reciting his usual litany of "No comment" and "Nothing to say at this time." Seconds after Galvin rang the bell and peered into the security camera, Ansel Kline opened the door.

Galvin was winded from his exercise. "I need to see Mrs. Kline," he said, still panting as he entered the foyer. "I'm glad you're here. Saves me a trip."

Ansel slammed the door in the reporters' faces. "We exist to accommodate you, Lieutenant."

Galvin's attempt at a smile faded. He could see that Kline was pissed off without even knowing the reason for his visit.

Galvin caught a whiff of scotch as Ansel said, "Stevie's upstairs, lying down. I'd prefer not to disturb her."

"Maybe she'll be rested by the time you and I are through."

"And if she isn't?"

"I'll have to ask you to wake her."

The two men went into the study. Ansel turned on a lamp and seated himself behind the desk, then gestured Galvin to a chair.

"I assume this won't take long."

"I hope not."

"Fuck," Ansel muttered under his breath.

"What's that?"

"Nothing. What can I do for you, Lieutenant?"

"I'll need a sample of your handwriting and your wife's, and I'd like you both to print the words exactly as they appear on this copy of the ransom note." He opened his briefcase and took out the sheet of paper. "Forensics has been going over the original, running some tests."

"And?"

"No results yet."

"Sounds familiar." Ansel reached into the bottom drawer of his desk and withdrew two manila folders. "So Madden was right."

"About?"

"Stevie and I are still under suspicion." He almost threw the folders at Galvin. "Help yourself, Lieutenant. Choose whatever paper you like while I copy the note. Do you prefer pen or pencil? Maybe crayon? There's a brand-new box upstairs in Todd's nursery. It's hardly been touched. Just pick a color!"

Galvin waited, then spoke matter-of-factly. "Ball-point, Mr. Kline. Black ink. And try to understand."

"I know, I *know!*" Ansel grabbed a pen and scribbled the words across a piece of stationery as he spoke. "You're only doing your job! Spare me, Lieutenant!"

"I can't do that. But the handwriting check might help clear you."

Ansel handed the sample to Galvin. "What might help is talking to the messenger who gave the note to Stevie!"

"He's a bellhop at the hotel. He found the note in the jacket pocket of his uniform. The envelope was addressed to Stephanie Kean, so he took it backstage and delivered it to her."

"Then it's someone who had access to the employee lockers!"

"Could be. Thing is, the bellhop had his dinner in the hotel kitchen—caught hell for that, also for leaving his jacket hung over a dining-room chair while he ate. Point is that anyone could have planted the envelope without being noticed."

"Including me!" Ansel exploded. "Oh, sure, that makes sense! I'd certainly want to collect a million dollars—from myself!"

"Mr. Kline, this is just one angle we're investigating. After we eliminate you and your wife as—"

"So!" Ansel interrupted. "You're trying to tell me this is ultimately in our best interests? Thanks, Lieutenant, but I've got a slew of excellent lawyers to look after our best interests. Should I call them?"

"Not yet," Galvin said after a long pause.

"Why not? I've had it with all the bullshit!" Ansel yelled. "You've questioned me—both of us—until we're blue in the face! Give me a lie detector test, for Chrissake! Let's just get it over with!"

"A polygraph test isn't admissible evidence, Mr. Kline."

"Will it get you off our backs? Will it get you to stop wasting what little time my son has left?"

Galvin shrugged. "It would be of your own free will. You understand that I'm not requesting it, that you're volunteering?"

Stevie entered the den before Ansel could speak.

"We're both volunteering," she answered for him.

Thirty-seven

Friday, July 26

Ansel had picked Stevie up and together they'd driven to police headquarters; neither seemed eager for conversation.

Now, several hours later, the polygraph tests were over and they were on their way back to the Canyon. The atmosphere was subdued but not relaxed. Stevie hadn't expected the truth to induce stress, but Ansel seemed as tense as she was. She sensed that his silence, however, was due to something besides the questions he'd been asked and the answers he'd given during the test.

He'd behaved like this before, and although Stevie never openly sought confrontation when it could be avoided, she hated this tacit agreement that encouraged their mutual silence to continue.

When they reached the house and were inside the entrance foyer, Stevie glanced at the floor below the mail-drop. She dreaded, but half expected, to find a second note with further instructions.

She found nothing.

Of course. Whoever had masterminded Todd's kidnapping wouldn't simply slip a note under the front door with the press rooted outside as witness. No important messages had been left on the answering machine. Carolyn had called, but Barbara would see to her. Or Ansel could, later. There was little to do but wait.

Stevie made a pot of coffee as Ansel slid into the corner of the kitchen banquette. He ran his fingers through his hair, then folded his hands in front of him. He wasn't looking at Stevie.

She couldn't bear it. And told him so.

He reacted with surprise, as though he'd just realized there was someone else in the room.

"Remember when we didn't need words?" he asked.

She did. "It's six years later, Ansel. We're not the same."

"I am."

"I don't think you are. I know I'm not. Especially after the past week." She sat down beside him, and he moved his folded hands away, out of her reach. She hadn't touched them.

"Ansel," she continued, "the phone isn't ringing. There's no meeting to attend. They don't need you on the set. And Todd . . . isn't here. It's just the two of us, alone. Let's take what little time we've been given. I miss my best friend."

He stared at the well of his coffee cup rather than at her.

"I'm not speaking because I'm afraid of what I'll say, Stevie. Or how I'll say it."

"So you'll hold it in until you say it by screaming

242

at me! It's like a storm building, Ansel. Or like waiting for the other shoe to drop. And I can't take it! Not on top of everything else!''

"Who's yelling now?" The almost paternal half-smile had charmed her in the past.

"I'm not yelling," she said. "And you're not directing the scene."

"I suppose *you* are?" Ansel pushed his coffee cup aside and leaned back against the back of the booth seat. "You do your own share of controlling."

"How?"

"By lying to me."

"I've *never* lied to you!"

"What have you told me about your life before we met? You're very good at keeping things from me, Stevie!"

She hesitated, then said, "I know."

He waited for more, but she added nothing.

"That's all?" he asked. "We spent a whole morning telling the truth to a fucking machine, Stevie! If you want to talk now, then let's talk! But both of us! Not just me!"

Stevie's hands began to tremble. She didn't answer immediately, and when she did, she wasn't looking directly at him.

"I did lie to you, Ansel. By omission." Her mouth went dry. She took a quick sip of her cold coffee. "The alarm system wasn't on."

"Thank you," he said without surprise.

"You knew?"

"Not until I was asked about it this morning. And about Jill's problem with numbers."

"I intended to tell you. I didn't mean for you to find out the way you did."

From outside, the sounds of the press cars and media vans revving up alerted them. By the time Stevie and Ansel reached the living room, the drive leading down to the road was deserted, except for a single squad car.

Stevie's heart seemed to stop. "Ansel, something's happened."

The phone rang. The private line. Ansel grabbed it.

Stevie watched his face turn ashen. Tears filled his eyes as he listened.

Then he hung up and came to her. "They've found a body," he said in a choked voice. "They think it's Andy Landau."

Thirty-eight

Within the hour, while a voracious press converged on the Landau estate in Brentwood, a more familiar yet equally hungry convergence was descending on the house in Beachwood Canyon. Lyle Hemmings arrived with two studio executives, Barbara Halsey, and Fran in tow.

Madden had to park his car at the foot of the road. He did a quick count on his way up the walk. Certain principals were absent, at least for the moment. Galvin was undoubtedly at the crime scene, and Eppie Goldwyn was just as undoubtedly dogging his steps with her tape recorder. The discovery of Andrew Landau's body offered Stevie and Ansel a temporary media reprieve, but they had to know it would be shortlived. The Landaus would be out of the spotlight within forty-eight hours, and the Kliegs would shine once more on the more famous parents, Stephanie Kean and Ansel Kline. Their child, after all, was still missing.

The implications were more ominous than before. Andrew Landau was dead. His parents had paid a ransom, and it hadn't saved their son. Madden and the Klines had five days—with no assurance that Todd Kline was still alive.

Madden was prepared for anything when he rang the doorbell. Stevie and Ansel must be going through hell, and Madden wasn't sure he could do anything to help.

Barbara Halsey answered the door. She was only a few degrees warmer than she'd been at their lunch date.

"Ansel's in the den with Lyle," she said. "And Stevie's upstairs." Madden opted for the latter.

She was sitting on the floor of Todd's nursery, hugging the lifesize toy lion and combing his mane with her fingers.

She looked up when she saw Madden.

"His name is Bert," she said. Her eyes told Madden that she'd been crying, although her voice was so expressionless and flat, she seemed to be in a trance. "He's named after Bert Lahr, the cowardly lion in *The Wizard of Oz*, you know?"

Madden nodded from the doorway without coming closer.

She continued in the same, distant tone. "When I was a child, it was my favorite movie. I used to wish that I were Dorothy—not Judy Garland, but Dorothy. All I'd have to do was click the heels of my ruby slippers together three times and I could go anywhere, be anyone I wanted to be."

"It happened, didn't it?" Madden asked gently.

246

She didn't answer, but went on as though he wasn't there.

"I played Dorothy in school. I even got to wear a pair of red shoes, except the rubies were really sequins." She pulled Bert-the-lion closer. "I'll tell you a secret, Joe. When the show was over, I stole the shoes. I'd never wanted anything so much in my life." Her eyes, rimmed with tears, were on the lion's mane, which she'd begun, absentmindedly, to braid. "And you know, after Todd was born, I couldn't find the shoes."

Madden was concerned about Stevie's babbling and wondered if Ansel should be with her. But he could see that she needed to finish the story, even if it made no sense to him.

"Funny, isn't it, Joe? You can lose something precious, something you thought you'd give anything to find again. But then, when you do find it, you realize it isn't that important after all, because you've lost something far more precious."

She reached behind the lion's rump and produced a pair of red-sequined shoes. "Look, Joe, I found them just this morning."

Then, in the whisper of a five-year-old child, she asked, "Does that mean Todd is lost for good?"

She burst into convulsive sobs as Madden ran across the room to her.

When Ansel entered the nursery, he found the cop-turned-PI seated on the floor surrounded by stuffed animals and rocking a half-sleeping, half-whimpering Stevie in his arms. A pair of glittering red shoes lay beside her. Ansel wondered where they'd come from; he was certain he'd never seen them before.

Madden had offered to carry Stevie to her bed, and Ansel had remarked—pointedly—that Stevie always slept in a fetal position, that Todd's bed was long enough. Madden got the message.

They came downstairs to find that Carolyn Kline had joined the entourage. Madden decided to let Ansel deal with her; he had more important matters to attend to.

First on the list was a call to Galvin. Forensics would have compared the Landau and Kline ransom notes by now. And they'd have arrived at the expected conclusion: that different paper, pen, and wording style meant a different MO—and a different perp. Galvin would have to surrender his obsessive belief that Todd Kline had been kidnapped by the cult that had taken Andrew Landau.

Something didn't add up. Why had the cult sent a ransom note to the Landaus if they'd planned to kill the child anyway? Well, that was Galvin's case. His task force could figure that one out. Madden, instead, was tired of being jerked around. Whoever had Todd Kline not only wanted, but had been damned sure, that the cops, the FBI, and the media would jump on the cult-theory bandwagon. It had to be someone with a logical mind, someone who knew the in's and out's and the habits of the principal players. And someone who needed money—unless the ransom note sent to Stevie was a hoax designed to throw everyone off track.

A logical mind. That all but eliminated Tammi Reynolds. Of course, she might be working with someone else—if anyone else in town was crazy or desperate enough to take her on as a partner in crime.

Madden laughed. Crazy or desperate might limit the suspects to a handful in someplace like Fargo, North Dakota, maybe. But in La-La Land? You had to be crazy or desperate just to drive on the freeway.

Motive, however, was another matter.

Motive had kept Madden from seriously considering Tammi. Sure, she could use the ransom money—who couldn't during these times?—but Madden had met countless misfits like Tammi over the years. Her idea of winning the lottery was finding a few hundred bucks to hide under her pillow. But a million? She wouldn't know how many zeros to write on the ransom note.

Tammi Reynolds, in her exclusive interview with Eppie Goldwyn, had hinted to Eppie—and half of LA—about a chauffeur. Now, in addition to the stars' kids, Tammi was missing, too.

Madden's call to Galvin yielded what he'd expected: zilch. Forensics hadn't finished going over the Honda, but all the prints they'd found so far, except for Stevie's prints on the door handle (which she'd explained) matched those on the steering wheel. Tammi Reynolds's, most likely. There were a few loose terry-cloth threads stuck to the blade of the butcher knife, which had probably been wrapped in the toweling. But no blood anywhere, and no signs of a struggle. The lab boys were working overtime, and even they admitted it was unlikely that they'd strike gold.

"The perp's no amateur," Dan, the lab chief, told Madden. "We could do handstands for another week and still come up empty."

Madden didn't have another week. Neither did Todd Kline.

Madden grabbed a roast beef on rye at a deli on the way, then drove to the crime scene. Galvin was in a more-constipated-than-usual mood. It was obvious that he was stumped. Madden decided this was not the moment to lock horns on who was right or wrong about the cult. He was here for a specific reason, although he'd anticipated the answer in advance.

He was right about that, too.

"Madden, you know I can't get a search warrant for Tammi Reynolds's apartment. She hasn't committed a crime."

"C'mon, Galvin, we both know there are ways around that."

"Such as breaking and entering? No way, José. And don't screw yourself and your PI license by ignoring me and playing Mike Hammer."

"Hey, Galvin, would I do something like that?" He was in his car and gunning the motor before the lieutenant could reply.

According to the note on the building manager's door, the super was at a funeral and wouldn't be back until four.

That gave Madden an hour. More than enough time.

His Mastercard, which doubled as an unofficial search warrant, usually required several minutes of concentrated work. This rattrap's locksmith deserved to have his own house broken into; the door to Tammi Reynolds's room swung open after thirty seconds of easy "credit."

Madden's first impression, when he saw Stevie Kean's movie stills taped chronologically on the wall, was that the room belonged to a star-struck runaway teen. His next impression was that someone had been here ahead of him and messed up the place. But a subsequent glance at Stevie Kean's personal history framed in silver told Madden that the room was probably in the same disarray as when Tammi was there.

He found himself studying Stevie's past through the pictures. In one she was dressed in gingham checks. Her long hair was styled in pigtails, and she was holding a toy Scottie. The candid shot was in black and white and clipped from a cheap fanzine. Nonetheless, Madden guessed that the pinafore's checks were blue and white, that the puppy was black, and that the sparkling shoes on the budding young actress's feet were the red sequined slippers she'd worn in the school play. Madden glanced toward the door, although he'd closed it behind him, and slid the photograph out of the frame. It was half the size of a postcard and fit easily into the breast pocket of his shirt.

He examined, but didn't take, the picture of

Stevie as a bride and Stevie as a young mother. Movie Cameras didn't do her justice.

But admiration wasn't why he was here. Madden set about a routine check of the premises, his mind open to anything his eyes might pick up.

They picked up a lot.

There was a paring knife in the sink; rotted orange peel was stuck to the blade, the remains of the fruit sitting alongside it. A filthy T-shirt with the M-G-M lion and logo had fallen or been tossed onto a broken end table. Madden watched as a cockroach scurried by and disappeared under a crack in the linoleum floor. He lifted the T-shirt to reveal a stack of unwashed breakfast dishes. Leo-the-Lion had been left—literally—with egg on his face.

Madden looked but didn't find signs that Tammi had been in a hurry to depart. The clothes rack behind a folded sheet had two pairs of faded, worn bluejeans tossed over hangers, and a denim skirt. The pressed-board dresser in the corner had three drawers. In the top drawer were two dirty acrylic sweaters; in the middle, four clean T-shirts, each with a different studio logo. The bottom drawer held the only surprise: a champagne flute wrapped in a soiled white towel. There was a pink lipstick smudge on the rim of the glass, but the surprise was in the quality of the crystal. Not something Tammi Reynolds could afford, let alone appreciate.

But nothing else seemed out of place in a room that, had anyone else been its tenant, would have suggested everything out of place.

A heavy, tattered suitcase that no doubt had seen

many luxury-liner ocean crossings before coming into Tammi's possession was propped against the wall next to the unmade Murphy bed. But except for back copies of fanzines, the suitcase was empty.

Madden had hoped to find a handbag or purse. Tammi Reynolds struck him as the kind of person who would carry her most personal belongings with her at all times, unless something had happened to make her leave them behind.

So wherever she was, her keys and wallet and anything she knew were with her. No help to Madden or the Klines.

Where had she gone? People like Tammi Reynolds appeared and disappeared without leaving a trace. Unless they were found dead in an alley, nine times out of ten they never made or left a mark.

Madden looked again at the homage-to-Stevie wall. Was there a clue in the photographs Tammi had chosen for her collection? He didn't feel closer to an answer, but he did feel closer to Stevie, and it touched him in a way he couldn't explain. Perhaps it was the same for Tammi. Maybe through a vicarious life she'd found importance, a way of not being written off.

"Well, seek and ye shall find!" came a caramelized voice as the door swung open.

Madden turned, and colored. Eppie Goldwyn. Exactly what he didn't need.

Thirty-nine

Eppie's relief, when she saw that the intruder was the Klines' private detective, was audible. She only regretted having left her tape recorder at the office.

"Caught in the act?" she asked, stepping farther into the awful little room.

"I might say the same," he replied. "Busby at the Guild?"

"I pay him." Eppie smiled.

"Ever been here before?"

"No. And you could save me the time and trouble of looking this place over by telling me if there's anything juicy I can use."

"We're probably not looking for the same thing, Ms. Goldwyn."

"Good point. But then, you never know." She came a few feet closer. "Madden's the name, isn't it?"

He nodded, and her smile broadened. It was stifling hot in the room, but Eppie didn't loosen the gracefully draped pink chiffon scarf that hid, until her next visit to Dr. Vogel, the crepelike folds in her neck.

During the aftermath of Stevie's outburst at the SOC benefit, Eppie hadn't noticed how attractive Madden was. It was the beefy, rugged look that Mort Kline had possessed. "I didn't recognize you without your tux," she said.

Madden returned her smile. It amused him that the first woman in a long time to undress him with her eyes should turn out to be Eppie Goldwyn. "No one's ever said that to me before. By the way, Stevie's holding up. I'm sure you were wondering."

"Of course." Eppie knew her face had reddened, and suddenly felt like an old fool. She became all business when she said, "I haven't tried to break through that media fortress at the Kline compound. How's Ansel taking the news?"

"By news, I assume you mean the Landau boy?"

"What else could I mean?"

She was fishing for the rumored ransom note, but Madden wasn't biting. "Ansel's handling it well, considering." He gestured to the mantel. "Seen this?"

Eppie needed only a glance at The Stevie Kean Wall to guess its meaning. "Even on a hot day, this could give you the shivers," she said.

Madden didn't comment on something else he'd just spotted. The lines of "The Serenity Prayer" were printed in flourished calligraphy on a piece of yellow paper that was set into a cheap plastic frame. It, and a much smaller card, also framed, lay haphazardly against the bed-table lamp. The card said, *Coke is God's way of telling you you're mak*-*ing too much money*. In red Magic Marker, *Ha Ha* had been added in a childish scrawl.

"Your article mentioned she'd been hospital-ized," said Madden. "For what?"

"Treatment," Eppie replied over her shoulder as she perused the bizarre gallery. "Nervous break-down, I imagine."

She was studying the photographs to find con-crete evidence of the baby Tammi had mentioned. The tie-in to Todd Kline was too good not to ex-plore. But she saw nothing so significant as the collection itself; the wall was a shrine to a wor-shiped goddess, but the goddess was only an ac-tress named Stephanie Kean.

Madden opened the door to the bathroom. On white wicker shelves were an assortment of jars, mostly acne creams. They had collected a thin layer of dust. On the shelf above, a dimestore se-lection of cologne and eau de toilette stood neatly in a row. Separate from the rest was a single, tiny bottle. He lifted the frosted crystal stopper and brought it to his nose. It was perfume, and it was expensive. The scent Stevie Kean wore.

In the medicine cabinet's mirror reflection he saw another framed motto. Madden didn't have to turn to read the words: *One Day At A Time*.

"Lonely," said Eppie from the bathroom door-way. She nodded toward the single toothbrush bow-ing over in its holder. It was pink. "She wasn't what I expected."

"How so?"

"From her voice on the phone, I thought she'd be younger."

"But you'd seen her before—at the baby shower, certainly."

"She didn't matter then. Anyway, both times on the phone, she sounded like some Valley Girl who'd seen *Private Benjamin* too many times."

"And you're still certain it was Tammi?"

"It's what the police think. So did you, Wednesday night." Eppie turned to give the room a final check. "Well, I've seen enough. I've got to write this up. And don't worry. I won't mention that you were here."

She didn't say, "You don't matter, either," but Madden could hear it in her tone of voice. He followed her back into the room.

"How long do you plan to milk this angle?" Madden asked.

"I beg your pardon?"

"Tammi Reynolds could be dead. What then?"

"She's important only with regard to Stevie Kean and Ansel Kline."

"And their son."

"And their son. You seem to resent me."

"You don't exactly make life easier for the Kline family, do you?"

"Look, Mr. Madden, my paper exists for the sole purpose of selling advertising space. Stories such as this ensure a wide readership. Greater circulation. As long as Stevie Kean is a star, she's news."

"And public domain."

"Precisely. The Klines are glamour, like it or not."

"You talk as if they weren't divorcing."

"They're seeing more of each other now than when they were married. Their names are linked to each other again, and fans everywhere are rooting for them as a couple. This whole thing might even bring them together again."

"Quite a price to pay."

"What doesn't have a price, Mr. Madden?"

"I doubt that Miss Kean would agree."

Neither would her mother-in-law. "You're awfully protective of *Miss* Kean, as you call her. But I suppose you have your reasons. I mean, I'm not the only one who benefits from this tragedy, am I?"

"Not all of us are exploiting it, Miss Goldwyn."

"And not all of us have climbed up on some sanctimonious high horse, either. It's a living, Mr. Madden."

Eppie strode to the door and slammed it in an exit worthy, she was sure, of Susan Hayward.

Once on the freeway, she began to calm down. The exchange had raised more than Eppie's hackles. Joe Madden was good-looking and smart. Any woman who spent more than five minutes with him would know that. Eppie doubted that Madden's obvious interest had gone unnoticed by *Miss* Kean. Was he servicing more than just the investigation? The divorce was, after all, still on.

Eppie's curiosity was strictly personal. Carolyn Kline would love to see Ansel rid of Stevie. Therefore, Eppie would do anything within her considerable power to aid a reconciliation. In print.

Besides, who was this Joe Madden? Nobody.

Eppie readjusted the silk chiffon at her throat and made a mental note to call Dr. Vogel the moment the story was concluded and she could spare a month off.

Madden gave the room a final check. He'd never visited before, but the territory was familiar. He and Tammi Reynolds had probably shared more than he cared to admit.

He glanced once more at "The Serenity Prayer." It reminded him about the eight-thirty AA meeting every Friday night in Echo Park—*where there were fewer drunks than cokeheads*.

He hadn't seen Tammi there last week, but if she was still alive and lucid, by now she could probably use a friend.

Forty

Maybe it was the heat. Or maybe the mayonnaise on his roast beef sandwich that afternoon had turned. More likely, though, it was the inescapable fact that time was running out for Todd Kline. Whatever, Madden couldn't shake the feeling of impending discovery—and not necessarily the kind that would lead to a solution.

His uneasiness increased at the meeting. It took thirty seconds to see that Tammi Reynolds wasn't there. Just the same, Madden stayed.

By the time he got back to his place it was after ten. The only signs of life in the neighborhood were inside his house: the red light on the answering machine was blinking, and the parakeets were singing.

He looked forward to a shower, followed by an hour or two with the wooden seagull that was close to hatching. His work had progressed more quickly than he'd anticipated; at this pace, the bird would be finished in another few days.

He'd been living high on the hog, and with the air outside wet with humidity, the A-C was worth every penny; it was actually cold indoors. The chill made Stanley and Blanche trill so loudly that Madden had to cover the cage to hear the message on the answering machine.

What he heard chilled the room even more. The call was from Galvin.

"We've found Tammi Reynolds. And she won't be talking to anyone." There was a number. Madden recognized it as Galvin's, but didn't pick up the phone. Instead, he was out the door and back into the sauna of Silver Lake. He was in such a hurry, he forgot to uncover the birds.

"We'll know more after the autopsy," Galvin was saying after Madden had made a positive ID. "So far, Byron thinks she OD'd on booze or drugs—or both." The lieutenant hadn't acknowledged Byron's presence, although the pathologist was standing next to Galvin and the opened drawer with Tammi Reynolds's covered form beneath the sheet. But Byron wouldn't take offense. Madden was convinced that forensic pathology required a special personality; homicidal maniacs aside, anyone else who spent his days cutting up corpses would lose his mind.

Madden wasn't blessed with Byron's detachment. He was on the verge of losing his lunch. No matter how many times he visited the morgue, he reacted the same way. And when the victim was someone he'd known—even as superficially as he'd known Tammi Reynolds—it affected him more.

Madden mentally corrected his mistake. After

half an hour in Tammi's room, he'd come to know her intimately. Now she was gone and she'd taken with her the information she'd been saving for Stevie Kean.

"Where did they find her?" asked Madden.

"In an abandoned gas station," replied Galvin. "No visible signs of violence, although finding her at dusk made it hard to tell. We'll examine the scene for trace evidence as soon as the sun's up tomorrow. Then we'll know if she went there on her own or was escorted."

"How long has she been dead?" Madden asked Byron.

"From the state of rigor mortis, I'd estimate the time of death to be a couple of days. Can't be sure until we do the autopsy."

Madden's gut was already sure. Tammi had made it as far as the Hollywood Bowl, and someone had seen to it that she wouldn't make it any farther. He glanced down at the fan who had seemed so eager for attention. She'd be getting that now. Eppie Goldwyn would be only one among the many.

"What about those bruises?" Madden asked, indicating the marks on Tammi's arms.

"May be postmortem lividity," said Byron. "Often confused with bruises. The autopsy will determine which." To Galvin he added, "Bruises would have occurred while she was alive. Of course, someone who's drunk or freaked out often needs to be forcibly moved from one spot to another."

"That's all you can tell us?" said Madden.

Byron scratched his head. "Well, on what we've got so far, I'd say she was either so drunk or coked up that she tripped and fell, or somebody wanted her to appear that way."

"What about the Honda?" asked Madden.

"What about it?" answered Galvin. "The car could have been stolen. Like I said, she could have been partying—with or without friends. We found a coupla empty scotch bottles."

"She was clean," said Madden.

"You know that for a fact?" said Galvin.

"Yeah."

"We've gotta talk," said Galvin.

"Tell you what," said Byron. "You guys go talk and I'll go eat." To the body, as he slid it back into the drawer and closed it, he added, "Tammi, we have a date—as soon as I finish dinner."

"What is it with you ghouls down here?" asked Galvin. "Dead bodies rev up your appetites?"

"You forget, Lieutenant," answered Byron, adjusting his wire-rimmed glasses, "I'm a vegetarian. I never eat meat."

He and Galvin laughed, but they both sobered when they saw Madden's face going green.

"So, what about the bruises?" asked Madden after he and Galvin had parked their cars and settled into a booth at the rear of a nearby coffee shop.

"You heard what Byron said. Besides, my sister-in-law has weak capillaries. Touch her—even lightly—and she's black and blue for days."

Madden couldn't argue with the logic; Tammi

Reynolds's neck, wrists, and ankles were free of marks; she hadn't been bound or strangled.

"But she hadn't OD'd, either." He repeated this aloud.

"Yeah, so you said." Galvin paused while the waitress set menus in front of them. Without opening his, the lieutenant said, "Bring me a cheeseburger, rare, fries, and coffee."

Madden's stomach had almost stopped churning, but not completely. "I had a late lunch. Just a diet ginger ale for me."

"Bring him a house salad with thousand island dressing," said Galvin. He turned to Madden. "I'll eat it. So tell me. How come you're so sure that Tammi Reynolds was clean?"

"Let's just say I know."

Galvin leaned in across the booth. "Were you the last person to see her alive?"

"We both know I wasn't."

Galvin had brought out his lighter and, partly because Madden wanted a smoke and partly to keep the lieutenant's lid-clicking from driving him crazy, he pulled a cigarette from the pack in his pocket.

Galvin lit it for him, then said, "And we both know you're stalling."

"Off the record?" said Madden.

Galvin let out a sarcastic half-laugh. "Allow me to guess. When you couldn't get me to cough up a search warrant, you let yourself into Tammi's place."

Galvin was staring at Madden as if it was a con-

264

test. Madden tried not to blink, but he'd been better at this game when he was a kid.

"I stopped by her room. I wasn't the only one."

"No?"

"Don't get excited. It was just the Goldwyn girl out doing her job."

"Either of you find anything?"

"Nothing that would interest you."

"No . . . paraphernalia?" said Galvin.

"I told you she wasn't into drugs."

"I'm talking about other things."

At first Madden didn't understand. But Galvin's inflection explained what other "things" he meant.

"You *still* think Tammi was part of the satanic cult you're investigating?"

Their food orders arrived, and Galvin waited until they were alone before he answered.

"Look, Madden, if the autopsy says homicide, that'll mean Tammi knew something she wasn't supposed to know. Either that, or somebody thought she did. And from what we've learned, she kept some pretty weird company for a while—*before* she got so clean."

"Any suspects?"

"I'd like to talk to this guy who calls himself Perry Fang."

"He could be calling himself the witch's tit by now, Galvin. Is that all you've come up with?"

"Listen," said Galvin, ignoring his food and pointing a finger at Madden, "you may think we've been jerking off on the taxpayers' money, but there have been four kidnappings and three, possibly four, murders in the past six months. In the beginning we didn't have diddley-squat to go on. It's taken me and my task force working night and day, seven days a week since January, to put the pieces together. And they spell *cult*. You think I *like* looking at decomposed bodies of children who have been murdered by these fucking cannibal freaks and left to rot in the woods? I ask the parents what their kid was wearing when he was last seen, and I tell them it's to help us in the search—and all the time I know the *real* reason is because without the kid's clothing, there isn't enough left of the kid's *body*, goddammit, to make a positive ID! You think I get a charge out of that, Madden? Or that I enjoy fending off the press, the mayor, and every ass-kissing politico in this town who wants to exploit these murders to advance their own careers?"

He stopped, but only for breath. "You can do me a big favor, Madden, by letting me do my job. Take my word for it, when we stop the cult, we stop the killings!"

Madden exhaled a huge plume of smoke. "I believe that, Galvin, except in the Todd Kline kidnapping. I still think you've got a copycat on the loose."

"For what purpose?"

"Find that and you've got the perp. And I'll bet you ten to one it's someone close to home." Madden took a sip of his ginger ale and frowned. The fizz had gone flat.

Galvin had bitten into his cheeseburger, and the meat's juices oozed out and dripped on his plate.

"You look like I feel," said Madden, stubbing out his cigarette.

Galvin reached for his wallet. "I need some air." He motioned for Madden to put away his money. "The drink's on me."

"You're springing for my ginger ale? You must really feel rotten."

"A trade-off, Madden. Once we're out of here, you're gonna tell me everything you know about Tammi Reynolds, up to and including the last time you saw her. And I want a full description of whatever you found in her room."

"Hey, Galvin, you don't need me. You can search the premises now that Tammi's dead."

"I plan to, Madden. And afterward, your detailed description will confirm whether anything is missing."

"This is a waste of time, Galvin."

"Look at it this way, Madden. Being booked for breaking and entering would be an even bigger waste of time."

Madden shrugged and muttered something under his breath.

"What was that?" asked Galvin.

"Oh, nothing. I was just reminding myself there's no such thing as a free lunch."

Forty-one

It was going on midnight when Ansel accompanied Carolyn to the hallway. Even in the dim light she was visibly exhausted. Only once before, at his father's funeral, had Ansel seen his mother's energies so thoroughly depleted. Tonight, her recent facelift notwithstanding, Carolyn Kline looked her age, and it distressed Ansel to see her growing old so suddenly. Then again, after the past week, they'd all grown older suddenly.

"I'll see you to your car," he said.

"No, don't. The press might be outside. I can move more quickly alone."

She offered her cheek. When he kissed it, Carolyn's arms went around him in an uncharacteristic gesture of affection. She held him to her for an unsettling moment, which he broke by saying, "I'll call you as soon as we . . . hear."

"Please do." Carolyn went to the door, hesitated, and said, "Ansel?"

"Yes?"

She turned toward Todd's room at the top of the stairs, where Stevie lay sleeping.

"Never mind," she said.

Outside the air was heavy. Carolyn walked cautiously past Barbara Halsey's Cadillac, all the while fearful that some snooping paparazzo would spring out with a camera from behind the car.

None did, and Carolyn knew why. They were stationed for the night at the Landau home. It was easy to envision the circus unfolding there.

A lone squad car was parked at the foot of the road. In the darkness Carolyn saw the glowing ember at the tip of a burning cigarette. But the presence of the police offered little comfort.

She glanced back at the house. The lights were out on the second floor, although Carolyn was sure she'd seen movement at the window curtains in Todd's room. She wondered how much longer this hell would last. For all of them.

Stevie stood at the window of the nursery and watched her mother-in-law's Mercedes pull away.

She and Carolyn couldn't avoid each other forever, but the parameters would be different, now: husband and son no longer in the middle, son and grandson no longer shields. When the two women spoke again, they would share nothing except the uncertainty of coping with change.

Stevie hauled Bert-the-lion onto the mattress and placed his head on Todd's pillow. Bert's mane was braided. She didn't remember doing that. Oh, wait. Yes. Joe Madden had come into the room, they'd talked, and she'd felt better.

She tripped over the sequined slippers before she saw them sparkling in the glow of the baseboard nightlight. Clicking the heels together wouldn't take her home, even if she knew where that was. Home had been here, with Ansel and Todd. Without them, it was just a house.

She shoved the shoes to the back of Todd's closet so they'd be easy to forget. She was sorry she'd ever found them.

Ansel had returned to the living room, where Barbara Halsey, her head resting on one arm, her eyes closed, was curled up on the sofa.

"You awake?" he whispered.

She opened her eyes and freed her arm, shaking it to restore circulation. "Yes. I've been doing some thinking."

Ansel lowered himself into the club chair near the unlit fireplace and reached for the tumbler on the coffee table in front of him. He took a sip of tepid tonic water and what was left of the ice cubes at the bottom of the drink he hadn't wanted. He looked up at the sound of movement on the floorboards above.

"Stevie's awake," he said.

Barbara raised her head and studied him. She'd been waiting all evening to tell Ansel, but the house had been filled with people. Stevie would be downstairs any minute.

"Ansel, there's something I haven't told you. Or the police."

"What?" His anger was resurfacing. More information had been kept from him. What the hell was it with everyone, anyway?

"I almost told your detective, but . . ."

"But you don't like him. I know. What *is* it, Barbara?"

So she told him about Manny's visit to the studio. "Lyle was really upset that the guy showed up. He tried to hide it, but he was jumping out of his skin."

"And later?"

"I didn't see Lyle till the meal break. He seemed fine by then. It's not hard to figure out why. Oh, yeah . . . that was when I noticed the cut on his nose." She shrugged, relieved to get it off her conscience. "I wasn't sure I should tell anyone."

"Why not?"

"Some kind of screwed-up loyalty, I guess. Although to whom or what, I don't know anymore. I just didn't feel it was anyone else's business."

"Not even mine?"

"You've had so much to worry about already, Ansel! But then I thought, what if it's important?" She paused. "Do you think it is?"

They heard footsteps on the stairs. "I want you to tell this to Joe Madden," Ansel said quickly. "Just don't mention it to Stevie."

Entering the living room, Stevie had no doubt that she'd been the last subject under discussion. It had happened a lot lately.

Barbara and Ansel made it more obvious by filling the awkward silence with small talk. Stevie complied, if only to assure them that she hadn't lost her mind.

She poured herself a sherry, but the taste was too sweet. She left the cordial glass on the top of the bar and, empty-handed, sat down beside Barbara, who hugged her.

"Thanks for staying," said Stevie. "I'm better now."

"Good. Then I'll get out of here. You two should have some time alone."

Without looking at each other, Stevie and Ansel both offered a short, wry laugh.

They were saying good night when the telephone rang. It was the private line.

Stevie jumped from the sofa and bolted for the study. Ansel and Barbara followed.

Stevie remembered to press the Record button as Ansel reached for the receiver and lifted it to his ear.

"Ansel Kline?" asked a woman's voice.

Madden was already worn out by the time he got past the cop in the squad car and parked the Toyota in the Klines' driveway. Next to his repair-shop loaner was the black Caddy he recognized as Barbara Halsey's.

He'd stopped here on a sudden impulse. Maybe calling ahead would have been a better idea. Ms. Halsey wasn't his biggest fan, and it was late.

He sat in the dark, collecting his thoughts and

thinking about Tammi Reynolds. Her murder had affected him. So had her life, unhinged or not.

Galvin had promised to keep the media's noses out of it until morning. But Madden didn't want to risk the news reaching the Klines secondhand. And it wasn't something to tell them—*her*—over the phone.

Barbara Halsey came to the door. She was carrying her purse and briefcase. Her eye makeup was streaked and she looked as though she'd been crying.

"I'm just leaving" was her greeting.

"Tammi Reynolds is dead" was his answer.

Barbara leaned back against the wall. "Well," she said after several seconds' pause, "then I guess it wasn't Tammi Reynolds on the phone."

"When? What do you mean?"

"Five minutes ago. Isn't that why you're here?" She didn't explain, but gestured with a nod toward the study. "They're waiting for you. I'll call you in the morning."

"Okay. But—" Madden's visit was expected. Had his beeper gone on the fritz, too?

"Tomorrow, then." Barbara beckoned him inside as she left. "And Madden . . . I'm sorry I behaved like a bitch."

Stevie and Ansel both began talking at once the moment they saw Madden.

"Have you notified Galvin?" he asked.

"It just happened. We wanted you here before we did anything."

Under the circumstances it seemed crass that Stevie's words should gladden him. But they did.

Ansel pressed the Play button. Stevie retreated into a shadowy corner to listen again to the woman's muffled whisper.

"Monday," said the voice. "Nine A.M. Unmarked one-hundred-dollar bills. Location to follow."

There was a rustling sound, as though the phone was being passed to someone else.

Then the small, frightened voice of Todd Kline cried, "Mommy! Mommy!"

And the line went dead.

Ansel stopped the tape. He and Madden looked first at each other, then at Stevie. Her eyes glistened with tears as she came forward.

"He's alive, Joe," she said, her own voice somewhere between a laugh and a sob. "Our baby is alive!"

Forty-two

Galvin hung up the phone and reread his notes, although Byron had promised to have hard copy of the official autopsy report on his desk before noon.

It was early, and relatively quiet for the morning after a hot, dank Friday night in summer. One of the guys had mentioned a shooting over on South Rimpau Boulevard, but that was typical; the locals spent Friday and Saturday nights partying and playing with loaded shotguns; every so often, someone was bound to get hurt.

Galvin sipped his coffee from the chipped mug he hadn't had time to replace. He'd already visited the crime scene, the gas station where Tammi Reynolds had been found. He glanced down at those notes, too.

The inside of the shack had been dusted, but Galvin didn't expect a lot from a place that had once seen so much traffic. They might get something from the bits of terry-cloth fiber that had adhered to the fabric of Tammi Reynolds's jeans. If it matched the fibers on the butcher knife, that would cinch it.

But what would it cinch? They already knew that the knife in the car hadn't killed her.

The empty booze bottles were smudged with prints. Ten to one the scotch had been imbibed by grease monkeys working at the gas station before it and the road had gone the way of the mastodons and the tar pits.

What else was there? Latent prints on the body would be run through the files. The marks on her arms were indeed bruises; the lack of postmortem lividity on the right side proved that she'd been moved to where they'd found her after she was dead.

Byron, in his inimitable way, had saved the best for last. "Oh, Galvin," he'd said, "it's possible your buddy Madden may have called it right. Tammi probably OD'd—not willingly, though."

"Possible. May have called it. Probably. How about something more definite, Byron?"

"Well, I checked for needle marks."

"And?"

"And, in all that plentitude, there was evidence of just one single hypodermic injection. Either the late Ms. Reynolds wanted to go out like Monroe, or someone wanted it to look that way."

"What the fuck are you talking about?"

"Marilyn. The needle mark under her breast. Galvin, don't you read?"

"Look, Byron, I want to know if this is a suicide

or a homicide investigation, so for Chrissake, get to the point!"

"Right. The point is, there's a needle mark under Tammi Reynolds's left breast. Hard to find at first. She was pretty zaftig, and—"

"What was she injected *with*, Byron?"

"Dunno yet. You'll be the first to hear when I do. For now, let's just say whatever it was probably did the job, and I doubt that it was self-inflicted, because as your pal Madden says, the deceased was clean."

Galvin had gone over the notes three times, as if repetition would force the lightbulb to go on in his head. When it didn't, he finished the dregs of his coffee and turned to the message pad on his desk. The call had come moments before Galvin's arrival, but Byron's report had taken precedence.

Now he addressed the contents of Madden's message. Okay, so a woman had called about the ransom payoff. They had the date for the drop, but not the location. A voice analyst would go over the tape, but if the woman was a stranger acting for someone else, what good would a voice check do? How could they make a match?

The second half of Madden's message perplexed Galvin on two counts. First, what was so important about a cokehead like Lyle Hemmings's ex-chauffeur making noises at the studio, unless there was a link connecting Manny Perez to Tammi Reynolds? Or to the Kline case and the cult? There was a chance Manny Perez had led Madden to Perry Fang, but that wasn't part of the message, and Madden wasn't one to beat around the bush.

Personality differences aside, Galvin and Madden were, after all, working on the same side. And they both knew it.

It was time for Galvin to make a few calls of his own.

"Lyle!" Carla yelled from the kitchen. "It's, like, that police lieutenant friend of yours on the phone!"

"Take a message, for God's sake!" He'd been more hyper than ever since last night.

"But, he's on hold! I mean, like, he knows you're here!"

Lyle threw the loose sheets of typed revisions across the room and watched them scatter as they hit the den floor. Hell, Carla could pick them up and put them back in order; it was her fault he was in such a snit to begin with.

He pressed the button and lifted the receiver. "Mike! Hey, babe, you're a mind reader! I was gonna call you this afternoon!"

"Yeah?"

"Right! Listen, Mike, I know it's last minute, so if you've already lined up something special for tonight, we can take a raincheck—"

"Hey, slow down, Lyle. What's tonight?"

"Saturday—and I'm making good on that invite to dinner. As soon as you get off duty—so go solve a case and get your ass over here!"

"Hey, Lyle, that's not why I called."

"Yeah, yeah, I know, you just wanted to see how I'm doin'. Well, I'm doin' great—never better—and

I want you to see the palace!" They'd agreed on seven o'clock and hung up before Lyle realized that he'd said *palace* instead of *place*.

Lyle unlocked the desk drawer that held his private stash. What the hell? One man's home really *was* another man's castle—and this was Lyle's castle!

"Carla!" he bellowed, heading toward the kitchen. "Gotta clean up the *palace*"—said purposely this time—" 'cause we're having company tonight!"

"Company! Are you crazy?"

He went to the cupboard and took out a bottle, from which he withdrew two pills. "Sure, I'm crazy! Here—catch!" He tossed the bottle to her, but he'd forgotten to cap it, and the little blue uppers went flying in all directions.

What Galvin had expected was a house like Norma Desmond's in *Sunset Boulevard*. Or a sprawling estate like the one in Bel Air where he'd investigated an only-in-Hollywood case a dozen years ago. The house, a Spanish four-story white stucco, had been bought and furnished by a famous cosmetics heiress as a wedding gift to her fifth husband, a part-time nightclub singer, full-time gigolo. The groom turned out to be a cross-dresser, and the bride turned out to be a double-crosser. After they'd formed a Romeo and Juliet suicide pact—with Romeo keeping his half of the bargain—Juliet reneged. No charges, no community property. The bereaved widow resettled on Ibiza. End of story.

Cases had been easier to solve in those days, the

answers usually closer to home. No random snipings on freeways, no serial killers on the loose, no satanic cults kidnapping and murdering helpless children.

Galvin was so engrossed in sweet reminiscence, he almost missed the turnoff.

But nobody could miss the turrets, even from behind the walls of the fortress.

Jesus! The last time Galvin had seen anything like this was on his six-year-old niece's birthday. The place looked like a goddammed Fantasyland, right out of Disney—and Galvin wasn't even past the gate!

Carla had ordered from Lyle's favorite caterer. She'd set and reset the sleek banquet table in the dining hall three times, and still it didn't work. Finally she'd opted for the cozier atmosphere of the conservatory. She set the round glass table for two; her stomach was too upset for food. Besides, she was too strung out to spend an evening seated next to the head honcho from the homicide squad and not make a slip.

What about Lyle? He'd been telling her all afternoon to relax. But how could either of them relax? Why had Lyle invited the detective here, anyway? To play games? To play God? Was it all the drugs messing up his brain, or had he always had a screw loose, even when it was just ludes and small stuff at school? She'd idolized him then because she'd thought he was a genius. She'd been willing to do anything for him; all he'd had to do was ask.

Lately, though, he'd started asking too much.

"Carla!" Lyle shouted from the library.

"I'm coming!" she called back, placing the gleaming silver bowl of flowers at the center of the table. Some of the ferns were hanging too low on one side, and she tried to rearrange them, but her hands were shaking.

"Carla!" Louder this time.

She abandoned the greens and hurried down the hall. She'd do what he wanted, but with each passing day, with each new demand, she was growing more fearful of Lyle and of what he might ask of her next.

"Something special for dinner instead of burgers and fries," said the clown, entering the room with a tray.

"Look!" The metal dome was removed from the plate. "Doesn't that look wonderful?"

"I'm not hungry," said Todd in a small voice.

"That's because you haven't tasted it. It's from a very good restaurant. See? Boeuf Wellington, garlic mashed potatoes, Caesar salad. You've gotta try it."

"I don't want any." In a smaller voice. But he did peek at the thick slice of rare filet in its pastry and paté shell.

"No? Not even a little bite?"

Todd shook his head. "I want my mommy."

"Well, I tell you what, Todd," said the clown.

"You eat your dinner and be a good boy, and you'll be back with your mommy in just a few more days. I promise."

"I want to go home *now.*"

"Y'know what, Todd?"

"What?"

"I want you to go home, too."

Lyle poured himself a brandy while he contemplated his malachite-and-gold cigarette lighter. He hadn't had time to run over to Cartier—Christ, he was a busy guy, right?—but he felt the need to make some kind of overture to Galvin, especially since tonight's invitation had been so long in coming. What the hell? The gesture would be even more heartfelt if he gave Mike *his* lighter. Lyle could pick up a replacement for it on Monday.

Monday. The prospect of Monday made his head spin. He went to the rectangular gold box on the lacquered table and took out a couple of pills, which he washed down with the brandy.

He felt an immediate buzz and thought at first that it was his reaction to the pills. Then he realized it was the sound of the buzzer at the main gate.

A glance at his watch. Seven o'clock sharp.

"Yeah!" he cried, running down the hall to trip the automatic gate release. "I'm coming, don't wear it out! Everything's gonna be great! Oh, yeah!"

* * *

"No, Todd, I can't stay," the clown was saying. "But aren't you glad you decided to eat? Isn't it yummy?"

Todd nodded; Mommy had taught him not to talk with his mouth full. The food *was* good, much better than McDonald's, and the clown—this one, anyway—was trying awfully hard to be nice, especially since last night after the other clown had yanked him away from the telephone.

There was a loud knock on the door, and an angry voice yelled, "Hey! Company's coming up the drive! What the hell is taking you so long?"

Todd could see that the clown's eyes, visible through the cutout holes, were filled with fear.

"I have to go, now, Todd. I'll try to come back later." And then, leaning closer and pressing the painted rubber lips against Todd's cheek, the clown kissed him.

Todd's little hands reached up in response, and before either of them knew it, his fingers were lifting the edges of the mask.

The clown offered no resistance as the rubber face came off.

"Carla . . . ?" Todd's eyes showed wonder, and something more.

Something heartbreaking.

"Todd!" Carla whispered. "Whatever happens, *don't* let him know that you've found out!"

Forty-three

Lyle stood at the end of the hall near the top of the staircase. He watched Carla as she locked the door and dropped the key in her pocket.

"What the fuck have you been doing?"

"D-don't talk to m-me that way," she said, trying unsuccessfully to keep the quaver out of her voice.

"You spend too much goddammed time in there with him!"

"I like him!" She removed the clown mask she'd replaced before leaving Todd. "And he likes me."

"He likes me," Lyle mimicked. "Just make sure it's the clown he likes, not Carla. Otherwise, we're dead—and so is he."

It was impossible to control her hammering heartbeat as he led—almost shoved—her downstairs. Lyle was talking nonstop. He was *always* talking nonstop lately, and the more he did, the less she heard.

"W-what did you say, Lyle?"

"I *said*, is the dining hall set up! Have you gone deaf?"

"No! To both questions! There's only one guest, Lyle! The dining hall seats forty!"

"That's what I want! Big! Like the jigsaw-puzzle scene in *Citizen Kane!*"

Carla pulled her arm free, careful not to lose her balance on the stairs. "In the conservatory you won't have to scream at him like you're screaming at me! If you need anything, you can ring the little bell on the table and I'll come running."

"You're joining us! I want you there!"

Sure he did. Having the cop in charge of the investigation dining right under the room where Todd was imprisoned wouldn't be half the gas if Lyle didn't have an accomplice to witness the fun.

"I'll play your maid, Lyle. You're, like, into that."

"Yeah!" He clapped his hands together. *"Okay!"*

The doorbell chimed. "Answer it! Stall for a minute, then bring him into the Casino!" He was halfway down the stone-tiled entrance hall when he turned. "But for Chrissake, get rid of that clown suit!"

Carla unzipped the costume and threw it behind the carved footlocker in the foyer. She reached the door just as Lyle, in a manic voice, called, "It's showtime!"

Galvin was glad to see Carla Franzen at the door. Nothing like scoring two birds with one stone.

"Hi! Like, uh, c'mon in!" Her greeting was too cheerful, but he'd give her points for trying. Galvin couldn't be sure if her shivering was from nerves, drugs, or the frigid temperature inside.

The entrance hall resembled a hotel lobby. Lyle's former address and Galvin's current digs could fit in here—together.

Carla seemed in a rush. She hurried him past the winding staircase and beyond what looked like a formal drawing room. Purposely Galvin slowed his steps. "Seen anything of the Klines?"

It stopped her dead. "Uh . . . no. I thought maybe they needed some time alone."

"Must be rough," Galvin said with what he hoped sounded like genuine sympathy. "You took care of their child once in a while. You must have gotten to know him pretty well."

"Y-yes," she stuttered. "Uh . . . Lyle's waiting."

"He won't mind. Tell me, what about Manny Perez? Have you seen him lately?"

It didn't matter what she answered. Her body language told him before she said a word.

She made an attempt nonetheless.

"Uh, n-no. Why?"

"What about Lyle?"

"Well, like, I wouldn't know. You'd better ask him."

"Oh, don't worry. I plan to."

Carla left the doors to the Casino opened and stood just outside, listening.

Over drinks, the forced laughter of the two men rang out. The lieutenant was asking Lyle questions, too. About Manny, and about someone named Perry Fang.

He also had news. Carla's knees turned to rubber when she overheard that Tammi Reynolds was dead.

Why wasn't it in the papers? Was it really because they wanted to wait for her killer to make a slip? Tammi had mentioned Manny in that dumb interview! If he'd snuffed her just for that, what would keep him from coming after Lyle? After her, too?

No. Manny knew he'd have his money by Monday night. She and Lyle would be safe, and Todd could go home. She didn't care what happened after that—even if Todd spilled all the beans. She'd rather face jail than die. Running away was no longer an option. She wouldn't leave Todd. Not anymore. Not with Lyle, who had definitely gone off the deep end. If she had any remaining doubts, what she was overhearing right now squashed those for good.

"How about the grand tour, Mike? We can start upstairs and work our way down in time for dinner!"

Lyle saw Carla's shadow disappear around a corner as he and Galvin reentered the main hall.

The news of the nutso fan's murder had momentarily shaken him, but by offering to show off the Palace he managed to steer Galvin off the subject of Manny Perez—and back on to the cult.

"Weird, isn't it," Lyle said offhandedly as he led

the way up the staircase, "about there being only two ransom notes and four kidnappings, huh?"

"Two?" Galvin was behind him and Lyle couldn't see his face.

Christ! Did I just fuck up? Don't act too cocky for your own good. Gotta watch it, ripped or not. "Yeah, Mike," he answered quickly. "Ansel told me about the note for the Landau boy." He ventured a glance over his shoulder. "Shouldn't he have?"

"No, he shouldn't have." Galvin was puffing from the climb. "I'm not surprised he did, though. And it's too late now, anyway."

"I guess so, Mike!"

Lyle let out a deep breath and hoped Galvin would think it was from the steep flight of stairs and not from sliding off the hook. Lyle also hoped he wasn't taking a stupid risk but something had been bugging him since the day he'd "borrowed" his godson from the nursery in Beachwood Canyon.

"You know," he said, growing very serious, "it's lucky no other kid's been nabbed."

"Excuse me?"

"Since Todd Kline. There haven't been, right?"

"Haven't been what, Lyle?"

"Other kids—nabbed!" He ordered himself to calm down. *Mustn't make it too important.* "I mean, if the first ransom note was kept from the media and so was the murder of Tammi-what's-her-name, there hasn't been another kidnapping you guys are keeping under wraps, too, has there?"

"We figure August one is the date for the cult's

288

next sacrifice. We think it's the reason Todd Kline was taken."

"Oh, yeah! Like I said, weird!"

Jesus! Recovering Todd—alive—would blow the cult theory to hell, but Lyle had no choice. The insurance company wasn't paying up anytime soon, and Manny's "business associates" weren't willing to wait.

Thank God Ansel had told Lyle about the Landau ransom note. It had set the precedent and given Lyle his brainstorm after the insurance suits had put him on indefinite hold.

The question was, of course, why the cult hadn't snatched another kid. Unless they had, and no one knew about it yet. Or maybe the August 1 black mass was being canceled because the heat was on. Whatever, it was a lucky break. Galvin—everyone— was still locked into the devil-worship angle.

Yeah, Lyle could relax. He was almost home free. Just a couple of days, and he'd have even more than he had now. He'd have it all! Yeah!

Galvin stopped to catch his breath when they reached the second-floor landing. He leaned over the banister and looked across the railing at the enormous crystal chandelier suspended from above. He glanced down at the stone-tiled floor some twenty-five feet below. He hated heights almost as much as he hated stairs. He hoped the grand tour didn't include the third floor.

* * *

Lyle was on the landing with his arms spread wide. He could feel the adrenaline pumping through his veins. To his right were four of the guest suites. He'd tell Mike they weren't furnished yet, even though the truth, despite what he'd led Ansel to believe about his excessive spending, was that he'd sold off the costly antiques, one by one, to pay for his habit. Maybe it was smarter to avoid the empty rooms altogether and thereby circumvent an explanation.

The alternative was a tour of the "game" rooms to the left—the model-railroad room, the sound-proofed stereo-listening room, the movie-projection room, and the F-X room—with Todd Kline.

"Which way?" asked Galvin.

It was too delicious. How could he resist? "You're my guest, Mike—you choose!" *Yeah!*

Lyle was dizzy with anticipation by the time Galvin gestured to the left and said, "Let's see what's on this side."

"You've got it, Mike!"

At the foot of the stairs Carla clutched the newel post to hide her attack of the shakes. Teasing Lt. Galvin wasn't like teasing some rookie! Lyle might as well be playing Russian roulette with a bullet in every chamber of the gun!

The two men were momentarily out of sight, but she could locate them from the sounds of creaking floorboards under their feet. They were in the west wing, and at first, the fading voices and footsteps told Carla they'd gone into the projection room.

Seconds later, however, a door closed. Their voices and footfalls grew louder as they came closer to the room at the top of the stairs.

The F-X room!

"Betcha can't guess what's in here, Mike!" she heard Lyle exclaim.

Galvin had tired of oohing and aahing. Okay, the place *was* spectacular. With the kinds of things he hadn't been able to buy for the ex-wife who'd wanted it all. But by now he knew the tour was calculated to point out not only what Lyle had, but what Galvin lacked. It didn't provoke envy. It provoked something else that Galvin couldn't put his finger on just yet.

"Go ahead," said Lyle, nodding toward another massive wooden door. "Open it!"

Galvin forced a smile, shrugged, and turned the knob.

The thin sliver of light under the door was blocked by two shadows. Todd sat on the edge of the bed and hugged Bugs even more tightly. He could hear the muffled voices of grown-up men.

Was one of them Daddy?

Todd scampered off the bed and tiptoed across the room.

He stopped when the fancy glass knob began to turn. Todd was ready to cry "Daddy!" He'd wait just till the door opened.

But it didn't. The knob clicked back into place.

And Todd recognized the laugh of the mean clown.

If I'm real quiet, thought Todd, maybe he'll go away. Maybe Carla will come instead. Her clown friend wasn't very nice.

Carla's friend.

That's what Mommy had called . . .

Uncle Lyle!

Lyle had never felt so powerful. Been so powerful. Every nerve ending in his body tingled. Only three inches of oak stood between Lt. Mike Galvin and Todd Kline! Goddammit, this was great!

"It's locked," Galvin said.

"Oops!" Lyle, wearing a secretive grin, took Galvin by the arm. "Carla!" he bellowed.

She was standing in the same spot at the bottom of the stairs. She looked very small.

"Yes, Lyle?"

"The F-X room is locked, and I wanted to show it off to Mike! Will you get the key?"

He could see that Carla was fighting tears. "I . . ." she began.

"You what, Carla?" He waited, but then decided she might lose it and screw things for them both. *"I* know! I'll bet you forgot to call the locksmith after the key snapped off this afternoon. Right?"

"Uh . . . r-right!"

"What's the matter, Carla? Were you afraid to tell me?"

"N-no! I was . . . I was so b-busy all day. Uh . . . I'll put dinner on the t-table, now, okay?"

"Be right there!" he said, slapping Galvin on the back. "Hope you're hungry, Mike! I'm famished!"

He waited until Carla was out of earshot, then added, "You'll have to see the F-X room on your next visit."

"Pardon my ignorance, Lyle, but what does F-X mean?"

"Special effects, Mike! It's picture talk! And you've gotta see 'em to believe 'em!" Lyle put his arm around Galvin's shoulders. "Sorry there's no poker game tonight to make it like the old days."

"I guess they're gone forever," Galvin answered. "But why look back?"

"Yeah! Why? It's the top of the world, ma!"

Galvin turned and looked at him blankly.

"Cagney. *White Heat*. Christ, don't you go to the movies?"

Galvin's beeper went off during dinner. Carla was in the kitchen making coffee while Galvin returned the call on the phone Lyle had brought to the table.

Lyle's intense high of earlier had plummeted to a low so deep that it gripped him with fear. The paranoia was nothing new, but this time he wasn't sure his terrors were imaginary.

What was so important that it couldn't wait till tomorrow morning? Galvin was saying "yeah" over and over, while flipping the goddammed lid of his cheap Zippo.

Galvin had asked questions all evening long.

Had Carla been dumb enough to let the cat out earlier? What if she'd blown it?

What if I've blown it? Christ, if the kid had screamed while they were upstairs, that would have been the ball game! Talk about dumb! Gotta get off the toot, babe!

The entrance gates opened, and Galvin felt released. Coke was turning his old buddy into a schizo and poor Carla into a scared rabbit. Galvin's stomach was churning from delicious food that was too much and too rich.

Too much and too rich. It described Lyle Hemmings.

Galvin's too-rich host had insisted that back salary was the only reason for his ex-chauffeur's visit to the studio. Never mind that Manny Perez was a dealer, and Lyle Hemmings a user. Carla had suddenly swallowed her tongue, so obviously there was a lot that neither was saying. Of all the bullshit he'd listened to this evening, Galvin was convinced only that Lyle and Carla had never heard of Perry Fang.

He stepped on the gas and rubbed his thumb over the malachite-and-gold lighter Lyle had given him. It wasn't a bribe, but it could hardly be termed a gift. More like an expensive castoff. Did the Beautiful People upgrade their cigarette lighters, too?

Galvin pressed it. Nothing happened. No propane.

He dropped the fancy trinket into his pocket and

withdrew his trusty old Zippo. The striking wheel worked at a touch.

Somehow he still preferred the old days.

Lyle had done another line and was beaming once more.

"Hey, tonight was great, wasn't it?" he asked Carla.

She didn't turn from her position at the casement window that overlooked the English garden. After his descent into depression, Lyle was on his way back up to euphoria again. Carla knew she'd be dealing with both extremes until this was over, no matter how it ended.

"Hey, y'know what Mike said to me, Carla?" He sounded almost like a little boy. Like Todd.

"What, Lyle?"

"He said this place reminds him of Disneyland."

Forty-four

"The line has a police tap on it, Mother."

Ansel was standing by the fireplace and speaking into the cordless telephone. "Because, if the kidnappers call, Lieutenant Galvin's men can trace the number." He glanced at Stevie, who gazed up expressionlessly from where she sat on the sofa, then returned to that day's edition of *Scoop*.

"No, Mother," he continued, lowering his voice. "Galvin thinks we'll be given instructions at the last minute. . . . Of course it gives the police less time, Mother. No doubt that's the point."

Another pause. Another glance at Stevie. She didn't look up this time; she knew what Ansel was going to say next. She'd heard it a lot lately.

"Yes . . . Stevie's holding up."

Who was she holding up? Herself? Carolyn? Ansel?

Ansel covered the mouthpiece. "She'd like to talk with you."

Stevie's eyes stayed on the tabloid as she slowly shook her head. She listened to him lie to his mother again.

The curtains were drawn, but the sound of activity outside told Stevie another news van had arrived. Because of the autopsy results, Andrew Landau wouldn't be buried immediately. Neither would Tammi Reynolds. No funeral for the media to haunt, so attention was once more focused on the parents of the surviving child.

She felt pity for Tammi Reynolds, but most of Stevie's thoughts were with the mothers of the three murdered babies. If—*when*—Todd was returned unharmed, how would the three other women react? Surely each one had asked herself, "Why me?"

Stevie had posed the question only once. The answer had been too obvious: "Why *not* me?"

Hollywood was a small town. Eventually, the four mothers would meet at a party or premiere; it couldn't be avoided. How would they respond to one another six months from now? A year?

Ansel was still on the phone with his mother.

And Stevie was still reading the article in *Scoop*. Even though Eppie's story centered on the Landaus, she'd nonetheless managed to include an unflattering candid shot of Carolyn Kline and some nasty verbal swipes.

Stevie had never wondered about it until lately.

"I can't yet," she said to Ansel as he hung up the phone.

"I know. So does she."

Stevie tried to imagine him as the little boy she'd seen in his family album. There were pictures of Ansel at the same age that Todd was now. But

Carolyn hadn't had to deal with fears that included the kidnapping of her son.

Or had she?

Stevie gestured to the sofa cushion next to her, and Ansel sat down. She didn't resist when he took her hand. It felt cold.

So did his. At a different time, on another night, they might have made love.

"How is she?" asked Stevie. In nearly two weeks, this was her first show of concern for his mother, and she was embarrassed by the look of surprise on his face.

"In private, she's a mess. Of course, she won't let either of us see it. Or anyone else, for that matter."

"You grew up rich," Stevie said. "Did your parents worry about things like kidnappings?"

He shrugged. "While we were living in New York, a TV comic had received threats on his daughter's life. My father handled syndication rights for him. There was a scare. I was nine." Ansel gestured to the newspaper. "What's the sudden interest in this rag?"

"The women involved, I guess," Stevie said after a moment. "We're all mothers. Except for Eppie Goldwyn. Maybe if she was, she'd be kinder."

"To you?"

"No. She's made me out to be Joan of Arc." Stevie smiled. Shaw's *Joan* was one of the stage roles she'd allowed Ansel and his mother to talk her out of.

Allowed. The fault, if there was any, had been her own. Not Ansel's or Carolyn's.

"I meant kinder to your mother," Stevie continued. "Your mother and I have our reasons for disliking each other. But this campaign of Eppie's doesn't make sense."

Ansel let go of Stevie's hand and leaned forward, resting his elbows on his knees. "By the time I was fourteen," he said, "my parents had been taking separate vacations for some time. I was in New York, with Carolyn. One day when I got home from school, she was out. Our new maid said my father had called from LA. I called him back, and Eppie Goldwyn answered the phone. I hung up." He felt Stevie's hand on his shoulder. "I hated my father then. But Carolyn was never . . . demonstrative. I can only imagine what being married to her must have been like. Eppie was his mistress until he died. To this day, Carolyn doesn't have a clue that I know. But it explains this." Ansel slapped the copy of *Scoop*, then let it slide to the floor.

"Why didn't you ever tell me?" Stevie asked.

"It seemed very . . . private. Humiliating for her, even if I hadn't known. And as time went on and things never got any better between you two, I was afraid you'd think I was using it to gain your sympathy for her."

"So you've carried it around all these years." Stevie leaned forward and assumed Ansel's position of elbows on knees. "God, what we do to ourselves. And to our children."

To Todd.

They sat for a long time saying nothing. The house was quiet. The phone didn't ring. A whole day had come and gone with no further word.

It was eleven-thirty. Ansel rose and turned off the lights, then accompanied Stevie up the stairs. On the landing they stopped, and kissed tenderly. Stevie whispered "good night" and watched as Ansel walked slowly to the den at the end of the hall.

She knew that if she joined him, he would welcome her. But she'd have to pass Todd's room.

Instead, she entered the master bedroom and closed the door.

Forty-five

Lyle's high was making Carla more uneasy than depressed. He'd often referred to it as pressing the outside edge of the envelope. Like the astronauts, he claimed, quoting *The Right Stuff*. She'd never realized how much of what he said came from the mouths of movie characters. Maybe he thought life was one long movie. God, how had she ever gotten herself into this?

And how would she ever get out?

"Carla!" Lyle's manic voice cut in on her thoughts. "Grab your hat—we're going for a drive!"

She didn't own a hat. "A drive? It's past midnight! Where're we gonna go at this hour?" She just wanted to go to sleep.

"Hey, it was Mike's idea! We're going to Disneyland!"

Now she knew he'd entered the twilight zone. "Disneyland isn't open this late, Lyle. Besides, it's, like, an hour's drive from here. Can't it wait till tomorrow?"

He was wild-eyed. "No, it can't wait! We're steppin' up the action, folks! One whole day ahead of schedule, ready or not—'cause the point is, coming one day ahead, they're *not* ready!"

"Who's not ready, Lyle? What are you talking about?"

"The Klines, the cops, the *world!*" he cried, clapping his hands together. "Yeah! It'll work even better on Sunday!"

Carla didn't understand, even after he'd explained it twice. Okay, so he'd planned it all in advance. Bought a couple of old cars and changed the plates. That wasn't hard to figure out; he wouldn't want to make the ransom pickup in one of his custom-made Italian jobs that could easily be identified. But *buying* cars off the street, outright, and paying *cash?* What if they broke down on the road? If Lyle wanted so badly to get caught, why didn't he just call Eppie Goldwyn at *Scoop* and give her an exclusive?

Instead, she asked, "Why didn't you rent the cars?"

He didn't lose his temper, but Carla sensed that was because he needed her—for the time being. Just till he got the money.

"You can't rent cars with cash," he said. "Besides, rentals and credit cards can be traced. Did you ever see anyone in *The Godfather* or *Goodfellas* doing business with *plastic?*"

No, but did Lyle realize that he was sounding more like Manny Perez every day, except for the accent?

She didn't get the point behind why they were

driving to Anaheim in two separate cars—Lyle in the blue Vega, Carla in her brown Ford—and leaving the Vega in the parking lot of a motel right across the highway from Disneyland. Or why she was chauffeuring Lyle back to Beverly Hills in her Ford at 2:00 A.M. so he could pick up his Ferrari and drop it off at an overnight garage. All this round-tripping, when they'd be returning to Disneyland first thing in the morning? It was crazy. But she didn't dare question any of it.

She asked only why he'd pushed the deadline up by a day.

"I told you already," he said. "Everyone's expecting Monday. There'll be undercover cops swarming all over the place. Sunday will throw 'em off guard, don'tcha see?"

She didn't see. How could the cops be swarming *anywhere* on Sunday *or* Monday if Lyle hadn't decided on the payoff location till after Lt. Galvin's comparison of the house to Disneyland? Geez, why hadn't Galvin made it a *real* challenge—like saying it reminded him of Buckingham Palace?

She asked one other question during the drive back from Anaheim. "Why can't I call the Klines from, like, a phone booth in Beverly Hills? If the police are gonna trace the call anyway, what does it matter?"

"That's the point!" he cried, beating rap-time on the steering wheel with his ring. "They'll trace your second call right to where we want 'em!"

"Whaddya mean, my *second* call?"

The catlike way he grinned at Carla, even in the

darkened car, frightened her. So did the way he said, "What, haven't you ever heard about creating a diversion?"

Forty-six

Sunday, July 28

She did as she was told. On so little sleep she was afraid she'd forget something, so she wrote down, word for word, exactly what Lyle wanted her to say. She waited in the motel coffee shop until the clock over the jukebox and the watch on her wrist both read 8:25 A.M. Then, with five minutes to spare, she went to the telephone booth outside, took out a handful of change and the mohair mitten she would put over the mouthpiece to muffle her voice, and placed the call to Beachwood Canyon. When Ansel answered, she thought she would faint.

She didn't. The thought of Todd's safety didn't let her.

The sound of the phone ringing at 8:30 sharp had awakened Stevie. Ansel's heated voice from the den brought her quickly to his side.

"What do you mean, *today!*" he was shouting

into the receiver. "We were told Monday! How am I supposed to withdraw a million bucks on Sunday?"

"You have connections," said the woman. "Use them."

"What if I can't get my 'connections' to open the bank today?"

"The bank will be saving a day's interest on your money. They'll be happy to give you the cash."

Ansel could understand what it meant to be angry enough to kill. Stevie's handclasp helped him quell the urge long enough to get the necessary information.

"All right. Where's the drop?"

"Disneyland. The bench on Main Street across from City Hall. By noon."

"Disneyland! That's at least an hour from here! How the hell do you expect me to get the money there by noon?" His hands were so tightly fisted, he could have smashed a wooden board.

"Just do it!" And then, three final words that Lyle hadn't supplied, *Please! For Todd!*

Now Lt. Galvin and Ansel were on the phone. Stevie was grateful for the phone tap. She knew the call would probably be traced to a booth in the middle of nowhere or at the center of town, but at least with the tap, Ansel didn't have to repeat everything to the police. It wouldn't take much to make him explode.

"Look, Mr. Kline," Galvin was saying, "they figure that by throwing us a curve, we'll be caught with our thumbs up our—well, you get the idea."

"Are they right?"

"I'll tell you something, Mr. Kline. Maybe you've heard it before, but it's worth repeating, especially right now. We're dealing with the criminal element every day of the year. The perpetrator only gets one chance. If he slips up, he's dead."

"So is my son, if your guys screw up!"

"Try to take it easy, Mr. Kline. It's going to be a long day. We're already moving. Disneyland will be infiltrated with undercover men. And they'll all be wearing wires. The perps will get their money, and then we'll get the perps."

"Isn't Anaheim outside of your jurisdiction?"

"Look, Mr. Kline, why don't you do your job and let me do mine? You get the cash, and I'll have a copter waiting at your bank to deliver you and the money to Main Street long before noon."

"Anything else?" Ansel's voice wasn't without sarcasm.

"Yes. Have Joe Madden keep Mrs. Kline company. With so much attention focused on the grab, she shouldn't be unprotected and alone."

When Ansel didn't reply, Galvin said, "I can send one of my men to the house, if you'd rather. It's your choice."

Choice? Did Galvin really believe that any of this involved choice?

Ansel was put on hold for a moment while Galvin took an urgent call. When he came back on the line, he said, "They've traced the number to a booth in a parking lot near Disneyland. I'm leaving now. You should, too."

"I will," said Ansel. "As soon as I call Joe Madden."

Convincing Carolyn's brother, who was president of the bank, to open the doors on Sunday, was far easier than convincing Stevie to stay home on the sidelines. He grudgingly admitted that his call to Madden helped.

"Tell her the copter they're sending to the bank only seats two—you and the pilot."

"Is that true?"

"Beats me. But she'll feel less like the kid who's not invited to the grown-ups' bash. I'll be there as soon as I can. And Mr. Kline?"

"Yes?"

"Hang in there."

Was it Ansel's imagination, or had everything begun to sound like instant replay?

Forty-seven

Ansel had already left to get the money by the time Madden arrived at the house. At first Madden didn't see any paparazzi hanging around, so he wondered if the band of vultures had trailed Ansel to the bank. Then he spotted two of the more ambitious—or hungry—photographers watching the house from a car. Ansel must have made his departure for the bank seem like a typical Sunday errand. And the rest of the kingdom's media mavens must be sleeping in this morning, God love 'em.

She was the only woman he'd ever seen who looked even more radiant under stress. Either that, or Stephanie Kean was a great actress. She answered the door with a friendly "Hya, Joe, c'mon in," as though his visit, like Ansel's errand, was run of the mill for a Sunday morning in the Canyon.

Or maybe she was just super aware of the power of a telephoto camera lens.

* * *

His last guess was the right one. As soon as the
door was closed, Stevie's eyes gave her away.

"You okay?" he asked.

"Too many people have been asking me that,"
she said. "Frankly, Joe, I don't know what okay *is*
anymore. I feel as if I've been cast in a movie I
never wanted to shoot. What's worse, it's one of
those high-tech action adventures where everybody
else gets to do something while the leading lady
just stands around playing Vanna White!"

She was leading the way to the kitchen as she
spoke. Madden figured the best thing he could do
was follow along and listen. He understood what
she felt; at least she was the leading lady in this
picture; right now he felt more like an extra. It
made him think of Tammi Reynolds. Still no word
on who'd iced her. He'd check with Galvin. But
later, after they got through today.

"Funny, Joe," Stevie was saying. "Until all this,
I never really identified with Ansel's feelings of
being left out, you know, when I didn't share certain things with him."

"And you do now?"

Her back was to him as she poured coffee, and
she shrugged. "I'm beginning to. Especially this
morning. It's more than fear that something could
go wrong. It's that something horrible could happen to Todd"—her voice began to choke her—"and
to Ansel." She turned to face Madden, and this
time she couldn't control the tears. "It's not just
that I feel left out, Joe, it's that I've always been

310

so damned independent. I thought I didn't need anyone—and I was wrong! When I was a kid, I read about Barbara Stanwyck, and she became a role model. She was an orphan, too, and I thought, hey, look what she accomplished! If she can, so can I! She was tough and vulnerable, so I became tough and vulnerable. I didn't stab anyone in the back, but I didn't let obstacles get in my way, either. And I was proud of my ambition! The jobs I got were strictly based on my acting talent—no family connections, no screwing around, just me. God, did I wear my independence like a Girl Scout badge! But y'know what, Joe? Somewhere, deep inside, I felt like a fraud, like I was pulling a fast one on the world and if I was lucky—and careful—nobody would find me out."

She paused to reach into her jeans pocket for a tissue, and blew her nose hard. Then she wiped away a tear and took a sip of coffee. She smiled at Madden. "Stage business."

"What?"

"Sorry. I'm thinking out loud again."

"Hey, did I say I mind?"

"Thanks. You're a nice guy, Joe."

"*Nice* is a word that usually makes me cringe," he said, "but not when it comes from you." He almost colored at his admission. "Anyway, what you say is true for most of us. My personal concept of heaven isn't the prospect of spending eternity with a hundred Joe Maddens."

"Doesn't sound so terrible to me," said Stevie.

"Now who's being nice? But that's what I mean. We're all too hard on ourselves. It's like worrying over things we can't control." He immediately regretted the tactlessness of his words.

But she hadn't noticed. "Fate plays tricks on us, Joe. Otherwise, why did it take my son's life being put in danger to make me understand? Is it because when the chips are down, there's no room for anything but the basics?"

"You've just answered your own question," he said, touched by her toughness and her vulnerability. He'd always liked Barbara Stanwyck, too.

"What an irony," she said. "We're in a situation where all the analyzing on earth can't change the outcome. And yet it's forcing us to analyze what we never took the time for when it was ours to take. Does that make sense? You see what I'm saying?"

Madden didn't need his PI license for that one. The "we" and the "us" and the "our" said it all.

"What I see," he said, "is that you and Ansel, no matter what happens today, are a unit. A *couple*. You never should have split up to begin with. Believe me, Stevie, he feels it as strongly as you do. The two of you belong together."

She didn't answer. She was praying, silently, to Whatever Power kept the universe in motion. In the movies, the lovers were given time to make amends, to start over. But in life, would she and Ansel have a second chance?

Would Todd?

Madden was watching Stevie, studying her. Whoever said you couldn't be in two places at once? He knew she was here, with him, in her kitchen. But she was also at the Bank of Beachwood Canyon,

312

with Ansel. Or she was with him in the helicopter en route to Disneyland. And she was with Todd, wherever he was.

In the movies, right about now, Madden would be sweeping Stevie into his arms and kissing her, then carrying her upstairs and making wild, passionate love to her, their mutual excitement heightened by the drama they were living through.

But this wasn't the movies, and Madden, instead of luring her into his arms, was propelling her back into Ansel's.

Yeah, well, win some, lose some, Joe. He hoped by day's end, nothing more would be lost.

Galvin headed onto the exit ramp and felt his adrenaline slowly beginning to surge. His years of experience on the force kept him from becoming overconfident; those flights could lead to carelessness, and that, above all, had to be avoided.

He'd set everything in motion, but there was always the chance of Fate waving her finger in the form of a copter crash or an innocent bystander caught in crossfire. The latter was one of the reasons he'd instructed his men and Disneyland security to let the perp make the grab. The other reason was Todd Kline. The perp had to lead them to wherever the Klines' child was being held.

Ansel had been provided with a Day-Glo orange bag; even color blind, you could spot that in the crowd. His men were working undercover, wearing wires and earpieces so they could keep in contact with one another. Security had cordoned off a section of the parking lot so the copter could land. From there, it was watch and wait. And hope that no one—including Ansel Kline and the perp—fucked up.

He had to admit disappointment in not locating Perry Fang by now. Or Tammi Reynolds's killer, if it wasn't Fang. Certain facts still didn't add up. Galvin hadn't shared his thoughts with Ansel or Stevie Kline—or Joe Madden—but he had strong doubts about finding Todd Kline—dead or alive—once the ransom was paid.

And yet, refusing to pay would have been out of the question. Simultaneously, that would have signed the death warrant of a four-year-old kid and wiped out the possibility of solving this and the previous three cases.

Galvin had gone off the cigarette wagon at dawn. He'd tried to resist each time he lit another smoke with Lyle's extravagant toss-away gift. Maybe he shouldn't have refilled it; if it didn't work, there'd be less temptation.

But that wasn't what was nagging him.

He'd gone over and over his bizarre Saturday evening with the Odd Couple of Beverly Hills. Somehow—although it was Galvin's gut and not facts telling him—there had to be a link between Manny Perez and the kidnappings. One of Galvin's pet theories, that the cult might be a cover for a sophisticated drug ring, had come up dry. Nonetheless, he was reluctant to let it go, and the harder he held on to it, the more blanks he drew.

He was pulling into the entrance of Disney's city within a city when he got the call. It was on his mobile telephone instead of the radio, so he knew it wasn't part of the ransom-drop operation.

"We just got this from the FBI," said his sergeant, "and I figured you'd want it right away."

"I'm listening," said Galvin.

"It's about the latent prints on Tammi Reynolds. The Feds made a perfect match."

"And?"

"They belong to an ex-con named Manny Perez."

"No shit," said Galvin.

"You know the guy, Lieutenant?"

"Not personally, but I know someone who does."

Forty-eight

Lyle's watch read eight-thirty. He had finished pulling his disguise over short pants and a T-shirt, and he was sweating, partly from the heat of his costume, partly from the excitement. Each time he started to open the door of the men's-room stall, he heard voices and the sounds of flushing, or running water from the sinks.

He'd done his homework and knew the cops wouldn't arrive for a while yet. He also knew the public rest rooms were off limits to Disney personnel. But as each second ticked by, more and more people would be filling the park—and the men's john.

He rubbed the last of the powder across his gums and checked the baggy pocket of his costume. The remote detonator was set and in place. He felt good. Like a million dollars. Yeah—in hundreds!

He lifted the large head and slid it down over his own. It rested easily on his shoulders, and the eyeholes allowed him perfect vision.

Lyle grinned to himself and unlatched the stall door.

Bob Boshanski had just arrived at the park and already the weight of two cameras suspended on straps around his neck was growing heavy. He pushed one across his ample belly in order to zip his fly.

"Where you from?" he asked the man three urinals to his left.

"Akron, Ohio," the man answered with a smile.

"Pittsburgh," Bob offered. "Drove out. Long trip."

"Kids?"

"Two. Etna, she's my wife, is as excited as they are to be here."

"First time?" the other tourist asked.

"Yeah! For all of us!" He flushed and began walking toward the sinks. "I'm almost forty, but I finally made it to Disneyland!"

In the reflection of the mirror, Bob saw a clown emerging from one of the stalls. A lady clown.

She—actually, Bob could tell by "her" build that "she" was a "he"—wore a bright-green-and-yellow polka-dotted costume that covered an enormous bosom. The pink tutu around her waist matched the pink neck ruffle. Slung over a football-padded shoulder was a huge imitation tapestry carpetbag. The clown's head was painted white, with wide fuchsia lips fixed in a permanent grin beneath the requisite red nose. Black eyelashes sprouted from frames of bright blue oversize plastic glasses. They brushed against a fringe of bangs on the curly orange wig, which was the exact color of Etna's hair.

"Oh—I get it!" Bob cried. "It's Circus Month at Disneyland, right?"

The lady clown nodded vigorously to Bob and the other man, then gave them both a dainty wave and sauntered from the men's room.

"Boy, oh boy!" Bob said. "And to think those guys get paid to have that much fun!"

Carla was driving along Harbour Boulevard and trying to figure out where to go next.

She had more than three hours to kill before it was time to return to the motel where Lyle had parked the Vega last night. He'd been emphatic about her not attracting attention. She mustn't spend too long in any one place.

She hated this. Hated the awful sound of Ansel Kline's voice on the telephone, hated that Todd was frightened—and could be in danger. But he'd been good so far about not letting Lyle know that he knew. Manny would have his money by tonight, and Todd would be released tomorrow. "Then I can get away," Carla said aloud. There was no one to hear, but the words calmed her.

She pulled into the parking lot of the Best Western. Coffee and breakfast, if she could keep it down, would help. And it would kill forty-five minutes.

* * *

It was what Oz must have looked like from the wizard's balloon.

Sleeping Beauty's castle rose majestically from the center of the park. Near it, Space Mountain towered over the skyway. The railroad cars looked like toys. Mark Twain's steamboat moved lazily around Tom Sawyer's island, and the waters of the Jungle Cruise in Adventureland were stirred by elephants and hippos.

"Okay!" the pilot shouted. "We're here!"

Ansel leaned into the angle of the turn, his knees pressed up against his chest. In front of him, next to the pilot, a detective was yelling something that sounded like more instructions.

Ansel wished Galvin was here. Stevie. Even Madden.

Stevie and Madden. They were alone, back at the house. Christ, thought Ansel. This was one helluva time to get jealous.

He concentrated on the cement of the parking lot growing closer. The whirring blades cast a shadow over the cars parked around the improvised landing pad. Except for color, all the cars looked alike.

"That's us!" the detective yelled, pointing down. "The Department just bought a shitload of 'em! Every time I spot a Vega on the road, I figure it's one of us!"

The shudder and rattle of the chopper increased as it made a less than surefooted landing. Plainclothes police, their shirts billowing in the wind, were out of their cars and watching. Parents and children watched, too, clapping and laughing, obviously thrilled that the day's excitement had begun.

"If all of these people can see us, so can the kidnapper!" Ansel said.

"Mr. Kline, he knows we're coming—he's expecting us! You can bet he got here ahead of us. But we're gonna fool him!"

The detective climbed out first, clutching the bright orange vinyl bag against his chest. Ansel followed, ducking down below the spinning blades that had begun to slow.

There was already a crowd passing through the main gates to the park. Little trams, transporting still more visitors from their cars to the entrance, scuttled back and forth. Ansel checked his watch. It was well after ten.

"Yeah," said the detective, "too bad it took so long at the bank. But there's no guarantee the grab will be made right away, either. He'll be a bitch to spot in this mob. Your kidnapper is smart. And he's got balls!"

Galvin was coming toward them now. He wasn't smiling, but he never did.

"I'll take Mr. Kline in, Larry," he said, placing a hand on Ansel's arm.

Larry handed the orange bag to Ansel. A million dollars was heavy—easily twenty pounds.

"Put it over your shoulder, Mr. Kline," said Galvin. "And try to look casual. We can't afford to create a panic. So take a deep breath and follow me."

* * *

They walked to a shaded area just outside the gates.

"All right," Galvin said, wiping perspiration from his brow. "In addition to my men out here, I've got four teams of five each spread out in the park area. You won't know them, but they'll know you. They're all wearing wires and mikes so they can communicate with each other. We've got Anaheim PD cooperating. They won't transmit dispatches over our frequency unless there's an emergency."

"Shouldn't I be wired, too?" asked Ansel.

"No. You'll be in full view at all times. Now, once you're inside, go directly to the bench. You know which one it is?"

"We shot a picture here last year. I remember."

"Good. Place the bag under the bench and walk away."

"Walk away! Just leave? And go where?"

"Larry—Detective Angelo—will drive you back to LA."

"No!" cried Ansel. "I'm staying till it's over!"

"I don't want you in there confusing things, Mr. Kline." Galvin paused. "Okay, look. I'll have Larry stick around till the all-clear. But you realize that could be hours from now."

"I was told *noon* Lieutenant!"

"For your drop. They can take their own sweet time for the grab."

"How many do you think there are?"

"They only need one to make the grab."

"How will you know who it is?"

"We won't. All these goddammed tourists look

321

alike. But anyone who goes for that bag—man or woman—has us on their tail. We can follow him through traffic and"—Galvin pointed to the sky—"we've got the chopper for aerial surveillance to track the car and lead us right to your child."

"What happens then?"

"We tackle that later, Mr. Kline. If we're lucky."

Ansel's T-shirt was stuck to him. Sweat ran down his bare legs into his socks.

"The cutoffs are a nice touch, Mr. Kline. You fit right in."

"Thanks," Ansel replied. "Now?"

"Now."

He tried to loosen up, but Ansel felt stiffer than wood as he looked up and read the words on the wide entrance arch: *Here You Leave Today And Enter The World Of Yesterday Tomorrow And Fantasy.*

Forty-nine

"Let's ask the lady clown over there!"

The little girl let go of her mother's hand and ran to Lyle, who stood near the railroad station and ached for a cigarette.

"Which way is Adventureland?" asked the girl.

Gesturing with his forefinger, Lyle indicated for the family to follow him.

Hey, this was all right! Be a clown—yeah! He began improvising a hop-skip down Main Street and heard the little girl giggling while she hurried to keep up.

A few hundred feet ahead, Lyle stopped to spin a clumsy pirouette. The girl's parents were huffing and puffing under their matching white canvas hats, dark glasses, and sunblocked noses. They were interchangeable with the thousands of visitors swarming over the grounds. There'd be thousands more by noon.

Lyle pointed to the right and jiggled his head. The orange curls of his wig did a little dance. The father, taking his daughter's hand, called, "Thank you . . . Miss!" and sent his wife and child into gales of laughter. "Oh, by the way," he added, "what time does the circus parade start?"

In a gruff falsetto, Lyle exclaimed, "Right here at noon! Hurry back! It's gonna be great fun!"

"We wouldn't miss it!" the woman shouted, waving as they went. "See you later!"

Jerks. Lyle turned his attention toward the main gates.

Flocks of tourists were strolling in and out of the shops that lined Main Street. They mingled with the six-foot-tall Goofy and Pluto, Donald and Mickey, all of whom posed for pictures and answered questions.

There were other clowns, too, some selling brightly colored balloons and buttons. Lyle was impressed by his own cleverness. Pulling this off to coincide with the park's circus theme was nothing short of genius!

His eyes strayed to the end of Main Street.

And there, coming through the gate with fifty or more tourists, was Ansel Kline. He could have passed incognito, but the bright orange bag stood out, even from a distance.

Sure. The money had to be in something that could be spotted easily so the cops could keep an eye on it.

He watched Ansel move slowly, nervously, toward the railroad station and City Hall. The bag looked heavy—hey, a million bucks wasn't feathers!—but it would be manageable. No problem!

All that cash. What a shame it had to go to a third-rate dealer like Manny.

Lyle checked his watch. Ten past ten. No hurry.

He'd just meander up the street to make sure Ansel left the bag in the right place. The cops—because there had to be cops watching—would protect it for Lyle until the parade came through.

Meanwhile, they could just sweat it out. Literally—yeah!

Carla had dallied over a toasted English and coffee. Now she was pulling into the parking lot of the Hyatt.

This hotel was larger and busier than the one she'd just left. She couldn't face another cup of coffee, but there were gift shops to browse in, and a magazine store. She'd pick up a copy of *Scoop* and the current *People,* then sit in the lobby and wait. Only another hour to go—for her, at least. After she made the final call, she could return to Beverly Hills. And Todd. She'd already packed a bag and put it in the trunk of her car. As soon as Lyle returned Todd to his parents, Carla would be gone—for good.

Unless Lyle made *her* drop Todd somewhere.

Better yet! Then she'd know Todd was safe before she disappeared. That lifted Carla's spirits as she walked into the magazine shop.

Ansel's shoulder ached where the leather straps had dug into his skin. He felt relief as he placed the heavy orange bag on the ground and, with the heel of his foot, shoved it under the bench.

His eyes searched the crowd for whatever—whoever—was out there, waiting.

It looked like an ordinary day at Disneyland. Horsedrawn carriages, manned by clowns, moved across the busy turn-of-the-century square. Balloons were everywhere. And children.

How Todd would love it. Ansel and Stevie had wanted to bring him here last year. But they'd thought three was too young to appreciate Disneyland. Then he was four, and Stevie and Ansel were separated. Some things shouldn't be put off. Ansel gazed enviously at the hordes of parents who didn't know how lucky they were.

"Not so far under the bench, Mr. Kline!" a voice whispered.

Ansel turned his head to the left, then to the right. Nothing.

"The bag!" hissed the voice. "Pull it a little further out, Mr. Kline!"

Ansel did an about-face. Standing on the grass of the circle in the square was the huge figure of Goofy, leaning his gloved hands on the back of Ansel's bench.

"Don't turn around!" Goofy whisper-yelled. "Just sit down!"

The bench was hot on Ansel's bare-skinned thighs. He listened.

"Lean down and pull the bag out two inches. Galvin wants a clearer view of the money."

"Where is he?" Ansel demanded, facing forward.

"Never mind! Just do it!"

Ansel obeyed, then heard Goofy ask, "Is tha

better, Lieutenant?" A few seconds, followed by, "Okay, Mr. Kline. Galvin says that's fine. Stay seated for another minute, then get up casually and go."

Ansel watched as Goofy moved off and waved to Pluto, who stood near the Cinema. Immediately they were surrounded by children who started jumping up and down excitedly.

"Hey now, kids, don't grab at Goofy's ears!" the cop inside the costume exclaimed in the cartoon character's dumb-silly voice.

Lyle's fingers caressed the remote-control device in his pocket. He checked his costume. The sweat hadn't penetrated the baggy pajamas, but the over-size shoulder bag had crushed one side of the tutu. Fuck it.

Forty feet away he could see "Goofy" being ac-costed by a gang of brats.

It was obvious. Goofy was a cop. They were all cops. Some of the other clowns loitering around the area were probably cops, too.

In the crowd Lyle spotted Bob Boshanski, who now sported a Mickey Mouse beanie complete with ears. Beside him was a woman whose hair was brighter orange than the moneybag beneath An-sel's bench. She—Etna?—and the kids had bought out the stores. The family was weighted down with junk in shopping bags.

Lyle watched them yank their kids to the lockers by the Emporium.

"Can we finally go *into* the damn park?" Bob yelled.

"We have to be back for the circus parade!" one of the Boshanski kids shrieked.

"Yeah, yeah! After that, we're goin' back to the hotel to eat! Etna, gimme some change!"

They threw the bags into a locker, then started to run up Main Street. "We gotta cram in as much as we can before noon!" Bob called out.

Lyle leaned against a post. He yearned for the cigarette a tourist in front of the tobacco shop was lighting. Lyle looked closer. *Tourist, my ass! It's Mike Galvin!* Still using his Zippo, too!

Lyle began humming "It's a Small, Small World." He watched as Ansel slowly rose and headed toward the main gates. Pluto had broken free of the kids and was fifteen feet behind Ansel.

And the orange bag with a million bucks inside it sat under the park bench baking in the morning sun.

Fifty

Galvin stayed near the entrance. The heat was fierce for all of his men, but it was Team 5 he was most concerned about.

"O'Toole," he said softly into his lapel mike, "how're you guys doin'?"

The response came almost immediately through Galvin's tiny earphone. "Goofy's feelin' pretty hot, Lieutenant. Ditto Pluto and the others guys. We could use a few beers."

"They're on me, after the grab. Over."

Galvin surveyed the scene. Teams 2 and 3 were men and women mingling as tourists farther along Main Street near Adventure Land. Team 4 was selling ice cream and balloons in the square. Team 1 was in the parking lot, waiting to put a tail on the car. Overhead, the chopper made another round.

Galvin crushed his third cigarette under his sneaker. The Roman numerals of the pedestal clock read 11:30.

Come on, dammit! Make your move!

* * *

Ansel watched through the windshield of Larry Angelo's Vega as the helicopter flew by, turned, and headed back over the park. The radio squawked, and Ansel listened to the communiqués that passed from one undercover cop to another. He and Larry hadn't said much for the last forty-five minutes. There didn't seem to be anything worth saying.

Carla made the turn into HoJo's, and slowed as she passed the beat-up Vega.

The red police teardrop light, which Lyle had placed on the dashboard over the glove compartment, was clearly visible. Beside it, the PBA baseball cap told the rest of the story. It looked every inch like a cop's car.

It was parked as close to the boulevard as possible. Carla was thankful that the other cars were parked no closer than thirty feet. If it could just stay this way for the next half hour, there'd be less chance of anyone getting hurt.

She found a space near the entrance to the coffee shop. She could see two empty window booths with perfect views of the lot. A lucky break. Time for a second breakfast.

Lyle stood off to the side. He'd join the crowd only at the last minute.

C'mon, folks, just a few hundred more people and we're ready to rock and roll!

The storefronts were blocked by tourists; the

square was packed. The paraders had congregated and occupied the entire length of the street. Backed up as far as anyone could see were horsedrawn floats. On one, a woman dressed as Snow White was surrounded by seven huge dwarfs. On another, the sun glistened on the golden hair of Cinderella and her sparkling blue ball gown. With glee, children pointed to her glass slippers.

"I don't like this, Lieutenant," O'Toole said.

"Neither do I! Just keep your eye on that bench! Teams four and five, stay alert! This could be it! Over!"

Several kids were standing on the bench to gain a better view. They were too excited to notice the orange bag underneath.

Fathers lifted small children onto their shoulders. The press of the crowd and its noise increased. The spinning blades and motor of the helicopter, passing over a sea of mouse ears, added to the din. On one of the floats a red calliope struck up a fanfare, and slowly the parade started moving to the tune of the Mickey Mouse Club theme. Adults began singing the words.

So did the Lady Clown. It was twelve noon sharp when "she" reached into her pocket, withdrew the small remote-control device and pressed the detonator button.

* * *

Carla watched the parking lot from her window booth in the coffee shop. She checked the time again. According to the clock over the counter, it was one minute past noon. Had something gone wrong?

Her mouth was dry, but her hands trembled. She was afraid to pick up the warm lemonade for fear of dropping the tumbler. She glanced toward the pay phone next to the ladies' room.

She turned just in time to see the explosion.

Patrons jumped up, running outside or to the windows.

Carla gasped at the sight of the billowing black smoke and bright orange tongues as the flames engulfed the rear of the Vega. Carla waited to be certain no other cars or people had been hurt. Then she sprang from her seat, hurried to the pay phone, and made her call.

"Emergency!" she yelled over the commotion that had taken over the coffee shop. "A bomb, or something! The parking lot at Howard Johnson's on Harbour Boulevard, across from Disneyland! A car—a blue Vega—is on fire! I saw a policeman get into it just before it exploded!"

Every cop at the park heard the Anaheim dispatcher break into their frequency. "Over nine-one-one! Police officer needs assistance! All officers in vicinity respond!"

Galvin watched as the ice-cream and balloon vendors, Goofy, Pluto, and the rest began pushing their

332

way through the crowd and toward the main gate. Running on instinct. What they'd been trained to do when a fellow officer was down, he knew.

Maybe someone else knew, too.

"Return to your positions! Return to your positions!" he bellowed into his mike, no longer caring who in the crowd heard him. *Team One only, respond to call! Repeat! Only Team One respond!* All others maintain observation!"

"What do we do?" Ansel asked, as every undercover car went speeding through the vast parking lot toward the Harbour Boulevard exit.

"Until I hear otherwise, my orders are to stay here with you!" Larry Angelo yelled over the screeching of tires. "That's what we do!"

"Goddammit! Fuck!" Galvin heard in his earphone.

"O'Toole! What is it?" he shouted back.

"It's gone! The fucking bag is gone!"

"Shit!"

There were thousands of people between Galvin and the teams nearest the bench. Teams 2 and 3 were too far down Main Street, with another ten thousand people in the way.

And one of them had a million dollars in cash.

The rush Lyle felt was better than sex. It had been simple, perfect, and quick. He clocked it at six seconds.

He couldn't believe that a million in hundreds could weigh so much. But the orange tote fit into his tapestry carpetbag with room to spare.

Goofy, Pluto, and their friends were standing in the square, their great heads turning left and right, their arms waving. Lyle was tempted to wave back.

And just as he reached the exit, he saw Bob and Etna Boshanski screaming at their son and daughter.

"We're just goin' to eat and drop off all this crap!" Bob cried at the top of his lungs. "We'll come back this afternoon!"

Bob and Etna's daughter was about to burst into tears. Lyle minced over to her and said, "Excuse me, little girl, but I'm lost. Could you show me the way out?"

She giggled. The boy laughed.

"Hey! It's the clown from the john!" Bob exclaimed to his wife. "The one I told you about!"

The little girl took Lyle's hand and followed her brother and father.

"Thank goodness you came along," Etna whispered to Lyle as they walked to the exit. "You've certainly made this easier."

"Etna," said Lyle, "you'll never know."

Carla would have floored the gas pedal, but knew she had to take her time. She slowed down with the rest of the curious passersby and observed the scene through the black smoke that filled the air. The acrid fumes made her cough, and she rolled up the window.

She counted six cars—all of them Vegas—jumping the speed bump and barreling into the parking lot. Within seconds, a dozen men had drawn their weapons and taken positions around the flaming vehicle.

Carla turned onto the boulevard. Lyle had done it! But did he have the money? And did he get away?

Lyle said good-bye to the Boshanski family and ducked into the men's room.

It was crowded, but there were two free stalls. He took the last one, stripped off the clown costume, and stuffed it into the carpetbag. He left the clown head on the lid of the seat; that would *scare* the shit out of the next guy who opened the door.

He hefted the bag once more onto his shoulder and strode quickly, but not too quickly, out of the bathroom.

He'd made sure to park the Dodge a short distance from the rest rooms.

With the bag on the front passenger seat beside him, he moved the car into the exiting traffic.

He could see fire engines and a fog of black smoke in the HoJo's parking lot across Harbour Boulevard.

Lyle checked his watch. Eight minutes past twelve.

If it hadn't been so crowded, he could have done it in five.

He laughed all the way to the freeway.

Fifty-one

Ansel was still feeling like an overwound clock. Larry Angelo, who was driving him back to LA, kept trying to help, but the small talk that was supposed to ease the anguish—especially with the constant interruptions from the radio-phone frequency—didn't do a damn thing except remind Ansel that whoever had his child now also had a million bucks. Sure, they'd planned to let him make the grab—but they hadn't planned to lose him!

He only half heard Larry's suggestion.

"Sorry, what was that?"

"I thought you might want to stop for coffee. Or something stronger."

Ansel shook his head.

"Well, look, I've gotta take a leak. There's a gas station coming up in a few miles. Maybe you want to call Mrs. Kline. She's probably sitting by the telephone, waiting."

Sure, thought Ansel. With Madden waiting alongside her.

* * *

Stevie could hear the tension in Ansel's voice even before he told her that the trap had failed, that the kidnapper had gotten away scot-free.

When she hung up, she said to Madden, "Joe, it didn't go according to plan." Her own spirits had sunk lower than she'd thought possible.

"Stevie, that doesn't mean . . ." He didn't finish. Her eyes warned him not to.

"I know what it doesn't mean, Joe." They'd been talking over iced tea in the den. Stevie absentmindedly wiped several drops of sweat from her glass before they trickled down to the coaster. Then, picking up Joe's empty tumbler, she rose. "Look, Ansel's on his way back from Disneyland, Joe, and . . . it might be better if I'm by myself when he gets here."

They both knew they had nothing to hide. And they both knew she was right.

"You'll be okay?" he asked.

Funny, Ansel had asked her the same question.

"I'll be fine. And if I'm not, I'll call you."

"I have to pick up my rattletrap at the shop. The mechanic who promised to fix it by Friday quit on Thursday. Herb's working today as a favor to me."

She walked him to the door. "I'll check in with you later," he said. Then, an afterthought, "With you both."

"Thanks," she said, not sure how much of her gratitude was for his being there and how much was for his remembering to say "both."

* * *

Carla had stopped at a Burger King to pick up a Whopper and a milkshake for Todd. Only when she was back on the road did she realize what the extra fifteen minutes might have cost her.

What a fool! If she hadn't stopped, she could have reached Beverly Hills ahead of Lyle, gotten Todd safely out, and split. He'd have been safely home, and she'd have been halfway to Denver.

Wait a second. She was an even bigger fool if she believed that.

When this whole mess was over and the truth came out—because one way or another, it was bound to come out—she'd wind up in jail. So what if it was Lyle's harebrained scheme? She'd gone along, hadn't she? An accessory to kidnapping, doing drugs, hell, like, they'd lock her up and throw away the key!

Well, she'd wanted it to end; she just hadn't been smart enough to figure it would end like this.

But at least it would be over. Manny Perez would get his money and Todd Kline would be delivered safely to his parents. Todd was all that mattered to her now. He was an innocent kid, he should have a chance. Whether anyone would ever believe her or not, Todd was the only reason she'd hung around this long. It wasn't even the drugs anymore. She hated the stuff and wanted off as much as she wanted out.

Fool was right. The milkshake had probably turned warm by now, and the burger would be cold and taste like leftover oatmeal.

Well, she could heat up the burger in the microwave and, like, drop an ice cube in the shake.

Poor kid must be starving by now. Besides, it was too late for her to do anything else.

Lyle's curiosity was making him itchy. So was the bulging carpetbag on the seat beside him. The drive back to Beverly Hills was boring the hell out of him, especially after this morning's fun and games! Yeah! But he didn't dare risk speeding, even though his adrenaline was still pumping a hundred fifty miles per hour!

He should probably call Stevie, just to see how it was going at her end. The picture wasn't shooting today, so she'd expect him to be at home. It wouldn't be like him not to call. He opened the glove compartment of the Dodge and took out his cellular phone.

Wait. The cops had a tap on Stevie's private line. If he called and said he was at home, a tracer would tell them he wasn't and they'd want to know why he was lying.

Was it real or was it drugs talking? Whichever, he didn't dare take that risk, either.

So he put through the call, and when Stevie answered and said there was a lot of static interference, he explained, "That's because I'm in the car. You know, Sunday errands. I wanted to know if you need anything—or if you've heard anything." *Try to make it sound casual, babe, you've got an audience!*

Stevie filled him in on everything he knew.

"It's a lousy break," he said. "I keep thinking

of the little guy, all curled up in his bed with Bugs and those silly purple ears."

"It's his favorite toy," Stevie said. "Since the day you gave it to him."

"Hey, Stevie, Todd and Bugs will be okay, you'll see! And they'll be back before you know it!"

He heard a police siren, and even though he was sure it wasn't following him, it made him nervous.

"Bad connection! I'll check with you later!"

Stevie didn't know why, but after thirty seconds on the phone with Lyle, her head was pounding like a chorus of kettledrums.

Was it something he'd said?

Galvin was still furious. He'd figured out every detail, even allowed for leeway such as cars, floats, or people in the way. Wasn't his motto "Expect the unexpected"?

But who the hell had expected the perp to be a mind reader? To anticipate every move and plan for it ahead of time? If he didn't know better, he'd think the whole thing had been engineered by an ex-cop.

Maybe Madden was smart to have vested out before he was burned out. Maybe, but it took a certain kind of personality to hang out a PI shingle and become a legal peeping Tom.

No, that wasn't for him. This morning may have ended in a total fuckup, but there were other mornings, past and future, that made it worth-

340

while. Galvin only wished they would outnumber days like this more often.

The radio caught his attention as soon as he heard the name Perry Fang.

"He's been in the hospital all this time?" Why the hell hadn't anyone found him before now?

Never mind. "I'm on my way," he said to the dispatcher. He just had to get out of the bumper-to-bumper traffic jam. He reached to the dash for the teardrop, then opened his window and plopped the flashing red light onto the burning-hot roof. Cars began moving aside to let him pass.

Wouldn't it be a joke if the perp was in one of these cars stuck in traffic? A million bucks couldn't buy an uncluttered road on a Sunday in Southern California, but a fucking red teardrop and a screeching siren could.

Maybe it was funny, but Galvin didn't laugh.

Stevie had been pacing back and forth since her phone call from Lyle. She'd gone from room to room, trying to get a handle on whatever it was her subconscious already knew. She'd forced herself, at one point, to sit down and concentrate on the problem.

No, the problem was all the trying. And forcing. Which only pushed the answers further away.

Was it fear of her own intuitive powers? Of what she might discover? The last time, her mind had "seen" a dead baby. In the morning, Andrew Landau's body had been found.

The first time, she'd "seen" a rabbit. Bugs. Not Todd's rabbit, but . . .

"I keep thinking of the little guy, all curled up in his bed with Bugs and those silly purple ears."

Wait. How did Lyle know that Todd had painted the ears purple?

Ansel hadn't even known until . . .

Oh, God. There was only one way Lyle *could* know!

Lyle parked the Dodge on a side street and walked the two blocks to the garage where he'd left his red Ferrari the night before. Soon he was back on the road—in style! Yeah! The only way to go! Tomorrow, he'd have Carla pick up the Dodge. Then he'd drive Todd to a spot where a clown getup wouldn't raise eyebrows—maybe the beach at Venice. Better yet, he could drop the kid at the Beverly Center, make it look like part of a toystore promotion. Yeah! He could ditch the car right there in the parking garage and have Carla come for him with the Ford. Credit Manny Perez for that.

"You gotta just walk away from it, babe, and never look back." Yeah! Good advice, Manny! And a good thing it was the secondhand piece of junk Lyle would be walking away from, not his beloved Italian custom job.

Yeah, but he'd also be walking away from—well, handing over, same difference—a million bucks. After dreaming up such a gorgeous scenario! It wasn't fair!

Still, it beat welching and getting wasted.

And it beat running outa stash! Lyle checked his pockets the moment he reached the front gates.

All gone! No more toot!

Wait! He could *buy* more, now that his credit was good again. No such thing as all gone! *Yeah!*

"Sorry, Mrs. Kline," said Galvin's assistant, "the lieutenant isn't back yet. But he'll be calling in. Can I take a message?"

Stevie had just left one on Joe Madden's answering machine.

"Yes! Tell Lieutenant Galvin that Lyle Hemmings has my son!" Voicing it even once, for Joe, had set her nerves on edge. Repetition brought her nearer to hysteria.

"I'll try to reach him, ma'am. Will you be at home?"

Stevie knew she couldn't sit still and wait for Joe or Galvin to call. Or for Ansel to get back.

"Ma'am? Shall I have Lieutenant Galvin call you at home?"

If she didn't act now, she'd lose her mind.

"No! Tell him to meet me at Lyle's house!"

"But ma'am, maybe you should wait till—"

She cut him off. "Tell him to hurry!" She'd already wasted too much time. She hung up, scribbled a note for Ansel, and grabbed her keys.

She was at the door when she remembered. Lyle could be—what was the hackneyed movie phrase?—"armed and dangerous." She might have to protect herself. And Todd.

She took the stairs two at a time. Before the separation, Ansel had kept a gun in the left-hand drawer of the desk in the den. She had no idea what kind it was, except that it was a revolver. She'd never fired it, wasn't even sure how. With luck, Lyle wouldn't know that.

She rushed to the den and prayed that Ansel had forgotten to pack the gun when he'd moved out.

She opened the drawer. Yes! There it was!

She'd fired prop guns in films, but just now she was all thumbs. She fiddled with the cylinder release until her fingers were steady enough to snap it forward.

The chambers were empty!

With more luck, Lyle wouldn't know that, either. He'd called her from the phone in his car, hadn't he? Well, if fate was really on her side, maybe Lyle hadn't returned yet! She could collect Todd and run!

Stevie dropped the revolver into her totebag. Part of her hoped Lyle would be out; it would be easier that way. But another part of her hoped he'd greet her at the door.

Because Lyle Hemmings had a lot to answer for.

Fifty-two

Carla was tempted to sneak Todd out of the house when she realized she'd returned ahead of Lyle. But who knew how soon he'd be back? What if he caught her pulling out of the driveway just as he was pulling in?

Todd was eating his burger when the key turned in the lock. Quickly Carla pulled her clown mask over her face and whispered "Shh!" to Todd.

He nodded as the big clown entered the F-X room and set the large carpetbag down in front of Carla and Todd.

"Wanna see something, Todd?" Lyle teased in his high-pitched lady-clown voice.

"Sure," answered Todd.

Lyle bent down and opened the bag wide. Carla's mouth formed a silent "Ohhh!" at the sight of a million dollars in cash.

"Wow!" exclaimed Todd, jumping up. "Can we play with the toy money?"

"Toy money?" Lyle burst into laughter. "Play? Todd, baby, we can do anything we want to!"

"Can I take some of it home? It looks so real, and there's so much of it!"

Lyle's laughter erupted into a spasm. He tried holding his sides, but his ribs ached, and tears of release made his laughter sound like sobbing.

"Are you okay, Uncle Ly—" Todd stopped.

Carla's heart stopped, too. Or shattered.

Todd was holding the remote control in one hand. With the other, he covered his mouth and said, "Uh-oh, I didn't mean to say it!"

Lyle had risen to his full height, and now he stood towering over the little boy. Carla had moved closer to Todd, who was clutching her wrist for all it was worth.

"Take off that goddammed ridiculous mask," Lyle commanded Carla. "You don't need it anymore.

She obeyed, and the rubber face fell to the floor.

Lyle tore off his own mask, his eyes never leaving Todd's.

"Can I go home now, Uncle Lyle?" asked Todd, trying not to sound terrified and determined not to cry.

"Yeah," said Carla. "You've, like, got the money. We can pay Manny and send Todd home, can't we?"

"Are you really *that* stupid?" shouted Lyle, although he was only three feet away.

Carla, still holding Todd's hand, moved them both farther back.

"Well . . . what *are* you going to do?" she asked.

Jesus, thought Lyle. Kidnapping and ransom

were bad enough, but *murder*? Could he kill Ansel and Stevie's kid, the child they'd called his godson?

Yeah, well, what other choice did he have, right?

Right! But could he live with that?

It wouldn't be easy, but, hey, he'd handle it.

Fifty-three

The male nurse led Galvin down a dimly lit corridor to the opened door of number 412.

"He's in there." The nurse gestured and continued along the hall.

The stack of magazines on the night table told Galvin he was in the right room. Publications with the names *Screamer*, *Metal Shop*, and *World Bowhunter* were strewn atop the collection.

But what struck Galvin was the strong resemblance between the police artist's sketch and the patient lying in the bed next to the window. The bed near the door was empty.

As Rover Jarvis had predicted, the man's style and name were changed. The shaved head had given way to shoulder-length frizz. A patchy beard and mustache hid a strong jaw and full lips. But the face and the tattoos were the same as those described by Jarvis. The blue-and-yellow design snaked around both arms from beneath the sleeves of the hospital gown.

"Albert Ogden?" Galvin asked, approaching the bed.

The patient's head turned. There was a moment's panic in his eyes as he studied Galvin, who was still wearing his undercover tourist garb.

"Well, you ain't with the Forfars, anyway," Ogden said.

"LAPD," Galvin replied, holding out his shield.

Ogden looked at it carefully, then said, "So, what do you want, Lieutenant?"

"You're also known as Perry Fang?"

"Used to be. I ain't the head banger I was."

"We've been looking for you for quite a while."

"You and a lot of people. I never thought I'd say it, man, but I'm glad you got to me first."

"A hospital's a pretty good place to hide."

"Not that good. You found me. So could they."

"The Forfars?"

Ogden nodded. "They fucked me up, man. Spent a week in a hospital after the beating."

"When was that?"

"Late April. I'm here now 'cause of the damage they did to my kidneys."

"You want to tell me about it?"

"Like you don't already know."

Like I should have known all the time, thought Galvin. Seeing Albert Ogden, aka Perry Fang, suddenly made a lot of the pieces fall into place. Galvin took out his Zippo. "What did you do with the money?"

Ogden closed his eyes. Weighing his options, Galvin surmised. Shouldn't take long; there were only two: Ogden could confess now, or risk a trial and probable conviction. Unless the cult found him first.

"I hid the ransom," Ogden said finally. "I shoulda known they'd figure it was me. Lucas Cabot sent his guys out. Beat me till I handed it over. Left me for dead."

"Will you testify to that?"

Ogden blinked and stared at him. "I'm supposed to get out of here tomorrow, and I got no place safe to get to."

"I'll put a guard outside your door for tonight, and get you protection after your release."

"Immunity?"

"I can't guarantee that."

"Okay. Deal." Ogden was quiet for a while. When he spoke again, it was with obvious relief. "I was drinkin' a lot then. I wanted out after they killed the first kid. They wouldn't let me, man. I was fuckin' terrified. After they nabbed the next one, I thought, shit, if I send a ransom note and make the Landaus and the cops think it's from the cult, I can collect, split, and maybe they won't go through with the second sacrifice. It blew up in my fuckin' face."

"That was the only ransom note you sent?" asked Galvin.

"You mean there was another one—for the Kline kid?"

"Just answer the question."

"Hey, man, I can't help it if I read the papers," Ogden said. "Yeah, I just sent the one note. If there *was* another note, it wasn't from the Forfars. If they grabbed Todd Kline, it ain't for the money, it's for the blood."

"And what if they didn't?"

350

"Yeah, I thought of that."

"We figure the next ritual is midnight Wednesday. They'd need another kid to sacrifice, wouldn't they?"

"And no other kid is missing." Albert Ogden studied the serpent's head tattooed on the back of his hand, then looked up. "That's right, Lieutenant, ain't it?"

Galvin didn't answer.

He started the motor while he went over the facts.

The clown head in the men's john and the exploding Vega at the motel told the story. What a fiasco—clever, well planned, and artfully executed. A cheap piece of crap with just enough props to make it look like a cop's car. Galvin didn't need the analysis of the 911 tape: he knew the voice matched the woman who'd made the other calls. He'd bet the million on it.

The million that some clown had made off with under Galvin's nose.

Some clown. Perfect casting.

Galvin had three more days. With Ogden's info, that should give them enough time to close down Lucas Cabot and his freaked-out cult. And enough time to save Todd Kline.

Provided the cult *had* Todd Kline. If Ogden was telling the truth, someone else—someone who knew about the first ransom note—had staged the Kline kidnapping to extort money and pin it on the Forfars. And Ogden was scared shitless. He was too afraid to be lying.

But if the cult hadn't taken the Klines' kid, that spelled copycat and made Madden and Stephanie Kean right.

Galvin hated being wrong. He didn't have a problem about admitting it, but that didn't make him *like* being wrong. It made him more determined than ever.

He was driving out of the hospital parking lot when the call came in about Manny Perez.

Fifty-four

Traffic was unusually heavy for a Sunday afternoon. Craning her neck, Stevie spotted the stalled car sitting in the middle of the road up ahead. She couldn't see the driver.

Panic was making her nauseous. For a week and a half she had felt—and been—helpless to do more than wait by the phone. Now, when minutes could mean the difference between saving or losing her child, fate seemed hell-bent on placing obstacles in the way.

Ridiculous. A traffic jam didn't mean there was a plot against her. Maybe by now Lt. Galvin and Joe Madden had gotten her messages. Maybe they'd reach Lyle before she did.

But she couldn't count on that, and time was running out.

Time. What if Lyle had realized his slip about Bugs's ears? He'd know the game was up. He'd rush home. To do what—pack? He might run. He might leave Todd behind.

Except that Lyle was a cokehead. Coke was what

had led him to think he could do something this heinous and get away with it.

Car horns were blaring all around Stevie and making it impossible to think.

But she *had* to think. It was the only way to keep her sanity until these cars got moving!

All right, so study the scene from Lyle's POV. He calls from the car and accidentally lets the cat out of the bag. What does he do? Yes! If he's not back yet—and a phone call to the house can find that out—Carla should answer.

Carla! God, she's in on it, too!

Todd's substitute nanny and Ansel's partner.

The note! Ansel would read it and be out of his mind with worry! He'd look for his gun and find it missing. Would he know it wasn't loaded?

Stevie reached for the phone and made the call. Twelve rings and no answer.

What did no answer mean?

Had Lyle returned and done something horrible to Todd?

A scream was rising inside her. She wouldn't be able to suppress it much longer.

Her foot was on the gas pedal. She pulled her tote bag closer and with her fingers traced the out-line of Ansel's empty gun just as the traffic started to move. The deafening noise from the car horns lessened.

And Stevie's silent scream grew louder.

Just get to the house. Get to Todd.

Her hysteria was giving way to rage.

Get to Lyle!

Madden slammed the door of his old heap. The A-C worked.

BFD.

Stanley and Blanche started squawking the second he entered the house. The light was blinking on his answering machine.

What new hell was this? He'd checked for messages less than fifteen minutes ago and there hadn't been any.

"Joe!" came Stevie Kean's cry on the tape. "Lyle Hemmings has Todd! It's the only way he could know about Todd's toy rabbit and the purple ears! I'm going to get him back! Meet me there!"

Instinct and reflex prompted Madden to instant action.

He called the house in Beachwood Canyon. The machine answered and he hung up.

He called Galvin. No luck there, either. Madden left a message and ran back out to his air-conditioned heap.

Stevie was alone. What in God's name was she walking into?

Galvin knew he was too late when he turned onto the run-down street of the Mexican neighborhood and saw the body bag being carried to the police ambulance.

What a day. And it wasn't even three o'clock yet.

He elbowed his way through the crowd, flashed

his shield, and plodded wearily up the strawlike lawn toward the ramshackle house.

All the windows on one side were broken. Bullet holes had riddled the facade. From the look of it, he could figure out what had taken place. Nevertheless, he let the officer in charge give him the specifics.

Manny Perez had started shooting as soon as the police pulled up to arrest him for the murder of Tammi Reynolds. Exchange of fire lasted about two minutes. Perez was dead. Inside the house they found enough coke to get half of LA high.

Dammit! Perez was an important link in the chain of drug traffic. Without that collar, they were back to zero on busting his suppliers.

Poor, crazy Tammi Reynolds. Her killer was dead, but was that justice? Galvin felt robbed. Not only for himself, but for a pathetic fan who'd wanted to help and gotten in the wrong person's way.

Galvin returned to his car and sat for a moment, trying to catch his breath while he sifted through the input his brain was working overtime to compute.

The radio crackled and he heard his name.

"Galvin here," he answered. "What's up?"

"Two calls, Lieutenant. One's from Stephanie Kean. The other's from Joe Madden."

"Christ," Galvin muttered. "All right. What'd they say?"

* * *

Larry Angelo slowed to clear the cars and news vans that were parked, illegally, on both sides of the winding road leading to Stevie's house.

The media people saw that Larry's passenger was Ansel Kline. They began running on foot behind the Vega and shouting questions as they ran.

"Goddammit!" Larry exclaimed. "Is it like this all the time for you guys?"

"Since the kidnapping, yes," Ansel said absently as Larry pulled into the driveway.

"You want me to come in with you, Mr. Kline?"

"No. We'll be fine." Yeah. Sure. "Thanks, Detective Angelo."

"Larry. And look, I'm sorry about what happened today. But we'll get the bastard."

Ansel forced a wan smile and started for the house. In backing away, Larry nearly hit a photographer who was jogging up the driveway, his camera poised and ready.

"Hey, Mr. Kline!" he shouted. "If you're looking for Stevie, she split!" He shot half a roll of film before Ansel turned and saw that Stevie's Lexus wasn't in the driveway where it had been that morning.

Ansel let himself into the house and called Stevie's name, although he knew she wouldn't be there.

He found her note beside the phone in the study. It was scribbled, obviously written in a hurry, and barely legible. Even after he'd deciphered it, it didn't make sense.

Until it did.

He raced upstairs to the den and went straight

to the desk. The gun was gone. But Stevie had insisted it never be loaded with Todd in the house.

He pulled out his keys, fumbled with the lock on the middle drawer until it opened, and tore at the fresh box of bullets. There were none missing.

Stevie was on her way to Lyle's with an unloaded gun.

Ansel tripped twice running down the stairs and out of the house. He slammed the front door and within seconds was in the Jaguar, leaning on the horn as the car sped, in reverse, down the driveway. It didn't matter who or what was in the way. He couldn't think beyond finding Stevie and Todd.

At Lyle's.

Fifty-five

"What are you going to do, Lyle?" Carla asked.
"I'll give you three guesses!" he answered,
brushing her aside as he locked Todd inside the
F-X room.

"But the poor kid's too scared to tell anyone!
Don't lock him in, Lyle! Let him go home, where
he belongs! Kids know how to keep secrets—it's a
game to them!"

Suddenly he whirled about. "Yeah? What about
you! Were you playing a game with Todd! Were
the two of you keeping the secret from me!" His
questions were shouted at her, all of them with
the tone of accusation.

She couldn't answer. He'd know she was lying
if she tried to deny the truth. She followed him to
the landing and up to the third floor. She didn't
need to ask why. Lyle was headed for what he
called his prop room. Visitors jokingly referred to
it as Lyle's armory.

Most of the weapons in his collection were sou-
venirs from films Lyle had produced. There were
quite a few from medieval times, relics of slash-

and-tear low-budget quickies. But Carla knew that some of the guns—the 12-gauge Remington and the Browning automatic shotguns and the pearl-handled .32-caliber automatic, for example, were always loaded. She'd seen them in action only once, when Lyle himself had been "loaded." He was almost as wired then as he was now. Only now, he was wired *and* scared, which made him more dangerous. She had to convince him not to hurt Todd.

"Lyle," she said, following him into the prop room, "listen to me!"

"Why should I? You're gonna tell me to pick up the phone and call Stevie or Ansel and say, 'Hi, there, I've got your little darling. Come pick him up so we can all do dinner!' And you expect them to say, 'Oh, okay, Lyle, that'll be nice. And thanks so much for babysitting Todd while we've been frightened *out of our goddammed wits!*' Are you off your skull, Carla, or what!"

"Lyle—"

"Shut up and use your head! Or do you wanna try convincing me to take the money and run? I'm supposed to believe that you'll stay here like a good little girl minding the store and you won't tell a fucking soul where I've gone!"

"Why don't you?" she cried.

"Why don't I what?"

Suddenly Carla thought she'd found a way to help Todd. "Why don't you do what you said—take the money and run! We can both get outta here before Manny comes to collect!"

"What about the people he's making the collection *for?*"

"You'll be out of the country before they find out!"

"And what, I take you with me, just to be on the safe side?"

"Uh . . . no! Leave me here! Don't even tell me where you're going! I'll wait for you to call from wherever, then I'll take Todd home—"

Mistake. She knew it the moment she said it, before he cut her off.

"You'll take Todd home? Oh, goody! Todd tells his story about two clowns who locked him up, and when Mommy asks who they were, Todd answers, 'Why, Carla and Uncle Lyle, of course!'"

Quietly she said, "He won't tell if I ask him not to."

"Yeah, sure. Like I'm gonna put my life in the hands of a four-year-old kid and a ditsy broad I can't even trust!"

"You *can!* Look what I did for you, Lyle! I didn't want any part of this! If you can't trust me after the Vega business at Disneyland and the phone calls to the cops and that Eppie woman, if you *still* think I'd turn you in, then you're more fucked up than I ever knew! Take the money, Lyle, and get away! The longer you wait, the worse it'll be for you!"

And for Todd.

Lyle ignored her. Carla watched as he took out the clip of the .32, examined it, put the clip back inside the handle, and cocked it. Then he swung the door of the cabinet shut, locked it, and hurried from the room.

Carla hurried right behind him.

"Get off my back!" he yelled. "You're not my fucking shadow!" He pushed her aside and she fell against the stair railing. Lyle's rage was making him unsteady, too; he missed a step before reaching the second-floor landing.

Stevie glanced at the speedometer. She was doing fifty-five, although she felt as if the car wasn't moving at all.

Then, suddenly, Lyle's main-entrance gate came into view.

The gate! How would she get past the security-alarm system? Lyle had bragged that breaking the code was next to impossible.

"The only way is to crash through the gate!" he'd said. "And half of Beverly Hills's Finest will arrive within five minutes!"

If Todd was safe, it wouldn't take her that long.

Stevie put the Lexus into reverse and backed up. For the first time she was grateful that Ansel had insisted on a sturdily built car. She prayed that it was solid enough to open Lyle's gates without sending her through the windshield.

The car was in position. Like a movie stunt, it was now or never.

Even inside the fortress, they both heard the crash. Lyle's features were distorted from fear, and for a split second Carla recognized him as the clown he'd always hidden beneath the flesh-and-blood mask.

"Get out the back way!" Lyle ordered.

"But . . . who . . . ?"

"Who else, dummy? It's Manny—or the guys he answers to!"

"Wh-where are y-you g-going?"

"We can't get outta here without cash! I'll meet you in the garage! Go!" He was already standing at the door to the F-X room with the loaded pistol in his hand.

Todd had never felt his heartbeat in his ears before. But he'd never been so afraid before, either. Just now, though, he was so frightened, that while Uncle Lyle and Carla were gone from the room, and with Bugs clutched tightly to his chest, Todd crawled under the big wooden closet in the corner. He would have hidden inside it, but he'd seen a movie on TV where the bad guy did that, and it was the first place the detectives looked. The space between the bottom of the closet and the floor was too small for a grown-up to fit under, but it was the right size for him and his toy rabbit. It also gave him a clear view of the doorway and the wall on the left, where the robot animals stood at attention.

Todd heard the key turning in the lock. "Shh!" he whispered to Bugs. "Don't make a sound!"

* * *

Carla had reached the foot of the stairs. All she had to do was go through the wine cellar to the garage entrance. But the pummeling fists at the door stopped her. Manny Perez wouldn't knock. He'd shoot the lock off. So, like, who . . . ?

Curiosity made her peek. She was shocked to see Stevie Kean. So shocked, that without thinking, she opened the door. Their exchange was brief.

"Where's Todd?"

"The F-X room!"

Stevie was halfway up the stairs before Carla remembered. "Stevie! Be careful! Lyle's got a gun!"

Where was the little brat? "Todd!" Lyle called out, coming farther into the room. *"Todd!"* Jesus, the place would be crawling in another few minutes—Manny, his pals, the cops—this was one helluva time to play hide-and-seek!

Lyle's pulse was making him dizzy. He went straight to the armoire that faced the remote-control zoo. It was the only piece of furniture in the room where a kid was likely to hide.

He reached out to the carved pinewood knob.

And heard Stevie call out, *"Lyle!"*

Goddammit to hell—he'd left the door wide open!

Todd was lying flat—or almost flat, except for Bugs, who was scrunched beneath his tummy. His left hand still clutched the remote control, while his right hand was trying to pull Bugs just far enough out from under so the rabbit's nose wouldn't keep poking him in the ribs.

Then he heard Mommy's voice!

She was here! Everything was going to be okay!

Lyle whirled around to find Stevie in the doorway, her gun pointed at him.

Of course, his pistol was pointed at her, too.

"Mine's loaded," he said.

"Then we're evenly matched," she said.

"Not from what I recall, Stevie. 'Ansel and I don't want to take chances with a small child in the house.' Remember?"

"Ansel doesn't live there anymore," she answered. "Things change."

Just then, they changed once more. A sound—was it a child's whimper? Stevie couldn't be sure—issued from beneath the armoire.

Lyle darted to the wall and cried, "Todd, come out from under there—or I'll shoot your mommy!"

Todd could see that Lyle wasn't bluffing. And he remembered that Mommy never put bullets in Daddy's gun. He had to come out from his hiding place, but he also had to do something to save Mommy!

He shoved Bugs, then crawled out after him.

Mommy looked so beautiful. And so scared. What could he do?

Lyle was standing directly in front of the monstrous grizzly bear. Imagine! Todd had been afraid

of a silly robot, when all the time it was Uncle Lyle
he should have been afraid of!

Wait. Maybe there was a way. If he could . . .

But it was broken, wasn't it . . . ?

Well, maybe it wasn't always broken . . .

He looked down at the remote-control keypad
in his hand and pressed the number 5.

It wasn't broken now.

Lyle wasn't ready for what happened next. The
huge bear lunged forward and with a single swipe
of one furry paw knocked Lyle's gun out of his
hand and sent it flying.

It fell, slid across the floor, and landed at
Stevie's feet.

She grabbed it and cried, "Todd! Get out! Go
to Carla!"

"But, Mommy—"

"*Now!*"

Fifty-six

"It isn't loaded," Lyle said, as Todd went tearing from the room.

"Oh, come on, Lyle!" said Stevie. "If it isn't loaded, why are you standing there shaking like a leaf?"

"Stevie—you've gotta believe me! I was gonna bring Todd home and tell you everything—just as soon as I paid these guys off! I never meant for it to go this far—"

"Save it, Lyle!" Stevie was shaking, too, but from rage, not fear.

And Lyle could sense it. "Stevie! I was only bluffing. You know I couldn't hurt you or Todd! Just like I know you couldn't pull the trigger!"

She didn't lower the gun.

Joe Madden arrived seconds later. A half-hysterical Carla Franzen yanked the front door open. Her free arm still hugged the sobbing little boy and his toy rabbit.

"Mommy's upstairs!" cried Todd. "With Uncle Lyle!"

Siren sounds could be heard outside. Galvin! It was about time!

"Stay here!" Madden ordered Carla and Todd, drawing his gun and taking the stairs two at a time.

"Stevie, you've gotta listen to me!" Lyle pleaded.

She took two deep breaths to steady her hands. The pistol was still aimed at Lyle and she wasn't going to run the risk of dropping it.

"You don't know what it means to have a child, Lyle. If you did, you wouldn't have tried to rob me of mine! I've read that everyone has a breaking point. A person can live a whole lifetime without ever recognizing it. But just touch that point—violate it—and watch out!

"I've played killers on film—films you've produced, Lyle, isn't that funny?—and I always fell back on the actors' cliché that you don't have to commit murder to know what it feels like. Well, until today, I never understood what it *really* feels like!"

"Stevie, I—"

"*How* could you do this to us, Lyle! Pretending to be so concerned! Pretending to be our friend! You're Ansel's business partner! Is it the coke, or have you always been a monster?"

"Stevie, you don't see—"

"I *do*, Lyle! You're Todd's godfather, but you were ready to sacrifice him just to save your neck!"

"Stevie, I wouldn't have! I swear it!"

368

"Stop the lies, Lyle, or I'll stop them with this!"

She raised the pistol just as Joe Madden entered the room.

"It's all right, Stevie. Todd's safe. You can put the gun down."

She didn't.

Madden waited. He wouldn't blame her if she shot the bastard. But he knew what it would do to her. And to the kid.

"Stevie," he said gently, coming to her, "let the police handle it. Todd's downstairs, and he's okay. He's been through a rough time, but he doesn't know the danger he was in. He'll get over it."

She didn't move the pistol.

"Stevie, think for a minute. If you pull the trigger, you'll be the one—not Lyle—who'll be scarring Todd. Right now he's a four-year-old kid who's had a scary adventure. He can tell his friends about it. The legal system will put Lyle where he belongs. Don't do something you'll regret for the rest of your life. Think about Todd."

One last try.

"Think about Ansel."

Fifty-seven

Without taking her eyes from Lyle, Stevie lowered her arm. She hated being the one responsible for the obvious relief on his face as she allowed the gun to slip from her fingers and fall to the floor.

Joe Madden darted forward and retrieved both weapons. They could hear the sounds of heavy footsteps as Lt. Galvin's men raced up the stairs.

Neither Stevie nor Lyle moved. They stood looking into each other's eyes as the years passed between them, and ended.

Madden's arms went around Stevie, and she began to tremble, violently and uncontrollably, but without tears. She rested her head against his shoulder as Galvin and his men came through the door, guns drawn and trained on Lyle.

"We'll take it from here," Galvin said to Madden. "Mrs. Kline, you okay?"

Madden answered for Stevie, then led her past Galvin and his backup team, through more officers who crowded the doorway, and out onto the landing.

"Your boy's downstairs," said one of the police-men. "The medics are just checking him over."

There was noise and commotion coming from the ground floor, but upstairs it was strangely quiet.

Lyle took a long, last look at his beloved F-X room while an officer cuffed him and his former buddy read him his rights. On the floor between them lay the tapestry carpetbag filled with cash.

"Just one question, off the record?" said Galvin.

Lyle shrugged. What did it matter now?

"Why?" asked Galvin.

Lyle shrugged again. "I was running out of things to sell. It's an expensive habit."

"Your ex-chauffeur?"

"Yeah. Manny would've killed me."

For an instant Lyle thought he saw a satisfied grin wrinkling Galvin's crow's-feet. But it immediately passed and Mike once more assumed his pro-fessional cop's face. The poker face.

"Manny Perez is dead," said Galvin.

Lyle smiled. He hadn't imagined the smugness after all. "When?" was all he said.

"About an hour ago. A shoot-out. Perez killed the Reynolds woman."

An hour ago. Lyle could have been on his way to Mexico by now. "Carla was right," Lyle mur-mured.

"About what?"

"Everything." Lyle made a helpless gesture with his cuffed hands.

371

"Here," Galvin said, taking the malachite-and-gold lighter from his jacket and putting it in Lyle's shirt pocket. "It's not my style."

An officer took Lyle's arm and said, "Let's go."

Galvin was trying to fathom the expression on Lyle's face. He didn't have to.

" 'I'm dead behind these eyes,' " Lyle quoted. "Olivier. *The Entertainer.*"

The police photographers asked Galvin and Madden to step aside.

"Come on," Galvin said. "We're in the way."

They left the F-X room and headed toward the landing.

When they reached the stairs, Galvin stopped to reflect. He'd been up there only last night. Had stood right outside the F-X room during Lyle's "deluxe tour" of the second floor. And all the time Todd Kline had been imprisoned behind the door. Goddammed games some people played.

"I guess I owe you an apology," he said to Madden.

"I won't stop you, Galvin," Madden replied with a grin.

"I didn't think you would. I should have been more open to your angle on this." Galvin was studying the scuffed tip of his shoe. "And maybe on other things, too, while you were on the force."

"That's blood under the bridge," said Madden. "And the Forfars still have to be brought in."

Galvin offered Madden a brief update on Perry Fang, alias Albert Ogden. "I'll have Cabot and his

372

cult behind bars before the next sabbat. The heat's on. I doubt if there'll be a black mass Wednesday night. No other kids have been reported missing."

"So you got 'em, Galvin."

"Not before three children were killed."

"It could have been four."

"Yeah." Galvin thought about extending his hand to Madden. Instead, he reached into his pants pocket, took out his Zippo, and flipped the top once. "See you around, Joe."

He started down the stairs. From behind, he heard Madden say, "Nice work, Lieutenant."

"Sure," Galvin answered over his shoulder.

Lyle slowed when he and the cop reached the foot of the staircase. They could hear Carla's voice echoing from the parlor down the hall.

"The interrogation room," Lyle said, grinning.

The cop offered no reaction.

"I only made the calls to Eppie Goldwyn to, like, make everyone *think* it was Tammi Reynolds! I never meant for her to get killed!"

Lyle's grin widened into a laugh. Good old Carla. Always insisting that confession was good for the soul. And she wouldn't have opened her mouth if he'd taken the cash and split? Yeah, right!

Lyle and the cop were inches from the front door when it burst open.

"You goddammed sonofabitch!" Ansel Kline cried out, lunging at Lyle. "Where are Stevie and Todd?"

Ansel's fist flew forward and crashed into Lyle's jaw. The two policemen at the door jumped to restrain him.

"Take it easy, Mr. Kline! Your wife and son are fine!"

Ansel stopped struggling, but they didn't release him until Lyle had been led from the house.

"You can loosen your grip now," Ansel said to the officers.

They did, just as a group of two more uniformed policemen, a plainclothes detective, and two medics came out of the Casino and started toward the main entrance foyer. At the center of the group was Stevie, her hand tightly clasping Todd's.

"Daddy!" Todd cried out, letting go of Stevie and bounding up the length of the hall with his little arms outstretched. His left hand still clutched Bugs, whose skinny legs dangled while his oversize feet dragged along the stone floor.

Ansel knelt, nearly falling backward from the impact as Todd hurled himself into his father's arms. A sob escaped as Ansel repeated Todd's name over and over.

"Don't cry, Daddy," said Todd, wiping the tears from Ansel's cheeks with the tip of a rabbit ear.

Stevie was standing before them. She took a handkerchief from her tote bag and passed it gently across Ansel's face.

"You're all purple," she said through her own tears.

Ansel held Todd tightly with one arm and enfolded Stevie in the other, gently rocking them both back and forth.

They didn't notice Galvin, who had paused at the center of the staircase to avoid intruding on the scene taking place below.

Two officers emerged from the parlor with Carla Franzen. She stopped in front of Stevie for only a moment. Galvin heard her say, "I'm sorry, Todd" before she was escorted out to one of the squad cars.

Galvin continued down to the bottom of the stairs to meet Stevie, who had broken away from Ansel and Todd.

"About Carla," she said quietly. "Please treat her kindly. She did everything she could to help save Todd."

Galvin nodded, then turned his attention to the child. "So! This is the guy all the fuss has been about!"

Todd giggled and waved Bugs at him. "I'm Todd! Who are you?"

"Oh, just someone who was worried," Galvin answered.

"I'll be in touch tomorrow," he said. "Take care of them." He indicated Todd and Bugs, and for a moment his features softened. Then the customary gruff demeanor returned.

"We'll arrange to have your car towed. And I'll

have a police escort see you home. The three of you have no more reason to stay."

Ansel put Todd down so he could shake hands with Galvin.

"Thank you, mister," said Todd, offering his hand and Bugs's paw. Stevie noticed the color rising in Galvin's face.

He opened the front door, and they all stepped out into the hot afternoon light.

Ambulances and police cars with spinning red lights were everywhere. Barricades had been set up at the gates to keep back the media vans and curious onlookers and fans who already were trying to enter the grounds.

At the gates, Barbara Halsey was yelling for attention and order. She was drowned out by the shouting voices of reporters and photographers who had gone into a frenzy at the sight of Ansel and Stevie with Todd.

"Where did they come from?" Stevie said. "So many people! And Barbara! How did they all know?"

"A radio news bulletin," Ansel explained. "I heard it in the car. They didn't say whether you and Todd were safe. It's amazing I got here in one piece."

They were interrupted by one of the paparazzi. "Hey, Stevie! Give us a smile!" He headed a group of a dozen or more who had broken through the barrier.

"We'd better let them have a picture or we'll never get out of here," Stevie advised.

Ansel picked Todd up on his shoulders and for

the next ten seconds, the sounds of camera shutters filled the air. Ansel and Todd waved to the photographers, while Stevie waved to Barbara Halsey, who gave her a thumbs-up sign before returning her attention to the reporters she was trying to control.

"Okay, people, press conference—tomorrow!" Barbara shouted over the din.

A gunmetal-gray Mercedes was being given permission to pass through the police roadblock. The car pulled up and stopped directly behind Ansel's Jaguar.

Carolyn Kline alighted from the driver's side at the same moment a figure in a shocking-pink flowered hat came barreling past Barbara Halsey and hurried across the manicured front lawn.

Eppie Goldwyn scurried up the first few steps leading to the house. Beads of perspiration were visible beneath the rose garden covering her head. Behind Eppie, Stevie saw Carolyn struggling in her high heels to negotiate the cobblestone drive.

"Todd, honey!" Eppie cried out, shoving the microphone of her tape recorder toward the little boy. "What have you got to say to Auntie Eppie!"

"G'andma!" he cried, as Ansel lowered him to the ground. The child raced past Eppie and leaped into Carolyn's arms.

Eppie didn't waste a second. She set her microphone on Ansel and Stevie. "Darlings! As a longtime friend of the family, let me just say that—"

"Friend, Eppie?" said Ansel. *"You?"*

Carolyn and Todd were standing less than three feet away from Eppie. Stevie left Ansel for a moment and came forward. She and Carolyn embraced briefly, then Stevie turned to Eppie.

"Print what you like about Ansel and me, Eppie," she said. "But keep your distance. At least twenty yards."

"Stevie, I—"

"One more thing. If you ever write another syllable about my mother-in-law again, I'll sue you. And I'll win." Stevie turned her back to Eppie and reached for Ansel's hand.

"Come on, G'andma!" Todd cried, sliding out of Carolyn's arms. "I'll race you to the car!"

He was off and running. Carolyn was laughing as she followed behind in her spindly, ungrandmotherly high heels.

"Your police escort's ready anytime you are," a uniformed officer told them.

Stevie glanced at Ansel and followed his gaze across the lawn to the parked automobiles in the driveway. Among them she recognized Joe Madden's heap. A moment later, the heap's owner was loping toward it.

Stevie called his name. He looked about, saw them, and waved.

"We have to thank him," Stevie said.

Ansel brought her hand to his lips and kissed her fingers.

"You go," he said.

Stevie knew this wasn't easy for Ansel. And she'd never loved him more.

"Ask Joe back to the house for a drink if you like," Ansel said. "Or a soda."

Stevie nodded and headed across the carpet of creeping-bent grass.

"Hi, Joe," she greeted him. "I see you got your car back."

Madden was lighting a cigarette. "Just in time to drive off into the sunset." He paused. "Todd's all right?"

"He's wonderful! Oh, Joe! You haven't seen him!"

"I did earlier." He gestured across the lawn. "And I see him now. He's happy. And I'm happy for you. For all of you."

"Come back to the house. Todd should get to know you."

Madden shook his head. "It seems to me that's a private reunion."

He was right.

"Well, then, maybe later in the week? Dinner?"

He'd have the seagull finished by then. "Sounds good." He looked at her for a long moment.

Stevie held the look, then gently rested her palm on his stubbled cheek. "Thanks, Joe. For everything."

There was nothing else to say.

She returned to Ansel, who stood watching Carolyn and Todd as they climbed into her Mercedes.

"Okay?" Ansel asked.

"Joe's not coming back with us."

Ansel placed his hands on her shoulders. "That wasn't what I meant."

Stevie glanced up at him. "It's still okay."

"Good. Todd's decided to ride with his grandmother."

"Oh, Ansel!" she exclaimed. "It's finally over!" She fell into his arms and they kissed until both of them were breathless.

Even after they broke the kiss, the camera shutters continued their whirring.

"That wasn't just for the photographers, I hope," Ansel whispered into her ear.

"That was just for you," she murmured. "Let's go home."

Madden sat behind the steering wheel and let the motor run. As the interior of the car began to cool, he glanced through the windshield at the media sideshow.

The spinning red lights. The empty ambulances pulling out. The police cars turning down the drive to take Carla and Lyle away. The reporters and photographers taping and snapping and recording Ansel and Stevie's embrace.

Carolyn Kline's Mercedes backed up. The top of Todd's head was barely visible in the seat alongside his grandmother.

Madden watched as Ansel and Stevie headed for the Jaguar. A beaming Stephanie Kean blew a kiss and offered one final wave to the cameras. Then she climbed into the car and closed the door.

The Jaguar moved in reverse until it drew up behind the Mercedes, which preceded it down the driveway and toward the gates. Madden reached into his back pants pocket for his wallet and took out a photograph.

It was a black-and-white picture of a girl in a gingham-checked pinafore. She was holding a toy Scottie. On her feet were sparkling slippers.

He brought his fingers up to the spot where she had touched his cheek. When he looked through the window again, the Jaguar was just disappearing from sight.

The dashboard clock read five minutes past four.

If he hurried, he could catch the four-thirty meeting in Echo Park.